BRO 2016
Brookins, Carl.
The Case of the Stolen Case
Carver County Library

The Case of the Stolen Case

OTHER BOOKS
by Carl Brookins

Sailing Adventures

The Inside Passage
Old Silver
A Superior Mystery
Devils Island
Red Sky

Sean Sean Private Investigator novels

The Case of the Greedy Lawyers
The Case of the Deceiving Don
The Case of the Great Train Robbery
The Case of the Purloined Painting
The Case of the Yellow Diamond

Jack Marston Academic novels

Bloody Halls
Reunion

The Case
of the
Stolen Case

Carl Brookins

Brookins Books

The Case of the Stolen Case

ISBN: 978-0-9853906-8-6
Carl Brookins
First Edition Copyright Brookins Books LLC 2016

Cover by John Toren
This is a work of fiction. Names, characters, places and incidents are the products of the author's imagination or are used factiously. Any resemblance to actual events or persons living or deceased is entirely coincidental.

1

When I turned right off Minnehaha onto Arundel I rolled the window down to let in some of the moist, warm, night air.

That's when I smelled it.

We were having one of those summers that people who live in Minnesota brag about whenever they encounter verbal jabs about our vicious winters. It'd been a summer to die for. Long warm and lazy days, blending almost seamlessly one into another. Cool romantic nights, the kind of days and nights poets wax poetic about. There'd been only a few scattered days of really muggy weather. Brief periods of rain kept things fresh, but it seemed to only rain at night or on weekdays and never in the evenings. Paradise. I was living in Paradise. Right.

Like a small military patrol, I was penetrating deeply into Frogtown, a neighborhood of Saint Paul that has seen better times. I was here because a friend of a friend had called me at home and asked me to meet him at an address that happens to be in Frogtown. Even though it was late enough that I'd been watching the ten PM news on television, I went. I like to watch the news. It's like research. When I know what's happening in my cities, I occasionally have an early warning about a case. Because I don't always sit around and wait for cases to sidle in the door. Sometimes I market my special services.

After the phone call I left my peaceful home in a northern suburb called Roseville and went into the city. I went because that's what I do—most times.

My name is Sean NMI Sean. Answering requests and pleas for help is how I make my living. Sometimes I even get to save a blushing female person from whatever form of dragon is in pursuit. That doesn't happen often, mind you, and I don't ride a pale horse. My current ride is faded blue, sired by Ford out of Detroit. Mostly I take jobs that require me to ferret out wrongdoers of low-level chicanery, the kind of cases the cops have too many of and too few resources to spend on. Occasionally, the requests for help evolved into something major. Not often.

Now I was answering the call. Actually, two calls. Earlier in the day I took the first call at my office from Sally Belassario. He had a friend in trouble and would I talk to his friend. Since Sally was who he was, I said sure, tell the guy to call me. I promised Sal I'd tell him when the appointment was, so he could be there too. The rest of the day, the guy didn't call. Actually, nobody called the whole rest of that day. Nobody called the next day either. My business wasn't what you'd call thriving at the moment.

But at ten-ten the next night, this night in particular, when the phone rings, it's Sally himself. Again. Would I come to such and such an address?

"When?" I asked.

"Instantly," Belassario said. His voice had a mournful, late-night, too-many-cigarettes back-of-the-throat scarred tone.

Belassario, being who he is, and who he knows, I agreed, silently mouthing my objections to having to leave the comfort of my house on such a nice, relaxing, night.

That was twenty minutes ago.

The smell got stronger.

I went left on Raney, following Belassario's instructions. I drifted along the street for a block, the finely tuned engine under the hood of my ride making barely a whisper. My ride didn't have a name. No loud hoof-beats. I saw flashing lights ahead. After cresting a small rise in the street, I could see the source, just two blocks away. My gut and my nose told me I didn't have to look at house numbers any longer. Good gut and nose reactions are useful things for a PI to have. That's what I am, remember? A PI, a shamus. A de-tec-a-tiff. I'm pretty good at what I do, in spite of certain physical shortcomings. There are those who have suggested the biggest part of me is my ego. It's also good for a PI to have a head, or at least a working brain somewhere close by.

Flashing blue lights atop a Saint Paul PD patrol car pretty well filling the next intersection led me to draw up to the curb. I carry an honorary Ramsey County Sheriff's badge which the county bestowed on me a few years back. Sometimes it gets me through auxiliary police barricades at parades, but that's it. So I parked and slid out. I didn't lock up. There was nothing in it to steal except the vehicle itself and if the doors weren't locked, nobody'd punch out a window. There were knots of people standing around watching the action. There was plenty to watch.

A house on the north side of the street was burning. Big plumes of steam and evil-smelling smoke rose toward the stars and wandered around the neighborhood. Yellow and orange flames shot up and then disappeared, beat down by tons of water from the high-pressure hoses. I ambled casually toward the burning house, hands in the pockets of my light-weight kakis, assuming the role of a neighborhood gawker. The house in question was located nearly at the end of the next block so it was pretty easy to figure it was the address Belassario had given me over the phone. The serious barricades were half a block closer to the fire. In the street, inside the barricades, were several shiny red and silver fire trucks, red lights flashing, their bright halogen floods trained on the burning house. I could see the same flashing red lights coming from between the buildings, so I deduced that other trucks must have been in the alley behind the burning structure. Loud com radios crackled and growled with a cryptic language I didn't understand. Gray hoses, like anacondas, extended out on the pavement from hydrants, crushing the grass on the boulevard. There were so many hoses the dark wet pavement was almost obscured. The big diesel truck engines rumbled and sometimes roared, their exhausts adding more stink to the already over-laden atmosphere. The floodlights focused on the house lent a surreal atmosphere to the scene. When a firefighter carrying an ax crossed in front of one of the searchlights, his huge distorted shadow was thrown against the roiling cloud of smoke and steam rising from the back of the building. To a small child's eyes, this was the essence of terror. I am a small child when it comes to big fires.

As I walked forward, avoiding the policemen scattered about who were supposed to maintain crowd control and keep civilians out of the firemen's paths, my eyes scanned the folks milling about. I was watching for a round human shape. If Salvatore Belassario was here, his shape would give away his location. It wasn't easy, my search. Like Sal, I'm what some people call vertically challenged, being a mere five-two. Bellassario was even shorter, but, whereas I could easily disappear behind a Minnesota Viking down lineman, Sal is what one might describe as a butterball, being that he weighs in at two hundred plus pounds.

The smell of the burning house was stronger. The firemen continued to pour gallons of water on the place, raising huge columns of steam, as they overpowered the smoke and flame I'd seen a few minutes earlier. I smelled burned wood, melted plastic, scorched paint, and something sickly sweet I'd never smelled before. I didn't like it. I wanted to be elsewhere. Anywhere.

"Flesh," murmured Sal in his cigarette-tortured voice. "Smell it? Burned human flesh." I looked over my shoulder to see Belassario waddling toward me. The damage to his throat and lungs that gave him his distinctive voice was from fifty-plus years of smoking the evil black Italian cigars he favors and their extra gift of emphysema. He wheezed closer and said again, "Flesh. Human flesh." In his hand was the inhaler he always carried somewhere on his person.

I stared at him. Wondered how he knew.

"Five kids. They think maybe. They were in there earlier, according to witnesses. No one can find them now."

"Not any of them?" I shuddered.

Sal shrugged his fat shoulders. "It's for sure someone died in there. You can smell it."

I shook my head. "Is that the address you called me about?" I knew it was and I already knew this was something I wanted to stay away from, whatever Sal had in mind. But I asked the question just the same.

There was a groaning, crackling, crunching sound from the house.

We turned to watch as the ridge timber gave way and the remainder of the roof crashed into the interior of the house. Ash and dirty black smoke bloomed out of the windows facing us. What had once been a home was now a roofless hulk of blown out windows and sagging walls. And stink.

"What am I doing here?" We turned away and began to walk slowly back up the street toward my car.

Sal shrugged. "You're here because I asked you to come."

"Come on, Sal. You know what I mean. Why did you call?"

"Sean, you are one of the few guys in this town I know well enough to trust completely. You have a clean reputation. An' you almost never give me grief."

Sure, I thought. I'm a damn saint. I wear a white robe and I bathe regularly. I stared at Sal, saw the flashing lights from fire trucks dancing off his shiny round cheeks. He stared off along the street, stage right, at nothing in particular.

"My company owned that place," he said. "We rehabbed a big duplex into smaller apartments and rooms for rent after it got run-down by the previous owner. Neglected, you could say."

Uhhuh. There were stories on the street about Sal's real estate company. About how they located suitable properties, fixer uppers some people called them, and bought out the owners. Very cheaply. Then the properties seemed to change hands rapidly over only a few weeks or months until they could be sold at amazing profit. It was called flipping, and it wasn't legal.

"You mean you kept this one instead of running the appraisal through the roof and unloading it at an inflated price to some unsuspecting civilian?"

Sal just looked at me. "C'mon, Sean. Never mind about that. There's been a real tragedy, but this fire now is just a coincidence. This is not why we're here."

I leaned against the hood of my car, wishing I was home in bed, or better yet, home in Catherine's bed. "Yeah? Well, you called me. I was having a nice evening minding my own business. But you called me. At home." I wanted to make a point. He had my home telephone number, which was known to very few.

"C'mon. Sean, you know me. This is Sal. Do I look like a firebug?"

Bug maybe, firebug, no. Not Sal's style. "Okay, so it's a coincidence this place is burning and people are dead, and we're here. Together. I guess you didn't know the place was burning when you called. Just tell me again, why I'm standing on this street with you."

"Do you remember the pharmacy robbery over on Grand six years ago?"

How could I not? It had been in every paper and was the lead story on the tube for several days. It wasn't just a robbery. Two innocents had been murdered. It was still, so far as I knew, an open case.

"There are two things you don't know about that. One, the reported amount of money that was stolen was way too low and two, one of the guys who did the heist lived in this building."

2

I stared at Sal for a minute, wondering where this was going. I remembered the robbery very well and it was linked in my mind to another incident of some significance. One of my Saint Paul PD acquaintances had ended his career of protecting and serving that same night as the result of an unrelated crime on the other side of town. The cane he now used in court to ease the discomfort of his bullet-smashed knee probably helped to remind jurors that the streets had to be made safe for us ordinary citizens. Six years ago, that same summer night, Jerome Ford had been a patrol cop on the midnight shift.

"Okay, Sal. You apparently have something else you want from me. Let's go somewhere for coffee. Unless this can wait until tomorrow?" I said with a hopeful question in my voice.

"There's a Dunkin' Donuts over on University. Meet me there in ten." Sal turned away, not waiting for my reaction. He knew what it would be. I'm a shamus, you see, a private investigator. I don't take every job that comes through my office door, but I take a lot of them. Sal and I go way back in a casual sort of way and he knew that I'd at least listen to his story. He's connected in some manner I don't want to know about to what used to be called the Mafia, the Mob, the families, OC. I didn't know how connected and I didn't want to know. I did know there was hardly any organized crime in the Twin Cities.

I hoisted my five-foot two-inch frame into my Taurus and

snapped in the shoulder belt. I'm one of those people you read about who sits too close to the steering wheel for an airbag to be anything but dangerous. As I wheeled out and started toward the all night fat factory that masqueraded as a Dunkin' Donut coffee shop, I probed my memory cells and dredged up the Grand Pharmacy event. The robbery and killings six years ago had happened on a night very like the one I was currently driving through.

It was a dark hour, a witching hour, one of those wee hours of the night when mists swirl; when shadows collect around the narrow pools of wan yellow light cast down by the street lights that march in soldierly rows along the boulevards and avenues of the city. It was that time of night when strange rustlings are heard in the trees, when bats and owls drift on silent wings through the urban forest searching for their unwary prey. It was a time when other predators stir and skulk. It was a time when active imaginations sometimes go into overdrive. It was a time when everyone but fools, nightshift workers and evildoers are tucked up in bed behind locked doors and barred shutters.

Nuts. What it was, it was about two-thirty in the a.m. of an extremely hot, still and sticky summer night. As I recalled it, everybody who had a window air-conditioner or a big fan was running it full blast. Which is probably why no one in the neighborhood heard the shots and the screams. There are three million souls in the Twin Cities, give or take, and just three or four all-night pharmacies to serve them. In the saintly city, there're only two. One of them was called the Grand Pharmacy, because it was located on Grand Avenue, not too far from the Mississippi river, which mostly separates Saint Paul from Minneapolis.

Traffic in the store after the bars closed, after two a.m., was usually sparse. There were two people working that sticky Wednesday night, the forty-five-year-old Caucasian night pharmacist and an African-American female at the counter who was only eighteen. She had to be at least eighteen to work those hours.

They were the only humans in the store at around one-thirty when two clichés appeared. In spite of the heat they both wore dark stocking caps and long dark raincoats. You can see what I mean about clichés. I knew this much from the published pictures taken off the security camera tape. The last useful frame on the tape, a view from above and slightly to the rear of the second walking cliché, showed the perp holding a long gun, a shotgun, and swinging it out from under the coat.

Then they shot out the cameras—there were two—and the counter girl screamed. We know this because she told the police that before she died of her wounds. And because the lone witness said so. Then the perpetrators blew away the pharmacist and in a very few moments, trashed the pharmacy, stealing a quantity of drugs. They also picked the cash registers clean and smashed open a lock box in a back room where some extra money was kept.

The hoodlums were very fast because neither counter person nor pharmacist was able to reach one of the alarm buttons. A few moments later, they ran out of the store and leaped into a car which had conveniently drawn up to the curb in a no parking zone at the entrance. We know this because the surviving witness, some citizen, was across Grand, walking his dog. Fortunately for him, Grand Avenue is four lanes wide at that point. If it had been a normal street, the thugs might have seen him and added to the death toll. Unfortunately for the cops, the citizen didn't get the license number of the getaway car. But he saw the two perps run out, one with a dark, probably plastic, trash bag. The plastic bag held, it was assumed, the drugs. The second man also ran out right behind the first. He was carrying a silver or gray aluminum case, in which, it was also assumed, was the couple of thousand dollars from the registers. The dog-walker described all this to the cops who arrived several minutes later in response to the citizen's frantic telephone call. The suitcase was described as bigger than an attaché case, but not as big as a standard suitcase. The citizen dog-walker could not describe the driver of the getaway car.

In spite of intensive efforts by the police, that's where the affair ended. The killers were never apprehended. Likewise, the money was never found. The trail, as they like to say, had grown cold. As cold as the unfortunate pharmacist and the poor counter girl. It had been six years and I probably hadn't thought of the crime more than a half-dozen times in those years.

Now, with the nasty smells of the burning house in Frogtown sitting in the back of my throat, and the images of the fire still imprinted on my retinas, I parked and went through the heat into the pastry shop where Sal waited. It was brightly lit, so much so, it hurt my eyes for a minute. There were six other customers, all sitting separate. There was a small Asian guy, two Blacks and a tall Latino-looking fellow. Plus one non-descript white guy. Sal got two doughnuts and I carried two cups of black coffee in cardboard containers to a booth toward the back. I looked around again and shook my head. Here I was sitting in a Dunkin' Donuts late at night with a man I didn't especially want to know any better. We were talking about one of the more notable unsolved crime cases in Minnesota history. I was not happy.

"First, I want to know why you called me to come down here," I said, blowing on my coffee.

"I called you from my office, you know. I didn't know the place had been torched."

"Uh huh."

"I just learned a guy living there was involved with the pharmacy robbery. Intimately involved. As in he did it."

"Okay, Sal, but why call me?"

"I was gonna go talk to this guy and I wanted a witness, somebody who could back up my version of what went down, should that ever be necessary."

"You mean the fire?"

"No, Sean, like I said, I didn't know the place was burning when I called you. I wanted to talk to this guy I heard about, a guy who lived in the building, and in case anything happened, anything unusual, I wanted someone else there."

"Yes, so you said, but why me?"

"You carry a big gun."

Right, I thought. Sean Sean, the runty PI with the beeg pistola.

"Sal," I said and fixed him with a squinty stare.

He shrugged. "Okay, Okay. I needed somebody with a clean rep. An independent operator. A standup guy known to be on the side of the angels."

Sure, I thought. A patsy, perhaps? I left it for the time being. "Next subject," I said sourly, frowning at Sal. "The one about the money?" I cocked one eyebrow. It was a practiced move. I sometimes practice cocking one eyebrow. I use a mirror when I practice.

He slurped some coffee. "One of the three guys who took down the pharmacy lived in my building—the building that burned tonight."

"Uhuh, so you already said. It's the other statement I'm curious about. The one where you stated more money was taken than reported."

"The cash was in the aluminum case that citizen said he saw one guy run out with."

"I see." I didn't really. There'd been much speculation from the usual range of sources, who knew little or nothing, about what was in the case the bandit carried out that hot violent summer night, but only the perps knew for sure, and they had vanished. "Suppose you tell me a little more, although I have to warn you, Sal, this does not sound at all like anything I should be hearing."

Sal took a bite of a doughnut and crumbs, many crumbs, sifted down onto his silk flowered shirt front. He took no notice. "Look, Sean, I need your help so I have to tell you some things. I'm gonna hire you to follow up on this fire so we can put this other thing to rest."

I opened my mouth to protest. What I should have done was just walked out, but Sal went on as if I hadn't reacted. And then it was too late.

"You ever run across a Mordecai Marsh?" Sal asked. I didn't react. "Well, he came to me several weeks ago to tell me a story about a guy named Beechy, George Beechy."

"So?" I'm good at that, zeroing right in on the main point. It's my investigator training.

"According to Mordy, you know, Mordecai? Mordy tells me he's pretty sure this George Beechy was one of the guys who did the pharmacy thing. Mordy used to live in that building an' he knew this Beechy."

"The building that just burned?"

"Exactly."

"The building that you told me you own?"

"Right. Me and some other guys."

"And the guy Marsh fingered is this George Beechy?"

"Right again."

"Sal, I like this less and less."

"Just hold on, Sean. Lemme lay it all out here. So I check out this Beechy. I do this because certain people I once did a little business with are innarested in the whereabouts of that aluminum case from the Grand Pharmacy. And Beechy looks like he could be good for it."

"So you think Beechy may have a line on the aluminum case. The one you say was supposed to contain an unspecified but large amount of money that you say was liberated from the pharmacy. Not just the take from the cash registers and the box."

"Exactly."

I looked across the table at Salvatore Belassario. The next question was fairly obvious, but did I want to ask it? I didn't, but I asked it anyway. Catherine says I should learn to exercise a little restraint at times like this. "How much money are we talking about?"

Sal glanced left and then right, just like you see in the movies and leaned in a little. "Around two mil."

"Dollars? Two million?" I had raised my voice a little and Sal waved his hands in front of my face to shush me. I took a deep breath and said, "What's a small all-night Saint Paul pharmacy doing with two million dollars in a suitcase?"

"It was a favor, that's all. The guy who was blown away was just holding the case for another guy, who was supposed to pick it up later that morning."

"The pharmacist," I said to be sure I understood, "was asked by someone he knew—" I paused to watch Sal nod in confirmation, "—to hold this case for him, I suppose because he didn't want to lug it around all night." I made one of my famous leaps of deductive reasoning.

"Right," said Sal.

"The pharmacist didn't know what was in the case, but someone who did know decided to steal the case for the contents. Whoever that was also robbed the pharmacy and killed the only two people in the place at the time."

"Right again."

"I dunno, Sal, this has the smell of a mob deal and you know I stay away from anything connected to the mob."

"This is not a mob deal. If it was, they would have sent in a crew and cleaned it up long ago."

I pondered, something else I do well. "What am I doing here?"

"This is a very cold trail. My associates and I want to find the money. The cops want to find the killers. Help us both out." He spread his fat hands and then sucked in some more doughnut. More crumbs cascaded down his front. "You got a rep, you know. You find out stuff. You're pretty successful. People know you are a standup guy."

"You swear to me there is no mob connection?"

"On my mother's grave."

I didn't like the sound of that, but I said, "Okay, Sal, I'll look into it, but I swear to you, if I find a link to OC, I'm going to come after you. And I'll bail." Sure, I thought, if I was still alive after I tumbled to the connection. By that time, bailing out would not be an option. One thing that bothered me was the fire, just when Belassario was closing in on one of the Grand Pharmacy perps. Somebody he thought was involved in the robbery and murders. The other thing was, I did know Mordecai Marsh. Not well, but I knew him. If it was the same person, he was a relative of Catherine Mckerney. My lady love, Catherine Mckerney.

3

"Good morning—"

"—Star shine," I completed the line from the "Age of Aquarius," the 60's song about peace and love and sunshine for all, while walking down the hallway toward Catherine's office in her lush three-bedroom apartment, my second home. We'd exchanged keys in small ceremonies a few months earlier, so I found her in her usual attire, peering fixedly at her computer screen. The mid-morning sun streamed in the window, lovingly highlighting her smooth naked shoulders and breasts. My heart went bump bump bump. But it did that whenever I saw her even after just a few hours of absence, so that wasn't unusual.

She turned her head and bestowed on me one of her bright welcoming smiles. It was one of Catherine's endearing traits. Whenever I showed up, she gave every indication of genuine delight in my presence. I walked over and bestowed a kiss on her bare shoulder.

"What doing?"

"Reading my morning email, at the moment, today's digest from DorothyL."

"Anything good?"

"Almost always. We're having an interesting discussion on justice, punishment and vengeance right now."

"Vengeance is mine sayeth the Lord."

"Verily, you speak truth." Catherine tapped several keys and the screen changed to a pattern of shimmering lines and patterns. "What's up with you, Boy Scout?" She swiveled on her chair and looked up at me. "Oh my, I see you are heeled this morning."

Although she was comfortable, mostly, with my profession as a PI, she didn't like the weapons part of it. "I have reluctantly accepted a new charge. Have I ever told you about a man named Salvatore Belassario?"

She looked thoughtful for a moment and said, "No, I don't think so. Is he another one of your low-life cronies, or a police person?"

"The former, I'm afraid. With a name like that, what would you expect?"

Catherine stood, straightening her long, gorgeous legs and twined her bare arms around my neck. Then she leaned down and kissed me—she's several inches taller than I am, even in bare feet. The kiss was soft, thorough, and lingering. "Now there's a prejudicial statement," she said when we separated an inch or so.

"I know," I said. "But in this case there may be a kernel of truth to it. I don't really know if Sal is connected and there isn't any active organized crime in this area, but, there has always been talk."

"So, tell me about this Belassario person."

As we walked back down the hall to the master bedroom, I described the rotund Belassario and some of the street talk about his connections. "Did you see the news reports about the fire in Frogtown?"

Catherine winced. "Yes, the house fire where that man died?"

"Man? I don't know about any man, but it was terrible. I was there last night. They said five children might have died in the fire."

"No, my love, not five children. The children have been found safe. They were staying overnight at friends. But the body of an adult male, according to this morning's news, was found in the rubble. The odd thing is that it was an odd thing."

I suddenly felt a weight I hadn't known I was carrying lift from my shoulders. It was bad that anyone had died in the fire, but the news that the kids were safe was a great relief. "That's wonderful news. But why do you sense an oddity?"

Catherine was standing, naked except for her panties, looking into her commodious closet. Finally she selected a tan dress that complemented her hair and laid it out. I sat on the edge of her king-sized bed and watched her. I knew I would never tire of watching her dress—and undress, for that matter. Moving to a chest of drawers, she selected a filmy bra and a half-slip. "It was an odd thing because of what they didn't say. It's just a feeling I got, as if they already know something about the man or his death, but didn't want to tell us."

"It's early times. Autopsy and investigation will take a few days. The news people will ferret out the gory details."

"I wonder." She slipped into the bra and straightened, catching my eye. She winked and said, "You like?"

I nodded and smiled. "Oh yes, I like very much." Then I reclined and returned to my narration of the night's conversation with Sal. "Anyway, I've agreed to look into the Grand Pharmacy thing. There's a ton of money missing and two unsolved murders."

"But you don't like the connections your client may have. And this is why you are carrying that big gun on your hip?"

Normally I don't carry a weapon. They are a nuisance in most of my work and the weight of the .45 in its hip holster was a drag. I'd never found a shoulder holster that was comfortable and even in the winter I favor casual dress, so I often don't wear a jacket. Walking down the street in the summer with a shoulder holster over my shirt would, I assumed, cause mass consternation among passersby. It would call attention to yours truly, not a good thing in my profession. I was looking into getting something smaller and lighter. Even though, as a smaller than average person, when I brought out my large gat, it earned me instant respect.

Respectably dressed, Catherine took my hand and we headed into the living room, about to depart the premises for the world of commerce. I put my hand on her arm. She stopped and turned to face me. "Is there something else?"

"I'm afraid there is. The man who gave Sally the tip about Mr. Beechy, the many who died in the fire, was apparently Mordecai Marsh."

"My cousin? That Mordecai?"

I sighed. "I'm afraid so. I doubt there's more than one Mordecai Marsh in the whole state."

Catherine was silent for several minutes. Then she said, "Well, even third cousins ought to stay in touch. I could invite him to dinner or something. To meet you."

"I don't think so, although it's nice you offered. I'd rather you not go near him, at least not until after I get this thing sorted out."

She looked thoughtful and then nodded slowly. "All right, I respect your instincts, you know that." We left her apartment and descended to the garage. In our parting embrace I respected the wrinkle tendencies of her linen dress. Catherine drove off to see her broker in one of the downtown Minneapolis towers and to visit the school of massage therapy she owns where she keeps an office. I slid into my gracefully aging Ford and drove to the near Northeast side where I had my own office.

It isn't much, my office, but it's adequate for my needs. Exiting the elevator on the third floor I went to my door. The plain black lettering on the glass proclaimed SEAN SEAN LIMITED, INVESTIGATIONS.

My full name is Sean NMI Sean. My mother was not of Irish lineage. But she apparently had a quirky sense of humor which, according to some, I have inherited. Giving me the same first name as her last name and no middle name at all had been the sum total of her bequests. I never knew my father. About him, my mother had been remarkably reticent, unlike her knowledge and opinions—freely given—about almost everything else under the sun while I was growing up. As far as that went, I didn't have a whole lot of information about her side of the family, either.

When she'd taken up with my father and thus become pregnant, either before or right after their civil marriage in some city hall or other, she'd become estranged from her family. They hadn't liked my father, apparently, not that they'd ever met him, you understand. I guess they'd been right, because he'd departed the scene shortly after impregnating my mother. My mother, Grace, had once told me he'd been in the service, and had gone to war, or at least overseas, I wasn't sure which, and he had not returned to her after that. I had no emotional attachment to the man, but still ... sometimes I did wonder who he was or had been and where he might now be.

But I digress. My office consisted of a single room, furnished with a few necessaries. I went to the safe in the corner under the window and placed in it my gun and holster. It was a small safe I had recently acquired. It was so small, a couple of really well-developed musclemen could probably carry it right out the door, but it was all I could afford. Catherine had offered to buy me a serious safe. She had many more resources than I—stock portfolios, investment counselors, and attorneys, multiple, and she had a real safe built into one of the closet walls at her home.

I'd declined her offer, preferring that she bestow more personal gifts on me when the spirit moved. She understood that very well, which was only one of the things I loved about her. I kept almost nothing of value in my safe. But it seemed to add a certain aura to the office. Helped with client relations, apparently, even though I do almost no real business from my office.

I sat down in the old desk chair I have. It's one of those wooden jobs with the shaped arms and curved wooden slats for a back. It had creaky wheels and a grooved steel spindle in the center so I could adjust the seat up or down. Since I'm only five foot two, I have the seat up pretty high so I don't bang my chin on the desk top whenever I sit down. But that means I have to keep a small box under my desk to put my feet on. Otherwise my feet wouldn't reach the floor and I'd be swinging my legs back and forth like a little kid. I judged that wouldn't make a very good impression on clients. Not that many clients came to my office.

In spite of the "Limited" on my office door, I was what's called a small businessman, a sole proprietor. With a staff of one. Besides my desk and chair with it attendant footrest, and the aforementioned safe, there was an ancient green four-drawer file cabinet and beside that an ancient bentwood coat rack I'd found at a flea market.

A modern typewriter stand beside my desk held my computer terminal. One window was partially blocked by my new energy-efficient air conditioner. The walls were pale, pale yellow, the floors were bare wood and the telephone had three lines, one for the computer and two for me. That way, I could impress a client on the phone by shouting, off stage, as it were, 'get my attorney on two!' I could also get rid of an obnoxious caller by telling her I had an important call on my other line. I suppose I could say that even without the other line, but that would be fibbing, right?

So much for my office. I'd picked up the last edition of the Star-Tribune, locally known as the Strib. It's the larger of our two dailies, the other being the Saint Paul Pioneer Press. There aren't any afternoon papers. The Frogtown fire was lovingly detailed. I was pleased to see a sidebar that confirmed the TV news that the five children thought to have been lost in the fire had been out of the house and were safe. Other residents, save one, had also escaped.

The paper identified the deceased as George Beechy, a man who occasionally intersected with our local constabulary, but apparently not frequently and he wasn't a heavy hitter. The profile in the paper didn't fit someone who would be involved in a double murder and a cash-heavy robbery. Beechy, the paper informed me, had relatives in North Carolina.

4

I considered what I knew and decided to call my friend, Ramsey County assistant prosecutor, Jerry Ford, the ex-cop. He was not immediately available. I love it in detective movies and books when the detective always finds a parking place right where he needs it, always finds the police lieutenant ready to see him, and the attorney is never in court or conference when the detective calls. It saves a lot of time, of course, but it isn't very realistic.

I called another acquaintance of mine, this one a member of the St. Paul PD. Since I work in this bifurcated metropolitan area called the Twin Cities, or more formally, Saint Paul on the east and Minneapolis on the west, it's imperative for me to have contacts in both police departments. In fact, I have contacts in several suburbs as well. In Minneapolis, a longtime friend, detective Ricardo Simon, was my contact and occasional benefactor. In Saint Paul, I usually called on Lieutenant Daniel Brooks. Both men had long strong careers in police work and were known to other authorities in the numerous suburbs. There's a lot of competition for my kind of work, even if Minnesota has rather strict laws about who can become a licensed PI. So who you know and can rely on is important.

Anyway, I drove over to the main Saint Paul PD building just off the freeway and there was the Lieutenant, frowning over some of many papers piled on his desk. He waved me in when I rapped on his door. "Hey, my favorite snoop. What's happening?" We shook hands and he pointed me into a chair.

I glanced around. His office appeared to have been recently painted, one of those innocuous, pale institutional colors. The picture of his wife and daughter sat in the center of the credenza on his left. "I heard the news a while ago," I said. "About the fire and the dead guy. I was hoping you could give me more details."

"Sure, Sean. This is all on the public record, whether the stations use it or not. I can get you a copy of the release if you want it."

"Just give me the details, my friend, that's all."

Brooks opened a file folder and glanced at the press release on top. "Okay, the Arson Squad is looking into it. 'Fire of suspicious origins' is the phrase. In fact, we know a little more now. The fire was deliberately set. Actually, the place was firebombed. At least four Molotov cocktails were tossed into the main floor rooms."

"That's a lot of gas. I guess they wanted to make sure. Witnesses?" I asked.

"A neighbor heard the commotion and looked out her bedroom window which faces the street. She says she saw four or five people, men she's pretty sure, fighting over something in the side yard and then running away. At the same moment she saw and heard explosions inside the house."

"Any IDs? Does she know what they were fighting over?"

"Brooks consulted the file in his hand. "No and no. It was getting dark, you know, and she's elderly, with not great vision."

"Twilight. When did the fire start?"

"Call came in to 911 at nine-fifteen."

"So, Sally wasn't lying," I mused.

"Excuse me? You have something to contribute?"

"Sorry, Lieutenant." I shook my head. "Go on, please."

"By the time the first trucks arrived the place was fully engaged. These old houses, even rehabbed like this one, have a lot of dry wood in them. Plus, construction can leave voids or air spaces in the walls and ceilings that contribute to rapid spread of the fire. The residents were out and the Battalion commander decided their best move was to try to keep the fire from spreading to neighboring houses. They were successful and after about an hour and a half, the fire was brought under control. The place is a total loss, however. The

Red Cross is assisting the people who used to live there."

"All of them?"

"Sure, at least, all of them who have asked. At first it was feared there were children in the place. Residents said five kids lived with their mom in an upstairs apartment. They couldn't be found and for a while we thought we were going to have five dead kids. Since the place was firebombed, it would have been murder. Fortunately, the whole family was visiting relatives in Minneapolis. Lucky."

"So, tell me about the unlucky dead guy."

Brooks's pale gray eyes bored into mine. "What's your interest?"

I stared back from my light blue ones. I didn't want the cops involved in my part of the investigation, at least not until I had gotten disentangled from Sal Belassario and had determined how Catherine's cousin, Mordecai Marsh, fit into things.

"C'mon, Sean, give. Or are you going into the insurance investigation business?" Brooks knew that was unlikely.

"Okay, look. This is all very amorphous. I was asked—"

"By your client who shall remain unidentified for all the usual reasons." Brooks, ever alert, pounced.

"Naturally, but I think we can help each other out here if we keep up a rational relationship."

"Okay. Continue, if you will."

I nodded. "Thank you, sir. My client asked me to meet him at the address that burned. I did. He insisted that he only called me to be a witness when he talked to a resident of that address. It was supposed to be a quick nothing sort of a job. A couple of bucks. Not something I do very often except once in a while, for one or two special clients.

"But the place was burning. I hooked up with my client—"

"You and he met at the fire?" Brooks scribbled a note.

"Correct. And my client then informed me that he had wanted me to be a witness to his meeting with a resident of the place, a man named George Beechy."

"The dead man."

"So I'm given to understand. The guy turns up dead in a felony fire which is murder and there is, apparently, something else about his death that has Saint Paul's finest bobbing and weaving. So here

I am, the seeker of truth, seeking answers."

"Though not just truth, I take it."

"Well," I acknowledged, "along with truth I'll happily accept speculations, observations, opinions and even a clue or two."

"I want to know why you think there's something special about the tragic death of this citizen. George Beechy."

"The eagle eye of my lady friend detected a certain shift in attitude in the video clips she saw on the TV news this morning, when reporters began to ask about Citizen Beechy. That was even before I told her about my sojourn to Frogtown. Could the identification be in question?"

Brooks grinned briefly, showing his white teeth. "Your lady friend has been reading too many detective novels. Definitely George Beechy. He died in a deliberately caused fire, after receiving several blunt force blows from assailants unknown. Because the fire was deliberate, it may be a question of murder. Beechy may have died before the fire reached him. He was a 40-year-old male Caucasian. It's Beechy, all right. He was a heavy dude, had a tattoo MOTHER on one shoulder and part of a finger missing from his left hand. He lived in that house for eight or nine years, and was apparently unmarried. At least, he lived alone for all those years, so far as we've determined. There are no known local relatives, although we are still checking. The investigation is continuing on several fronts. End of story." Brooks leaned back and smiled.

"See, now, Lieutenant, you're doing it." I smiled. "If that isn't an official brush-off, I don't know what is."

"What? What are you talking about?" Brooks spread his hands, palms up. Tried and failed to look innocent.

"Your voice changed, your delivery changed. All of sudden this wall appears between us. What's goin' on, Dan? Who is this Beechy? The TV did mention he'd had a few minor run-ins with the law."

Brooks smiled at me again. He had a nice smile. "I doubt the TV report said anything about his record."

Ever vigilant myself, I pounced. "So he did have a record. C'mon Dan, give."

"He had a short, very minor record. D&D, caused a fuss at a

grunge bar over on University, known to hang out with fringe characters, et cetera, et cetera. I don't think there's anything here for you."

I nodded and stood up, stretching. Brooks' side chair wasn't very comfortable, and I could feel tension rippling across my shoulders. "I know I don't want to go there, but I have to. Tell you what. You give me what you develop and I'll retaliate in kind."

"Retaliate is right." Brooks grimaced. He hesitated. He thought about it and didn't want to do it, but in the end he knew I might unearth some useful information that would advance whatever investigation they were running on this Beechy fellow. Even if it was just corroboration from another source, it would help.

"Okay, Sean. Beechy was last in North Carolina where he was involved in a real estate scam. Before that he has some smalltime stuff in California. The real estate scam sounds very much like similar stuff going on in Minneapolis. You probably read about it. Also, there are questions about where Beechy's body was found."

I raised my eyebrows.

"Beechy was badly beaten about the upper part of his body and one arm and one leg were broken. We'll know more after the autopsy, but it was very clear he was beaten up just before the fire."

"So you think what the woman saw from her window might have been the fire bombers beating on George Beechy?"

"Correct."

"Probably was, in fact, and Beechy was maybe not inside when the place was firebombed, but his body was found inside, correct?"

"Correct again."

"So how'd he get inside? Why would he, if he was that badly beaten, with a house going up in flames, go back inside? Where exactly was he found, by the way?"

"He was in the kitchen at the back of the house, lying in the door from the kitchen to the back stairs."

"Stairs which go where?"

"Up to his room on the second floor above the kitchen, down to the basement. It seems possible he was trying to get to his room to try to get something. Something important," Brooks said.

"Any idea what that might have been?"

"Nope." Brooks shrugged. His apartment is a total loss."

"Odd. Circumstances raise more questions."

Brooks shrugged. "Maybe you have some answers?"

I sat down again. "Not to those questions, but I may have some information that will help. There is a small-time scuffler on the ragged edge of the law in Minneapolis. His name is Mordecai Marsh. I think detective Ricardo Simon can help you there. He's a third cousin or something, of Catherine."

"Ah, I see."

"From his, Mordecai's, mouth to my client's ear came word about the aforesaid George Beechy. The word was Beechy's location and possible involvement in a most heinous crime here in Saint Paul."

Brooks leaned forward and drilled me again with his eyes.

"The Grand Pharmacy robbery," I said.

"Salvatore Belassario," he hissed at me.

5

After more conversation with Dan Brooks, I left the PD building. The sun was seriously heating up the day. It felt good on my shoulders while I walked up the street after the over-cooled air conditioning of police headquarters. I suppose it helped when they were sweating suspects in the holding cells.

Brooks told me that a couple of local gangs were most likely involved in some of the real estate scams then going on in Minneapolis. The cops were currently operating on the theory that a rival gang may have cashed in Beechy's chips, possibly in a turf war of some kind.

Except, I thought.

Except that the nice folks ripping off banks, S&Ls and ordinary citizens in such scams were generally non-violent. And except that Brooks hadn't told me everything he knew, or thought he knew. And why was Beechy found in the house, if he'd been beaten almost to death on the lawn? I speculated that Beechy had been trapped outside his house and beaten at the same moment the Molotov cocktails had been tossed. That meant the house was starting to burn while the fire bombers were working over Beechy. The cocktail throwers had then split from the scene, leaving Beechy on the lawn with a broken arm and leg and multiple contusions. I figured the thugs had miscalculated, they hadn't intended to kill Beechy, just mess him up. That could mean they were trying to send a message, or they had to split because the fire spread too fast. For me, the burning question was, why had he dragged himself back into the house? Or, had someone else dragged the man inside? That didn't seem likely from what I now knew, but I'd have to check it out. If I could. There was yet another possibility. That it wasn't retaliation at all, the was a possibility that the missing cocktail throwers were trying to beat some information out of poor Mr. Beechy.

If Beechy had gone back under his own power, considering the shape he was in, the obvious question was why? The cops knew, but couldn't yet prove, Beechy had been involved with real estate scams. Sal had information from somewhere that Beechy might have been involved in the six-year-old Grand Pharmacy case. The cops knew this also but were keeping that info close to their collective vests. All very tenuous. I decided to concentrate first on Beechy and real estate. It was fresh, a more solid lead, and I thought subconsciously, unlikely to have anything to do with Sal's mob friends. This way I could assure Sal I was working on his problem, while staying at arms length from organized crime, and the robbery, for as long as possible.

I walked the four blocks to Mickey's Diner for a succulent fried ham sandwich, some fries, and random conversation about the crowded field of democratic candidates for governor, the current state of the stock market and the Vikings' prospects for the fall. Mickey's Diner, squeezed onto a tiny corner of land in downtown Saint Paul next to a big insurance company, was a 1930's-style railroad car-diner. Mickey's was bright yellow with a flamboyant neon sign on its red roof and neon advertising in several windows. I didn't believe it had ever actually been rolling stock, but it was a nice fiction.

Mickey's attracted a noontime crowd of wildly varying types. It was nationally known, not only for its food, but also for the fact of its preservation by the upscale movers and shakers of local city government and business. That was one of the differences between St. Paul and Minneapolis. St. Paul preserved the old; Minneapolis tore down and built new. Then they said oh, sorry, we probably shoulda kept that. Like the late lamented Metropolitan Building, and the Times Arcade. But there were some signs that rambunctious attitude was changing.

I ate my sandwich elbow to elbow with an insurance executive on one side and a well-known tax attorney on the other. We didn't have too much to say to each other. After lunch I hopped on the freeway and whisked over the river and through the urban canyons to Kenwood and my lady love's apartment. My second home.

It was cool and restful and I helped myself to a T n'T. Tanqueray and Tonic. Then I sank onto the big comfortable couch, or divan, if you prefer, and cogitated, whilst waiting for Catherine to return from her daily labors.

"Ah, light of my life," I said when she came through the door. "I could be inveigled into broiling a nice steak and—" she stopped me with a kiss, leaning over the back of the couch.

"Hm, it tastes like you've already had your protein for the day. I have an alternative. We have the makings for a nice big salad. I'm sure you can use the greens, and I'll even throw in some mock crab. Deal?"

"How can I refuse? I know your salads."

"Good," she said. "Make me a drink while I shed these clothes and we'll share our day in the kitchen."

And so it was.

The night lights of the city bloomed through the tall bedroom windows of the apartment. I was lying face down on CM's portable massage table. I finished revealing what I had learned that day while Catherine's agile and educated fingers probed muscles and tendons in my shoulders and neck. Her skill as a massage therapist was well known in several upscale circles among those of Minneapolis who were so inclined. Her turn under my own less skillful hands would come later. She was gradually instructing me in some of her extensive knowledge of human anatomy and massage technique so I could reciprocate.

"So, that's the story so far. Lieutenant Brooks is not telling all, Beechy is still a cipher and the questions continue to mount." Catherine lightly whacked me on the ass to signal she was through. I leaned to one side and captured one of her hands, placing a quick kiss in her palm. She wiped her forehead and hands with a small towel and went out of the room.

"It appears you need some more background on this Beechy person," she said when I rejoined her in the bedroom.

"That is affirmative. I have no contacts in either South Carolina, where he last lived, or in California, where he has a small-time criminal record. And since my client doesn't care about those past locations, he isn't going to pay me to do that kind of background check."

"Even though it might help you solve the case?"

"Pity the poor P.I.," I said, "forever saddled with clients of limited vision."

"I bet I have some contacts in both states."

"Really?"

"Sure, and what's more I bet they'll help you—me actually—if I ask real nice."

"What kind of contacts? I wasn't' aware you lived in either place."

"Oh, I haven't, but remember the power of the Internet."

"Unnnh," I grunted. I have a computer and an Internet connection from my office but I am somewhat retrograde when it comes to the use of computer technology in my business. I can store stuff, copy it, even use my faxmodem if the occasion demands. That's about it, however. When something goes wrong, or the machine stalls, I throw up my hands, yell at it and call somebody. Besides, most of my business is collecting information and ideas on the street, face to face, as it were. I need to be able to assess the nuances of body language, glances, voice tremors. All right, so I use the telephone a lot. But I haven't yet succumbed to the cell phone craze. Now I waited for Catherine to explain.

"I'm a member of an on-line discussion group called DorothyL, remember?"

"Yeah, named for that woman who wrote a lot of popular classical mystery novels back in the thirties, right?" I knew about Dorothy L Sayers all right.

"There are around three thousand members scattered all over the world. We're a pretty bright group with lots of varied experience and I'll bet you if I ask someone will know how to get the information you need."

"I'll take the bet. But it seems like a pretty public way to do research."

"What? You think I don't know how to be discreet? Besides, I won't ask for the details right up front."

"Okay, I'm persuaded. How do we work it?"

"Come."

We rose from the bed. Catherine slung one arm around my waist and cupped her fingers over my right buttock. We went down the short hall, past the small Miro sketch hanging on the wall, to the third bedroom, the one that served as her office. Her computer was never off so it took a mere nudge of the mouse to bring the seventeen-inch monitor to glowing life.

"Sit," she said, pointing to the heavy, padded, executive-style chair in front of the computer table.

"Sit? I'm not doing this. I'll make too many mistakes, even if you're right here."

"Never mind that. Just sit." So I sat. Catherine then joined me, sitting on my lap with her fingers resting on the keyboard.

"Comfy?" she asked, wiggling her bottom. Her wiggles caused the light shift she was wearing to slide a little further up her thighs.

Not bad. I could get used to this. I swung my feet, which were a couple of inches off the floor, like a kid who's been turned loose in his favorite candy store. In a way I had. I cocked my head to one side so I could see the monitor around her shoulder, inhaled the sweet muskiness of her body. My lady used very little scent, and then mostly when she was hard at work doing therapeutic massage. I liked her that way.

"I don't remember any of my college instructors acting like this. Now what?" I murmured, swiping at her ear lobe with my tongue.

She wiggled her bottom again and said, "First we'll compose the question. I think we'll make it fairly comprehensive and innocuous at this point." Her fingers began a rapid tattoo on the keyboard.

"Um hum," I said. I'd discovered that if I let my arms down normally, with just a slight inward crook of my wrists, my hands landed gently on Catherine's upper thighs. Her warm, bare, thighs. I began a little gentle massage of my own, more a caress, I guess you'd say.

"Here. Try this, Sean."

I looked past her at the screen where she'd written that she was engaged in some research for a friend writing a book. Was there anyone on the list who could answer questions about criminal procedures in California and South Carolina?

"Seems okay." My attention was drifting to the sensations I was causing myself while my fingertips brushed the soft skin of Catherine's thighs.

"Slow down, tiger," she said, giving me a little bump. I lifted my hands from her hips.

Immediately, she took her hands from the keyboard and replaced my fingers on her thighs. "I didn't say stop, just slow down."

We chewed over the words for a while, eliminated any reference to writing a book and saved the message. "Now what?" I asked.

"Now, we send it off via my connection to the server in Ohio. In mere minutes, unless there's a glitch in the system, my message will appear in all those thousands of inboxes, or later on the daily digests of the message traffic. I'll be very surprised if there aren't some responses right soon after that."

"Sounds good." By now I'd found other soft places for my fingers to do the walking and it was becoming an effort for either of us to stay focused on the task at hand.

"Mmmm," Catherine murmured. "You do know how to give a girl pleasure, my love." With a few swift strokes she sent the message off, and disconnected from her email program. Then she twisted half around and placed her soft lips on mine in a long, languorous kiss. When we broke, she looked into my eyes from a couple of inches away and said. "Let's remove ourselves to a more comfortable location."

And so we did.

6

Neither Catherine or I had anything pressing the next day, so we had a leisurely breakfast. After that we went back to bed for a while. About ten, Catherine rolled over and placed her nose against mine. She said, "Let's look at today's email." We rose and covered our naked bodies.

Her computer obligingly revealed that the day's DL digest had arrived during the night and just as she'd predicted, there, toward the bottom of a substantial set of messages were her questions. There were even a couple of answers. Two suggested that county tax record offices in South Carolina would be good places to start.

From that information, I made a few telephone calls and soon learned some interesting facts about George Beechy's activities in Columbia, South Carolina. It was mostly petty stuff, but I was able to confirm that the man had dropped out of sight right around the time he was reported to have shown up in Saint Paul. We also heard from the other coast.

A woman in California, a court reporter, sent word that she freelanced in the system and could probably get whatever records Catherine might need. She explained that technically, once a case was concluded, a court reporter's records could be sold by the CR as work product.

"Obviously we don't know this woman, but I don't have any other contacts in California. Send her a message and ask her to give us a fee to do a little research for us."

The Case of the Stolen Case

Right after lunch we got another electronic response and a telephone number. I called her and we made a verbal deal. Hell, if it turned out she was incompetent, I could still hire an agency out of the telephone book.

But she wasn't incompetent. As it turned out, Annie—spelled i.e., no y—Flynn, was a paralegal working in a law firm in Glendale and attending law school part-time. She had a nice soft drawl. "Since the questions were posted by your lady friend, Catherine, per'aps I should be discussing this with her?"

Catherine got on an extension and broke in to assure Annie—no 'y'—Flynn that she'd been acting as my agent. I explained to the young sounding woman what I needed, and what expenses she could charge me for. We struck a deal. Catherine and I spend the rest of the day having a tasty and healthful lunch, having tasty and pleasurable sex, and then a tasty but not as healthy dinner at a good Minneapolis restaurant, the only one in town that came close to reminding me of the long-gone Charlie's Cafe Exceptionale. The one with pristine white table cloths, real silver utensils, prompt and discreet service from a formally dressed and gloved wait-staff. The one with subdued romantic lighting and an hors d'oeuvere tray to die for.

We decided to stay in Minneapolis for the night. In my closet—yes I had a closet in Catherine's extensive suite of rooms—I found an old sweatshirt and jeans I'd forgotten about. Living out of two homes, mine in Roseville and hers in Minneapolis was an interesting experience in the clothing division. It was interesting in other ways, too.

Catherine didn't like guns. She owned a small one and kept it in the safe built into one of her closets—I wasn't sure which closet, but I tried to respect her wishes on the matter and almost never carried a weapon to her place. My home in Roseville was a different story. In my years as a private investigator, I've never been particularly reticent about my address or my home telephone number, so I keep guns around. But whenever she came to my house, CM's nose wrinkled. She smelled my guns.

The next morning I called the Ramsey County Attorney's Office and connected with Jerry Ford. He could see me at ten. The Court

House in Saint Paul houses a lot of civic functions belonging to both the city of Saint Paul and to the county. It's a thirty-story tower set back a block from the river bluff. Maybe the builders were afraid the bluff might crumble under the weight. Or maybe the railroad would have objected. The exterior is sort of rose colored granite. The place was built in the twenties, and it strongly reflects the style of the times. Art Deco it's called.

Ford's offices were on the fourth floor. The bank of six elevators was grouped on the Kellogg Boulevard end of the big lobby, but I parked at a meter on third. I figured I'd be in there at least an hour, so I fished three quarters out of the dust and detritus-collecting cup holder built into the dashboard and plugged the meter. If it took longer, I'd need to come out and feed the meter more quarters. As I listened to the meter grind up my coins, I made a mental note to keep track of all my expenses. Normally on a case I just made reasonable estimates of piddling miscellaneous costs like parking when I submitted a bill to a client. But I knew from past not-particularly pleasant experiences that Sal Belassario was a stickler for details. His suspicious nature naturally assumed everyone else was just like him—fudging every possible nickel and dime out of every deal.

The many double glass doors to the Court House on the Third Street side greeted me with a whoosh and a small blast of frigid air when I hauled one open. Inside I was confronted with a huge space. The high-ceilinged lobby stretched up three stories into the darkness. I realized that although I'd been in the court house many times before, this was one of the few times I had entered through the north entrance, so the memorial lobby was not familiar ground.

Several elaborate brass and glass chandeliers, reflective of the period, hung overhead in the gloom. The lobby floor and most of the walls I could see were made of slabs of polished black marble. It was a very impressive space, but dark. Clients and workers scurried back and forth. Hard footfalls echoed around me. My rubber soles merely squeaked softly. At each level there was a balcony. I could see that office doors opened off the balconies. There was a stairwell at my left and right sides. I wondered how far up and down the stairs went.

Approximately two blocks away, directly in front of me was an enormous, imposing pale stone statue. The head of the statue brushes the ceiling. I have no idea how tall the thing is or how much it weighs. What am I, the tourist bureau? The statue is carved in a representation of what white folks in the twenties thought Indians looked like. I have no idea what Native American people thought of the statue, except I recalled they changed the name of the thing some years ago because it was felt the original name sent an incorrect message about native peoples. I knew it was also irreverently referred to as 'Onyx John.' I guess it's carved from onyx. Probably not. At one time city officials gave small cheesy plastic replicas to visiting dignitaries. I don't know if they still do that.

Anyway, I walked all the way to the statue and executed a curve around the rotating base of the statue and went to the other side, the side where the polished brass elevators were. The place was renovated in the nineties but they made a wise decision to retain as much of the original materials and design as possible. I could feel the eyes of the uniformed guard on me as I inserted myself into the gaggle of folks waiting for the next ride.

Hey I was normally dressed, wasn't I? I had on a lightweight dark blue jacket over tan wash pants that were reasonably unwrinkled. They even had a pleat. Maybe it was the bright red high top tennies with the white soles. They're almost the only shoe I wear. The elevator came and raised me to the fourth floor where I entered a light filled reception area.

"Hey, Sean," said Jerry when I entered his office.

"Hey yourself." I stretched my hand and we shook for a moment. He was standing in shirtsleeves, suit coat hanging from a rack behind him, wide elaborately tooled leather suspenders a sharp contrast to his white shirt. He had a big smile on his face. Jerry's desk was stacked with files, I assumed of cases he was involved in. I saw the head of a carved blackened cane hanging from a partially opened drawer beside his right hand. It was the same Black Walnut stick I'd handed him the day, six years earlier, he'd been released from the hospital. The bullet that shattered his knee one night, the same night as the Grand Pharmacy robbery, hadn't been very big. It was just a .22 short, but it passed through John's knee and did such damage that eventually he'll need reconstructive surgery again in order to ever walk without a pronounced limp and the help of the cane.

"So, Sean, how's tricks?"

"Tricks. I can still do a pretty good half-gainer off the board at the Y. Or so Catherine assures me. But that's about it. How goes it with you? I keep hearing good things about you. Rumor has it the County Attorney considers you a prime candidate for the top job when she retires."

Ford shrugged. "Well, you know it's an elective position and I've never been active in the party. Are we just gonna chit-chat or have you a more serious purpose for being here?"

I sat down and shrugged, "Haven't changed, have you? Always cut right to the chase." Until he'd been wounded, Jerry was on a steep track which would have led to a high administrative position with the Saint Paul PD, if not the top job. That small piece of copper-jacketed lead had sent him to a different place. "I'm looking for some information relating to an old case."

"The Grand Pharmacy murder/robbery, right?"

"And in addition to knowing which case, I suppose you are gonna tell me why?"

"Sure. Let me make it easy on you. Sal Belassario hired you to help him with a certain George Beechy, the same man who was killed during the fire in Frogtown a couple of nights ago. Beechy lived in the torched building and may be linked to the killing of the two people in the Grand Pharmacy."

Ford stopped and I waited. After a minute, I said, "And?"

"And what is it you want to know?"

I thought it curious he hadn't mentioned the two mil, supposedly copped from the store, but maybe he didn't know about the money. "Results of the autopsy?"

Ford looked down at the open file on his desk and picked out a piece of paper. "According to the ME, he died of smoke inhalation, lack of oxygen, and was observed to have multiple abrasions, contusions, and broken limbs. A good deal of blunt force trauma" He dropped the report back into the file and looked at me.

"Where was the body found?"

John nodded as if confirming something he'd expected and leaned back in his padded chair. "Beechy's body was found face up on the kitchen floor, his upper torso through a door that leads to the back stairs. The stairs go up to higher floors and down to the basement. It looks as though he wanted to get to his room, but then tried to escape the fire by heading toward the back door."

"He was attacked in the side yard, am I right?"

Ford nodded.

"So you think he then went into the house and tried to return to his room, even with a broken leg and arm, in a desperate attempt to get something from his room. Right?"

"Right."

"That something being—"

"No clue."

"Speculate."

Ford smiled. "Okay, I speculate he had some information in his room, perhaps a safe deposit box key. Maybe a family keepsake. Or, even a picture of his girlfriend. Sean, how the hell do I know? It happens that Beechy's room was totally destroyed."

"Really?" Was this a significant clue? I readied myself to pounce.

"Now don't get all eager on me." Ford knew the signs. "We assume the door to the back stairs was closed. By opening the door off the kitchen, Beechy created a chimney which sucked the fire into the kitchen and up those stairs more quickly than might otherwise have happened."

I scratched my nose. "The result was that the kitchen and Beechy's room, in fact pretty much the entire rear corner of the house, was gutted. Jerry, why do you think Beechy, already suffering grievous injury dragged himself back into the burning building?"

"Like I said, he must have wanted something from his room. On the other hand, we think it's possible Beechy got into the stair well and then tried to make it outside to save himself when the fire took off."

I got up and said, "Thanks for the info. Still lots of questions, don't you think?"

Ford nodded. "A few, but there always are. Take care. Thanks for the invitation to the party."

"Glad you can come. See you tomorrow night." I left thinking, Jerry didn't seem to have much more than the PD, unless they were carefully coordinating what was being left out. And yeah, there were several more questions. I'd work on those, particularly the question of why George Beechy died in the kitchen of his residence. Up or down, that was the question. Brooks figured Beechy was heading for his room to get something, Ford thought he might have been heading back outside to save himself. What about the basement? Me, I was keeping an open mind.

7

It was early afternoon when I rolled in to my suburban driveway. My driveway is located half a block south of County D on the north and east side of the central business district of Minneapolis. My paved driveway, wide enough for two cars side by side, runs right up to my single car garage. Since I only have the one car, that's all right until I try to sell to some upscale comer with two vehicles. But there are advantages to this place that might outweigh the single-car garage situation. Like lots of trees and almost no grass to mow. What I have here is a well-maintained, ordinary split-level with three bedrooms, two baths, a big hot tub in a glass-enclosed atrium, and a loaded slightly shortened double barreled shotgun over the door in the front closet.

There is also a pretty nice intruder-detection system around the outside. The security people I'd called in after a certain incident the previous year had recommended grubbing out all the ferns and bushes around the house--apparently they'd never heard of foundation plantings--losing several trees in my personal forest, and putting bars on the windows. Given my profession and the likelihood that more and more thugs and assorted bad guys would learn where I lived, the suggestions weren't out of line. But I just couldn't see myself living out my days in what amounted to a self-selected prison. So we compromised. An electronic web was woven around my abode and connected to various lasers, lights and motion sensors. They were all arranged to provide advance warning of intruders into the property whenever the system was activated. With the exception of the roof.

I figured if the Libyans or other gonifs wanted to send in a night helicopter assault team to break through my fiberglass shingles and sheet-rocked ceilings, they could have me. The system was adjusted to respond to critters larger than a small bear or a greyhound. I figured anything of lesser size, my killer cats would take care of. I live there alone, mostly. No wife, no children, no parents, no girlfriends, except for Catherine now, an arrangement I hoped would become permanent. I'm referring to Catherine. Not a verbally expressed hope, you understand. We were a tight couple, but I hadn't detected any desires on her part to legalize the bond between us. I once considered getting a dog. That was after I saw a friend's Springer. Buddy, the dog, not my friend, responded to odd commands. My friend would call, "Secure the perimeter," and the dog would run around the outside of the house several times. But I decided a dog was more than I was prepared to take on. Especially given my life style. Somewhat similar to previous relations with women. There were a few who'd thought my lifestyle was interesting and romantic, until I would not show up for a date or occasionally arrive still smelling faintly of the county morgue.

I slid the Taurus into the garage and tripped off the security system switch, a pressure plate I'd had installed under the sheetrock in my garage and in a couple of other places near outside doors. The switches were designed so they only turned the system off. That way I could deactivate the system when I drove in without having to leg it up to one of the touchpads at the front or deck doors before the timer sent the scramble signal to the local cop house. The special switches were concealed so bad guys couldn't subvert the system.

I opened the doors and windows and made sure the screens were secure. We hadn't had many bugs, but living as I did in a small forest, mosquitoes were usually present in large numbers. Forest or not, I am basically an urban dweller. I never cared much for the out of doors as a place to be, and I wanted the house as bug-free as possible for the small gathering I was hosting this evening. From my basement freezer, I pulled out ice cream and pizzas. A nearby deli would deliver several relish and *hors d'oeuvres* trays at the appropriate time. The party was intended to introduce Catherine to my fairly narrow circle of acquaintances and friends. By the nature of my work, I didn't have a large circle of intimates in or outside the business. But I did want several people to meet my companion, now that we appeared to be going down a longer road together. Hand and hand, as it were. Catherine had offered to help prepare some of the food, but I had demurred. I didn't want her to have any responsibility for the evening's festivities. What if nobody but me liked her? Nah. Not a chance of that. It was more likely I'd be busy fending off the lechers hitting on her and trying to entice her away from me.

I'd invited the usual crowd of suspects to this very casual affair. My long-time friend Perry-the-film-maker and his new bride would be there. So would Erin, the feisty Irish landscape designer. Recently divorced, she'd asked if she could bring a companion. I'd assured her that was fine, but later it occurred to me that if she brought her nubile daughter, we could have a hormonal riot. Daughter Jessica was nearly nineteen chronologically and rather inexperienced due to her mother's watchful eye, but considerably more mature in other attributes. To say she seemed usually to dress in a most provocative manner was an understatement. A vast understatement.

I checked my hot tub to be sure it was okay and then laid out stuff on the dining room table. I always made sure the hot tub was ready. Whenever I invited people to the house, someone always asked if it was up and running. Almost no one ever went in, you understand, but they always asked. Then I swept the day's accumulation of leaves and twigs and fallen bird seed off the deck. About that time Catherine arrived and parked in the drive against the garage door. I nipped upstairs to change into jeans and a summer-weight pullover.

The bell rang and the couple from the very end of the block walked in. Gene and Jean were born-again Christians who'd started out in Georgia as Southern Baptists. They almost always showed up at these rare affairs I threw, even though they heartily disapproved of smoking, drinking, coarse language and almost anything else that went on at my parties. I never entirely understood why they came, except that we were neighbors.

Who is that just flaunting it through the door?" Catherine's breath was warm on my ear.

"What?" I turned to glance toward the front of the place. Several of my immediate neighbors arrived in a group. I always invite the neighbors, both as a means to deflect complaints about late night noise, but also because we've always looked out for each other in this piece of suburbia. Besides, I truly liked them. Most of them.

Widower Ed Wheeler came in the back way. Our yards adjoined. He always had this grim expression on his face and walked as if he was wading through a huge pile of mashed potatoes. He was dressed in his usual dress shirt and snugged up tie. I think he mowed his lawn in a shirt and tie.

The crowd rearranged itself to accommodate new arrivals, and I glimpsed the object of CM's comment, the flaming red hair of Erin Anderson. Beside her was her daughter Jessica, nearly not wearing a tight black scoop-necked top that left no doubt she was unencumbered by anything so mundane as a bra. The black top contrasted nicely with her smooth, peaches and cream Irish complexion. The rest of her was clad in tight black pants and sandals with small heels. Her mother wore a bright green blouse and slim blue jeans, in keeping with the casual nature of the affair.

Bob Whitaker, looking dapper per usual and carrying what he called his dress-up cane limped through the door. I pressed a small glass of Glen Livet into his free hand. "John, how've you been since last we talked? Glad you could make it."

"Thanks for inviting me. When you have a free moment, I'd like a quiet word." I nodded, wondering what he wanted and then was pulled away by someone looking for ice to refill the depleted ice bucket.

By the time Ricardo Simon, the Minneapolis Police Homicide detective and his wife arrived, the party was in full and raucous swing.

"You are looking well, Mr. Simon," said Catherine when I guided her close enough to him that we could carry on some kind of conversation. I raised one eyebrow at him.

"Yes, sir, quite dashing, Mr. Simon," I chimed in. "Are you two by any chance already acquainted?"

The Case of the Stolen Case

Simon smiled and wiped his forehead with a bright white handkerchief. The temperature continued to rise from all the hot air being wafted about. "We are, as it happens." He smiled at her. "We met about a year ago, at the school. I was doing a license check and as soon as I discovered you were legit, I brought Sue in for a little help with her back."

Catherine nodded and took her hand. Sue Kelso continued to use her professional name in her accounting business. She was Simon's wife and it must have been right about the time she was due to give birth to the twins that she'd had some sessions with Catherine. Our conversation was interrupted by another casual friend, Dusty Larson. Dusty was a stripper, who usually worked out of town. I'd helped her with a little problem one year when she'd been unable to convince a would-be pimp that she "wasn't that kind of woman." She was, however, some kind of woman. Over six feet tall, she'd studied classical ballet and trained in modern dance as well. She sported a pile of flaming orange hair that clashed with Erin's. Dusty had a slender, hard body that barely jiggled at all when she moved. She was short-bodied with long gorgeous legs concealed this night under a spectacular ankle-length variegated silk skirt that swirled enticingly when she moved, and an abbreviated deep-blue top that was probably the upper half of a bikini bathing suit.

There were twenty or so people sitting or lounging around the place, drinking my wine and scarfing up food when Catherine leaned against my back and murmured, "Well, how's it going, mine host?"

"Pretty well, don't you think?"

"Yes indeed. I'm pleased to meet these friends of yours. Everyone seems to be having a good time. How are you getting along?"

"Just great." I glanced around the dining room. "Would you intervene with Erin and Dusty? I sense a certain tension developing."

Dusty had attached herself to Erin's daughter, Jessica. The pair was leaning against the end of the fireplace and Dusty had draped one arm over Jessica's bare shoulders so her hand swung dangerously close to Jessica's cleavage. Jessica looked enthralled with whatever Dusty was murmuring to her. Erin looked less than pleased. I headed for Dusty while Catherine took Erin's arm and drew her away.

"Jessica, will you excuse us for a moment? I need a word with Dusty here." We walked a few steps away.

"What?" demanded Dusty.

"Jessica's mother appears to have figured you out and was about to come after you with that wine bottle she's clutching."

"Now, Sean, you know I wouldn't try anything, especially in your home."

"I know that and you know that, but Erin doesn't. In fact, why don't you just dance around and have a little chat with her? Relieve her mind a little." Dusty grinned and pecked me on the cheek. Then she went after Catherine and Erin.

By now, people had started to drift out and the party was taking its natural course, winding down. Someone found my CD collection of blues pieces and selected a Lady Day album and then turned down the volume. The party segued into that early morning kind of sleepy, drifting mode, of small groups and couples talking earnestly in corners and sprawled on the carpet. The noise level gradually diminished and a few people carried paper plates and plastic glasses to the kitchen and the door opened and closed more frequently as guests made their slow departures.

I prowled through the house and found Bob Whitaker sitting in a corner deep in intense conversation with Ed Wheeler. Ed rose as I approached and shook Bob's hand. Then he turned to me. His face twitched in what I always took for a smile and he clapped me on the arm. "Good time, Sean, good time. I must be going now. Have an early date tomorrow." He nodded at us and waded across the room to the back door and disappeared.

"Bob," I said, "you wanted to have a word, to tell me a tale?"

"Sean, I'm concerned. Word is you're involved in something that could turn awkward."

"I am? Can't think what it could be."

"I can't say much because we have an open investigation going." That told me something right there, as John well knew. "Just let me say, you and Sally B ought to be careful. Watch your backs, as they say." He rose with the help of his cane and smiled briefly. "Thanks for inviting me. It was fun. You have some interesting friends." He went toward the front door then and let himself out. I stood with the grace notes of Billie Holiday in my ears and watched him go. The warning was clear, but where was the threat coming from?

No one had even asked about the hot tub, much less taken advantage. By two-thirty, the guests had departed and Catherine had gone off to our big bed in the corner bedroom. I was still wired from all the activity and decided a short walk in the cooling summer night was in order. It was something I did frequently, at least three seasons of the year.

The city created a walking path that began only a block from my house. I slipped into my shorts and nipped out the door. The path makes a nice fifteen-minute walk through the woods that line Langton Lake, a shallow pond of unremarkable character. Walking, particularly at night, lets me wind down, get a little exercise and sometimes helps me get my thoughts in order.

The night was dark and soft and I was feeling very good. Ten minutes into my walk, I encountered a new section of the path that was being dug out. Apparently, an ordinary gravel path wasn't civilized enough for the city, so pavement was being laid down. I stepped off the harder surface down a foot or so onto the trenched portion. It was very dark and the bushes and trees formed a solid barrier between me and the nearest house a block further on. Around me, the night critters sang their cacophonous off key songs. As I passed a large basswood—that's a tree—I heard a snap just off the trail. I paused. Nothing else, except for the hum of a mosquito that made itself known in my left ear. I took another step and this time, the sound I heard was not a twig snapping. It definitely was mechanical and not of the natural order of things.

What it was, was the sound of the slide on an automatic weapon being pulled back and released. It's the action that loads a bullet into the firing chamber. I stopped again.

"Mr. Sean."

The voice was low and firm. Authoritative. It came from behind the Basswood tree. I looked in that direction, dimly made out the texture of the tree trunk.

"Mr. Sean, please do not make any abrupt moves."

I felt the nudge of a gun barrel in the small of my back. It was just a touch and then withdrawn. So I knew whoever held the gun had stepped back in the soft dirt of the path, no doubt out of reach of my hands.

"What do you want?" I figured whomever had accosted me, with at least one companion, wasn't going to identify himself, so why ask?

The voice of a different person, a few steps away said, "You've had a very nice party, introduced Ms. Mckerney to friends, and even to some important people. Let's not spoil things with a rash move. I'd hate your party to end with a bullet in your spine."

Yeah, me too, I thought. "All right. What do you want?" I had a sense I could hear breathing, or anyway, a feeling of at least one, possibly two, other bodies close behind me. If I was right, neither was the man doing the talking. I figured I wasn't about to be shot, but the owner of the voice knew entirely too much about me and my business. Made me nervous.

"You have been engaged by Salvatore Belassario to investigate a certain George Beechy, is that not so?"

"Perhaps."

"It happens that others have possibly competing interests in the same George Beechy."

"Are you suggesting that I not take a job investigating this George Beechy? Assuming, of course, that some client or other hires me to investigate this individual."

"Not at all. I do suggest that you be extremely careful from now on."

"I'm always careful," I said. "Which is why I've lived this long."

"Thirty-six is not so many years, I would think. And one must also consider the comely Ms. Mckerney. Is it not so?"

The voice was making me increasingly uncomfortable. He was threatening me and even Catherine, although in an oblique way.

"I advise you to be most circumspect as you pursue various lines of inquiry. Otherwise, there may be unfortunate results."

Unfortunate results, I wondered? Covered a wide range of possibilities, none favorable.

"Now, Mr. Sean, I have delivered my message. You are now it, as they say. You will wait where you are for whatever time it takes you to count to 100. Then you may commence looking for us, if that is your wont."

I had no weapon, so looking for this trio, if it was only three, might not be wise. But I could engage in a little detection. I stood very still, breathed through my mouth and felt my elevated heartbeat begin to slow down. Yes, there were definitely two people walking away. Either that was the entire army, or the third man was still close, silently watching me. I suddenly crumpled to the ground and rolled off the path, away from the basswood tree. No shots, shouts or other alarms ensued. Cool.

The two guys had gone in the general direction from which I had come. I couldn't detect the third person. I suspected they'd go back down the path to one of the breaks in the brush on the right side, away from the lake. About twenty yards from the path was one of those commercial developments, lots of small light manufacturing and storage firms that did damn near everything imaginable. There was the building, with many doors leading to many separate units, surrounded by a paved parking lot.

Since I was presumably more familiar with the immediate area than my accosters, I could beat a direct line to the parking area, while my unseen friends were retracing the route they'd taken to the Basswood tree so as not to get lost. I stood up and jogged through the brambles and ran through the brush. Sure enough, three minutes later I was looking at a large, almost empty parking area, dimly lit by some of those ugly yellow low-pressure sodium area lights.

Just as I stepped out of the brush, I heard a car door slam. The vehicles I could see all appeared to be trucks or commercial vans. Then down the way a car engine started and headlights flashed. I faded back into the bushes and watched a dark green, late model, Buick roll toward me, swing left around the building, and then accelerate away toward the exit onto Cleveland Avenue. There was no rear license plate.

8

There was nothing further to be accomplished standing in the dark, except give up more blood to the local insect population, so I jogged my sweaty body the two blocks back home, took a quick shower and slid into bed beside Catherine. Morning would be time to assess the situation.

In fact, it was nearly eleven when Catherine roused me from sleep with a strong cup of coffee. I staggered to the bathroom, showered again and stuff and we congregated at the dining room table where I noted with deep appreciation that Catherine had already cleaned up the detritus from our party.

"I slept the sleep of the just, my dear," she said. "I didn't hear you come to bed."

"I was delayed. There are more players in the game." I related my encounter of the early morning on the dark path.

"What does it mean?"

"I don't know." So much for my superior detection skills. "Bob Whitaker gave me a similar message last night, although it was in a friendlier manner. I think somebody wants me to keep looking into the business with George Beechy and or the real estate scam, but they want me to be discreet. When am I not discreet? I am going to reach out to Mr. Belassario and find out what sort of reaction he may have. If he's been holding out on me, I may just cash in my chips and get out of this game. There's a possibility that there may be more than one band of players here. Sal and I might even be third in line."

I called Sal from home. It turned out Sally had no idea who the unknown figures on the path had been, or exactly what the purpose of the warning was, except the obvious. "I don't get it, Sean. Nobody else but you and me are looking at this thing."

"I'm thinking we're wrong about that, Sal. Besides the cops, there could be one or even two others."

After a minute of listening to Sal breathe in and out, I heard him grunt. Then he said, "You better watch your back."

"You too, Sal, you too. And remember what I said. Those thugs who accosted me last night may not be connected to the mob, but they sure smelled like it. A damn good imitation, anyway. I thought the warning was a little obtuse but there's some kind of game going on here that could turn deadly real fast"

"You could smell 'em?"

"Figure of speech, Sal, just a figure of speech." He grunted in my ear and hung up. I hadn't mentioned to him that the city of Minneapolis, represented by Bob Whitaker, was also interested in the matter, and not just the fire and Beechy's death, which was really a Saint Paul crime. I wondered if officialdom had made more of the possible connection between Beechy and the Grand Pharmacy murders. Was there more?

Catherine departed for home and her business day. I went to my office. I hoped the change of location would generate some ideas or lines of inquiry as we in the detection business call them, but it was no go. Then the phone rang.

"I have a message from the court reporter you talked to," said Catherine. "She's located the trial transcript for your Mr. Beechy. Shall I buy a copy?"

"Yes, have her overnight it to my office and include a bill." I called the man in North Carolina who had responded to Catherine's question on DL. After I explained my mission, he agreed to check out the public tax records of one George Beechy.

It was nearly time to pack it in after an unproductive afternoon when North Carolina called back. It was 6:30 in the evening on the East Coast when Ed Abbot called.

"It's supper time there, Mr. Abbot. I'm surprised you're still working."

"I'm not, exactly. But the chance to be involved, however peripherally, in a real case, after years of reading mystery fiction, was too good to pass up."

"What have you got for me?" What he had was interesting. George Beechy and several others had been active in urban real estate, buying and selling apartments, small commercial establishments, and a few homes in and around Raleigh.

"He and his partners were churning the market, raising prices, selling properties back and forth among themselves, and moving money around until they could take some tidy profits."

"Do you have any idea why they closed down?"

"Oh yes. It seems the word got out and the authorities began to take a hard look at their operations. Apparently whoever is running this crowd got wind of the investigation before things came to a head and closed it down. I also talked to an insurance investigator who was looking into possible fraud with some of the same properties. Seems a couple of places had mysterious fires that pretty well gutted the businesses."

"Interesting." I was beginning to see a pattern. "Any names associated with Beechy?"

Abbot read off a short list of names, Jake Larson, Annette Campbell, Eddie Talbot, Henry Talbot, and Mordecai Marsh. "Mr. Abbot, do you know if all those people were actually in North Carolina while their real estate game was running?"

"Well, Campbell, Larson and Beechy certainly were. They, Larson and Beechy, were questioned during the investigations. None of the others appear in any tax records. Of course, if the time frame was expanded, we might turn up something more. I might turn up something in law enforcement through my contacts."

He sounded eager to continue, but I knew that could be a large waste of time. "I don't think that's a productive avenue, Mr. Abbot. What you've given me is interesting and useful, although I can't say just how, just yet. What I'd like you to do is write it all down and put it in a letter to me together with a bill for your time and expenses. Thanks very much for your help."

"Sure, Mr. Sean, glad to do it. Please let me know the outcome, if you can."

"I'll do that. Oh, one more thing. Please don't discuss this on that digest you subscribe to, DorothyL? Or with anybody down there. We're still in a confidential phase on this."

"Certainly, Mr. Sean. You can count on my discretion."

Right. I certainly hoped I could. I didn't want to learn that my contact in North Carolina had suddenly died a violent death of some kind. I dialed Catherine and got her answering machine, left a short message to the effect that North Carolina was concluded. I didn't say what I'd learned, just that I was heading out for the night and we'd connect the next morning. Who knew, in this day of rampant electronic eavesdropping, who might be able to access her telephone, from Zambia, say. My mysterious nighttime encounter was making me more than habitually cautious. Which reminded me. I called my local electronics jobber, Mike the Mole. When I remembered it, I had him come in and sweep my office for bugs-not the six-legged kind-and telephone taps. He'd never found any, of course. Now we scheduled some twice-monthly debugging appointments to start immediately and run until further notice.

In the morning I finished a report for another client, a big law firm in town, Harcourt, Saint Martin, Saint Martin, Bryce, Bryce, et cetera—they had dozens of names on their fancy letterhead—and if I wanted to get paid, a not unusual concern in my business, I'd better get the report off to them. I hadn't invested in a copy machine, so I took a disk—floppies they're called, for reasons beyond my ken—down the hall to my neighbor entrepreneurs, the Revulon sisters. Big, Swedish, blond and buxom, Belinda and Betsey ran a high-tech firm using computers, scanners, modulators, demodulators, several phone lines, a DSL, whatever that is, and a lot of other equipment I couldn't put a name to, to create, recreate, dispatch, print and manipulate electronic documents for customers around the world. They also wrote specialized programs for their clients. I figured they might be a CIA front.

Over the years we'd had nearby offices, we'd developed a kind of mutual affection for each other, but the sisters' feelings had transformed into a sort of mission. Their mission was to take care of me.

Not in a personal or sexual way, but they sort of watched over me. I didn't ask them to, they just decided to do so and I was unable to resist or dissuade them. That they were both several inches taller than me and more than slightly heavier might have had something to do with it.

One way the sisters helped was to watch my front door. Frequently I got notes or calls from one of the sisters describing people who visited my office when I was not in. They also peeped out windows to keep an eye on the street for me when I asked. I suspected they would peep in windows as well. I never asked.

I went down the polished tiled floor, my red high-topped Keds squeaking the news of my progress every step of the way. Their door was open; an ordinary state of affairs, but only Belinda was present. She grinned her big white-toothed grin and jumped up to give me a high-five greeting.

"What's goin' down, dude?"

I stared at her and shook my head slowly. Her language never went with her image. "I have here a three page confidential report to a client. I need five copies."

"Cool." Belinda pointed her chest at me and thrust out a hand to take the disk.

"Whoa. I said. Confidential stuff. I just want to use your machines to print and copy."

"Honey, it'll take three times longer if you do it, an' then I'll have to reboot to clear out your mess-ups. I'll keep my eyes closed, promise." She grinned at me.

"Okay, but I stay while you do it."

"No prob, babe." She took the disk and slid into a chair before an idle computer. After she inserted my disk, her fingers became a blur on the keyboard and the images on the screen changed so fast I couldn't read the information. While she inserted, loaded, formatted, checked, moused, manipulated, and whatever else she was doing to my document, Belinda hummed an unrecognizable tune. After a few minutes, her right elbow rose, she mashed a key with her forefinger and lifted both hands off the keyboard in a manner reminiscent of the pianist Catherine and I had enjoyed at Orchestra Hall a few weeks earlier.

"Now we wait," she said, looking up at me. "You had a visitor this morning, bye the bye."

"Yeah? Did he leave a message?"

"No, but he had cute buns."

"I'm sorry, he had what?"

"Cute buns, Sean. A nice ass! Aren't I speaking English here?"

"Really."

"Yes, really. In fact, he was altogether a pretty fine specimen of the male animal."

"A body builder?"

"Nope, but nicely built." Belinda's hands described a narrow isosceles triangle standing on its point. Behind us the printer was humming its song. "He's about six feet, white, no hat, and straight, shoulder-length dark blonde hair, nice shoulders, flat belly, ordinary features. I couldn't see the color of his eyes, but he had a nice smile."

"How do you know that?

"After he tried to open your door, he turned and looked at me, you know? I waved and he waved back and smiled at me."

"Then what, Belinda?"

"Then nothing. He turned and went down the hall to the elevator." Behind us, the copy machine, connected to the printer connected to the computer, stopped its song. "Nice buns," Belinda said again, and went into the back room to get my copies. When she handed them to me, I flipped through the perfect pages and nodded. While I waited, I ran through the list of men I know, trying to decide if one of them could be carrying around the buns Belinda described. No joy. She handed me my disk and I said,

"Thanks. Send a bill."

"Sure, sweetie. You can pay me at my place, tonight at eleven."

"I look forward to it." It was another game the sisters Revulon and I sometimes played. They both knew and admired Catherine. Neither sister would think seriously of poaching on CM's playground, as one of them had put it. Even supposing I was open to such poaching. Which I wasn't. But they rarely resisted the risqué remark. Betsey said it kept the juices flowing and the skin firm.

I put the report to Harcourt, Saint Martin, Bryce et cetera into an envelope and called Silver Streak delivery service. While I waited, I jotted down Belinda's description of the man with the nice ass who had come to my door earlier. There was no particular reason to do so, except that he might be connected in some way to a case. Right? We PIs, do that, you know. We connect odd and random bits and pieces until the whole is made clear. After I jotted down the description of the man, and the messenger still hadn't arrived, I doodled and thought about Sally B and George Beechy.

Sometimes I play solitaire when I'm thinking. Sometimes I sling playing cards at a top hat I hide in my file cabinet. Today I doodled. When the messenger showed up I looked at what I had been drawing. Around the edge of the paper was a series of little houses with flames coming from their roofs.

9

I drove home and replenished the food in my cats' dishes and gave them fresh water. Then I checked the perimeter and had a brief conversation with my twinkly-eyed, retired neighbor on the north, Abner Larsen. He was watering his flower beds so I suggested he water the common border between our properties. In return, I'd be sure he and his wife got some of my raspberries. He agreed, but he reminded me that last year I'd missed nearly all the ripe raspberries, leaving them to the local bird population

I told twinkly retiree Larsen I'd be away for the night and the motion sensors might light up the place unexpectedly, if critters invaded. Although he and the rest of the neighbors weren't aware of my real occupation, they'd become accustomed to my odd comings and goings. I didn't tell him some of the invading critters might walk upright on two legs.

I locked up and hopped on the freeway which took me within seven blocks of Catherine's apartment. She was home when I let myself in and greeted me with enthusiasm. "See here, my wandering boy scout. I've had more information from my query to DL. I took the liberty of contacting that court reporter in San Francisco. A large coincidence has worked to our advantage."

"What's that? I leaned down and bussed her a good one, then went to the bar to mix a highball. That's what happens in a lot of old mysteries I've read. Somebody fixes somebody else a highball. I usually fix my own. Took me a while after I first read the word to learn exactly what a highball is. Anyway, I now knew, so I fixed one. Catherine already had one. I also drink scotch, blended, and single malt. I like beer too. I guess you could say I'm an eclectic kind of guy, drink-wise. But I wouldn't want anyone to get the idea I'm one of those hard-drinking, hard-bitten, womanizing, cynical kind of PI's who'd just as soon put a bullet between your breasts as look at you. That's not me at all. I haven't shot anybody in weeks.

"The coincidence is," Catherine said, patting the couch beside her in an invitation to sit close, "that this same court reporter had a case a couple of years ago that involved some people whose names you'll probably recognize, people quite possibly involved in this case of yours."

"The doubtless recognition being due to my perspicacity and general all around good looks?"

"Pretty much," she said and kissed me on the nose. "Our California reported emailed me the names from the transcript."

"She, your court reporter, has the transcript?"

"Yep. It's her property and once the information is in the public record she can sell it to anyone who wants to buy."

"So you bought me a copy," I nodded approvingly. "What names did she give you?"

"Annette Campbell, Jake Larson, my third cousin, Mordecai Marsh, and George Beechy."

"Ah," I said. "Mordy once again, and Campbell and Beechy once again. Jake Larson is a new player. Now we have these people working together in North Carolina, in California, and now here. It sounds like a ring of some kind."

"I thought so. They seem to be relocating just ahead of the authorities."

"I wonder if any of them are mob-connected." I was liking this case less and less. "Can I assume some of those people were named in the investigation, but weren't present and weren't indicted?"

"Right, Mordecai is one, Annette Campbell another."

"I'm going to have to talk to your cousin, you know."

"Third cousin. Yes, I do know and you are not to worry about it.

Family or not, if he's been involved in a murder you—"

"What if it's not murder, just thievery or other lesser crimes?"

"Well, I wouldn't object too strenuously, I guess, if you gave him a little slack over something like that, if he wasn't hurting people. But, you know where I come down on the ethics question. Remember our little spat during the Saint Martin investigation? The time you walked out 'cause I wanted you to tell Mrs. Saint Martin everything you knew right then and you refused?"

"Do I ever. Except my recollection is that you threw me out. Fortunately, we fixed things." I smiled at her, thinking that regardless of her protestations, any leaning I might have to do in the direction of cousin Mordecai, distant though he might be, was going to strain our relationship. "It's beginning to look as though these people are like those home repair gypsy con artists who prey on unwary home owners, only they buy and sell real estate instead. I guess I'm going to have to have words with Mr. Marsh. But I'll leave him for last."

"Why would that be? Come on, let's continue this in the kitchen."

"I think I am tonight's designated chef," I said, rising and following her. While I shredded some Romaine and Boston lettuce and sliced a tomato and a mushroom or two for the salad, Catherine uncorked a nice bottle of Merlot.

"I think I'd like you to talk to Mordecai as soon as possible."

"Why is that?" I switched on the broiler and peeled potatoes, putting them to boil.

"This thing worries me. It'd be nice to know sooner rather than later whether my cousin, my third cousin, I remind you, is involved in something seriously illegal." She poured a small gurgle of wine and swirled the glass under her nose, sniffed appreciatively.

"And how much," I amended.

The lamb chops were at hand in the refrigerator. After a few minutes of inconsequentials, other than a kiss or two, I finished my highball and switched to the Merlot. The potatoes were close to ready, the salad was marinating in its dressing, so I slid the herbed chops onto the oven grille. Catherine switched on the exhaust fan, which is why we didn't hear the telephone. It probably wouldn't have made any difference in the outcome, but I'll always wonder.

The chops were grilling nicely to a sizzling golden brown. I turned them with tongs and mashed the potatoes with a dollop of real butter and a little milk. Watching my machinations, Catherine sighed and said, "I can see I'm going to have to crank up my exercise routine."

I smiled and the buzzer signaled the chops were done—medium rare—just the way we liked them. I slid them onto plates and distributed the potatoes, sprinkling on some chopped dill and chives. Catherine carried the salad to the previously set table and we tucked into to a fragrant, healthy repast.

"How does all this stuff about the real estate scams relate to the thing you are investigating for Sal?"

"I'm not 100 percent sure, except that Beechy and Mordecai have turned up in all three places. Sal told me he's heard street talk that Beechy was involved in a similar real estate scam here in the Twin Cities."

"How reliable is that?"

"Not very," I admitted.

"Do you think the stolen money--?"

"Allegedly stolen money."

"Well, the money allegedly in the attaché case that may have been taken from the pharmacy was likely to have been stolen. At least, it was stolen from the pharmacy. If it was there in the first place." She smirked at me.

"Suppose," I said, taking a final sip of wine, "that there was something else in the case, with or besides the money?"

"You mean like records or something?"

"That's one possibility. It doesn't seem logical to me that this gang, or any gang, would run a real estate scam in North Carolina and another one in California and pull their profits together here in the Twin Cities. Why wouldn't the thieves just distribute the loot to the participants when they bailed out? Trust is never a big factor in these groups."

"Maybe something prevented them from doing that."

"Once I could buy," I conceded, "but not twice."

We cleared our places to the dishwasher and returned to the living room. On the way I glanced at the telephone and saw the blinking red light indicating a message had been received.

Catherine picked up and punched replay. A frown appeared on her forehead.

"Problems?" I asked when she took the phone away from her ear.

"It was Mordecai. Listen." She handed me the instrument pressed replay. I heard a high whinny voice. 'Hi cuz. It's Mordy. Mordecai. I—something's come up. I gotta go outta town for a while. Just wanted you to know. I'll be in touch."

"Do you have his number?"

"Sure." Catherine took back the phone and dialed. "No answer." She stared at me with a question on her face.

"Maybe he was calling from the airport, or the train station, or .... play the tape again." She replayed the recorded telephone message from Mordecai, but neither of us could hear any identifying sounds in the background. "How does he sound? I asked.

"Like always, I guess."

"No strain in his voice, no change in his usual octave?"

Catherine shrugged. "We don't talk all that much, you know. He sounds pretty normal. Completely normal. As normal as he ever sounds. I guess."

"I think I better try to find him before he skips town. Maybe he's still at his place. I need to talk to him about this pharmacy business," I said.

"I'll come along. Just let me get a light jacket." She hurried to the bedroom and returned as I reached the front door. We elevatored ourselves to the underground resident's parking spaces and hopped into my Ford.

We roared out of the garage and headed south on 35W. Fortunately, traffic was light and in no time we'd crossed Minnehaha Parkway and were off-ramping at Diamond Lake Road. A couple of quick lefts and rights and there was the address. I got out of the car and touched my right hip where my holster would have been if I'd been heeled.

"He lives upstairs in the third floor left front," said Catherine, closing the passenger-side door and pointing at a dark set of windows.

This was an older building, brick, with painted, double-hung windows. Apparently there were four apartments on each of the four floors around a central hall and staircase. There was no lock on the front entrance and no security to keep out salespeople, leafletters or other troublemakers. The double row of narrow brass mailboxes had no bells so we climbed the stairs. It was an aging dowager of an apartment building, like hundreds built in cities across the Middle West in the early part of the century. It was quiet and dimly lit and the stairs and hall were carpeted. I smelled floor wax and furniture polish.

When we reached the third floor landing we stopped and looked around. There were two doors with brass numbers close behind us, on either side. Ahead of at the end of the short hall were two more identical doors, the one on the right labeled 3B. Mordecai's place.

Catherine started forward, saying, "It's the door on—"

I put out a hand to stop her. My keen detective's eye had noted that the dark vertical line between door and jamb was wider than it should be. Marsh's door was slightly ajar. We crept closer. No creaks or squeaks from the carpeted floor betrayed us. Motioning CM to step behind me, I positioned myself just to the right of the door and pressed on the wood panel. The door swung noiselessly open a couple of feet. Since the room was dark, except for light from the outside streetlight filtering in, I couldn't see much. But I heard something. A snuffle, then a cough, then a soft groan. Throwing caution to the wind, I bent over and snaked a hand inside and reached up to the left, where I knew there ought to be a light switch. When I flipped the switch and retrieved my arm, soft light illuminated the narrow view. Since there was no movement or further sound, except another cough, I straightened and went through the door, my eyes sweeping left to right to take in as much as possible.

It was an ordinary living room with a couple of wingback chairs, some tables and a small desk with a telephone and a litter of papers on it. There was also a sofa behind a low plastic coffee table. Slumped in one corner of the sofa was the crumpled figure of a woman. I went around behind the divan and leaned over the back to press my fingers against her carotid artery. Her heart was beating strong and rapid. I didn't see any weapons nearby. Catherine made a distressed sound in her throat and knelt beside the woman. Alarms were ringing in my head. Was there anyone else in the apartment? I checked the kitchen, the bathroom and the two bedrooms at the end of a short passage. One of the bedrooms appeared to be a store room. All the rooms were empty of other living creatures. They were ordinary rooms, but they all looked as if someone had gone through them quickly. They hadn't been trashed—the one double bed was still made but the mattress was askew and I got an impression someone had made a hurried search for items in each room and then made a fast departure from the apartment. I went back to the living room and examined the desk. Here too, someone with a swift hand had pawed through the drawers and cubbies. Was it Mordecai before he left or someone else? Catherine was just placing a towel wrapped around ice cubes on the back of the head of the now-revived woman.

She held the ice to her head and peered up at us. "Who are you guys?"

"Friends of Mordy," I said. "Who are you?"

"Yeah? That's what the last guy said."

"What happened here?"

The woman sat up straighter and winced. She put a careful hand to her head and reapplied the makeshift ice bag. "Goddamn, that hurts. Who wants ta know?"

"Mordecai is my cousin," Catherine said in a low voice. "He's not here. I'm worried about him."

The woman grimaced and said, "Yeah? Catherine? I seen your picture in the bedroom." She pointed a trembling finger at me. "Who's he?"

Apparently Mordecai didn't keep a picture of me by his bedside.

"This is Sean Sean. He's my friend. He's okay. Who are you?"

She shrugged wide shoulders, which called attention to the tight fawn sweater she was wearing, and gave me a look. She was generously proportioned and had a lot of gold colored hair hanging in disarray around her face. Her skirt was very short and showed off her shapely legs in gray patterned stockings with some kind of sparkly stuff woven in. The sparkly stuff winked in the overhead light.

I bent closer to look at her eyes. She didn't appear to be high, but

I smelled the booze on her. There was an empty tumbler on the floor under the coffee table and the carpet showed a damp spot. "What's your name?" I asked, squatting down on my haunches so she wouldn't have to arch her sore neck to look up at me, and so I wouldn't have to smell the vapors. Her response was to lower her head until her forehead was almost touching her thighs. She mumbled something I didn't catch.

"Excuse me? What did you say?" I wanted to extract as much information from her as I could, while she was still groggy.

"I said my name is Campbell, you know? Annette Campbell?"

My internal antennae vibrated. A name from the reports out of North Carolina and California. I wrote it down in a little notebook I usually carry for that very purpose. I left out the 'you know.' "I'm sorry to push you, Miss Campbell, but time, as they say, may be of the essence. What happened tonight?"

She gave me that look again and said, "Mordy and me, we're just havin' a nice evening here, ya know? Then the phone rings. Mordy gets up off the couch an' answers it, ya know?"

Logical, I thought. That's what I usually do when the phone rings.

"So I'm still watching the TV, an' I don't hear Mordy sayin' much."

"What did he say? Do you remember?"

"He jus' mumbled somethin' I didn't catch. Then he banged the phone down. Then he headed for the bedroom. I called to him and said somethin' like where was he goin', you know? I thought maybe he just hadda pee. But what he said was, he hadda go someplace right away and I better go home, you know?"

Catherine sat down beside the woman and moved her shoes aside. The shoes were black with high spike heels. I couldn't remember the last time I'd seen a woman wearing spike heels like those. CM took the towel from the woman and added ice. Then she lifted the mane of brassy blond hair and tenderly replaced the makeshift icepack on the back of her neck. Campbell leaned back against the couch to hold the towel in place.

"You and Mr. Marsh are friends, are you?" I put a question mark at the end so she'd know I was asking one. There was a pause then and she looked at me like she knew I was really asking something else. I wasn't, at least not on a conscious level, but both women apparently got the same message, because Catherine threw me a glance that could have frozen blood.

"Me and Mordy was friends, good friends," she said. Then something broke inside and tears appeared in her eyes. "Sure, I usta be in the life. But not no more. Not for a long time." She straightened until she was sitting fully upright. Annette twisted her hips slightly and crossed her feet at the ankles, assuming a lady-like pose. She squinted at me and continued in a firmer tone.

"Me an—Mordy and I have been seeing each other for over two years now, ever since I moved to Minneapolis. He helped me get straightened out. He's a very nice man. I'm worried about him." Her chin quivered. The tears now trickled down her cheeks.

"How long have you been living in Minnesota?"

Annette raised one eyebrow, almost exactly the way I do it and said, "Don't you really mean, like, when did I move here from North Carolina?"

For a moment I just looked at her. How much did she know? For that matter, how much did I know?

"I'm not sure what you mean," I said.

"Sure you do. I mean, I may not have much education, formal like, but that don't mean I'm some kinda dummy, you know? I know who you are. Mordy tole me." She stopped and Catherine gave her a fresh tissue. Then, as sometimes happens, she began to talk.

"I was with George in Carolina. He knew the others before I did. He told me some of the setup cash came from here, from Mordy."

Although I didn't think this conversation was getting me any closer to Marsh, I didn't want to shut off the flow of information so I stayed with her theme.

"What happened when the authorities in North Carolina got onto the scam?"

"We did what we were told to do from the start. We closed down and split town, you know? Can I have a glass of water?" Annette looked up at Catherine, who nodded and went back to the kitchen. I heard water running in the sink.

"Then what?"

"I didn't like George—Beechy. He was too rough so I said I was splitting for good. George was mad, but Eddie, Eddie Talbot, said okay. They were all goin' somewhere else."

"To California?" I asked.

"I suppose so. After I said I was getting out of the gang, they didn't talk about their plans in front of me. So I called Mordy and told him I'd come to Minneapolis. Everything seemed okay. Then when I got to the airport, there was Eddie. I was picking up my ticket when he came up to me in the line and handed me a bag."

I felt a faint stirring in my innards. "What kind of bag?"

Annette shrugged. "How do I know? It was just an ordinary suitcase. Eddie said check it though to Minneapolis and either keep it or give it to Mordy." The faint stirring went away.

"So you already knew Mordecai Marsh."

"Naw, I dint. Not really. I knew his name. We'd talked a few times. He seemed real nice. Talbot an' George said he was part of the deal. I told you that. But I never saw him in Raleigh."

"What else? Oh, Eddie said he'd see me later in Minneapolis and left. When I got off the plane here, Mordy was waitin'. He had a sign and was dressed like one of those limo drivers. 'Cept he didn't have no limo, you know?"

"What happened tonight?"

Annette sighed and rubbed her neck under the ice pack. She took a long drink of water and then delicately wiped her lips with a tissue. "Mordy came back outta the bedroom with a small suitcase. He handed me the keys to his car and said he hadda go, I should get myself home and he'd call when he got back."

"How'd he look?"

"Worried. Scared maybe."

I nodded. "Then what happened?"

He kissed me and went out. I turned off all the lights but this one here and decided to finish my drink. Then the bell rang. I thought Mordy maybe changed his mind or forgot something, you know? I went to the door and bam!"

"Bam?"

"Yeah, bam. Some wisenheimer dropped a bag over my head and

the next thing I know, here you guys are an' I got this lump?"

"You didn't see who it was? You didn't look though the peephole in the door."

"Nah. Like I said, I thought it was Mordy. I pulled open the door and bam. It was too quick. I didn't see nothin'."

Sure, I thought. Bam. We questioned her some more and didn't get anything else relevant to the night's activities. I hadn't noticed a bag, the first time through, so I looked around again. No bag. Our man must have carried it away with him.

It was apparent Mordy's apartment had been searched, but not trashed. Some of the disturbances I'd noted could have been Mordecai getting out of the place, but the way the desk was left with the drawers all pulled out, suggested someone other than the owner had gone through the papers. So exactly what had happened? Was Marsh on the run? If so why and from whom? I stood up and looked down at the Campbell woman who had stopped talking and was just staring at the wall.

"I ain't stayin" here. I got to go."

CM picked up a key ring and held it out to Annette. "Aren't these Mordecai's keys?

Annette waved them away and CM said, "Didn't he give them to you, so you'd have a car to get home in?"

"Sure, 'cause I came in a cab. But, I have my own key to this place, you know?"

"But he wanted you to have his car," said CM, still holding out the key ring.

"Yeah, but see, he must of forgot. I don't drive."

10

We closed up Marsh's apartment and went to my car. Then we drove around the block and down the alley to the parking lot reserved for the apartment dwellers. Annette pointed out Marsh's ride. I got out and Catherine slid into the driver's seat of the Taurus. Marsh's car was a bronze, late-model two-door Pontiac. Not quite a pimp-mobile, but, like the owner, skirting the edges. I used my pocket flash and gave it a once-over from all sides. It didn't appear to have been tampered with. I hoped it hadn't been wired with a bomb or other fiendish device, but I wasn't going to call the cops and I didn't want to leave the car untended while I assembled a team of my own experts. So, I settled for a close examination of the hood latch, the trunk and door latches and the gravel around the car. Nothing jumped out at me. I slid the key in the lock, turned it and opened the door.

Nothing happened except the overhead light went on.

I waved at Catherine and sat down behind the wheel, pulling the door shut without slamming it. It snicked closed, reminding me of the arming of a switch. For a moment I imagined I could hear a timer ticking.

Nuts. I took a deep breath and blew it out. My pulse was running a little hot. Then I felt for loose wires around the steering wheel. All clean, although the plastic cosmetic shield around the column made it difficult to be certain. That same shielding, I reasoned, also made it difficult for a would-be bomber to futz with the wiring. So I put the key in the ignition and turned it, unconsciously holding my breath. Like that would do some good. The only thing that happened was the starter motor cranked and the big engine rumbled happily into life. I blew out my breath and waved behind me at Catherine. She pulled ahead so I could get out of the lot and I turned left, following the Taurus with CM and Ms. Campbell down the narrow, black-topped alley. We both turned left again onto the street and headed for Annette Campbell's apartment. Just as I made the corner out of the alley, headlights winked in my rear view mirror. It looked like a car turned into the parking lot we had just vacated. I debated going around the block to see what there might be to see, but remembering the absence of a weapon on my person, I opted for discretion and rolled off to the 35W northbound onramp. Catherine disappeared in the direction of Edina, to take Annette Campbell home. For a moment I wondered if I should have stayed with them.

    I had lots to think about on the twenty minute ride back to Catherine's garage. Annette Campbell hadn't mentioned Mordecai's call to CM. Either she forgot or Mordecai had called from somewhere else. And why had he called CM anyway? I was sure she was accurate when she said they weren't all that close. But maybe ol' Mordy didn't see it that way. Another possibility was that Mordy figured she was the most trustworthy person he could count on in his trouble—whatever that was. And how come whoever bammed Ms Campbell on the noggin didn't take Mordy's key ring? Maybe because he wasn't looking for car keys, especially if he a) was pretty sure Mordy had split in a hurry and assumed he'd drive or b) knew Ms Campbell didn't drive and didn't expect to find car keys on her person or in her purse. Interesting thought. Yeah, I liked it.

    Twenty minutes later the Pontiac was parked in a visitor's slot farthest from the entrance to the garage below Catherine's building. I didn't have much in the way of tools but the jack in Mordecai's trunk was solid looking and I was able to get it up high enough so I could maneuver under the vehicle with some ease. I forced visions of slipping jacks and falling Pontiacs out of my mind. Both car doors hung open. So did the trunk lid and the hood. I'd zipped upstairs and changed to some jeans and an old sweatshirt that was stashed in

Catherine's apartment. With my little flashlight, I was going over the car inch by inch. My scenario went like this. Someone called Marsh, and whatever they said persuaded him to split. Perhaps with the caller. Why? Something for later consideration. Another possibility was that whatever was said by whomever it was that called, scared Marsh enough to get him out of his place in haste, quite possibly to protect Annette. There were other possibilities, of course, but they were more remote. As he left the apartment, Marsh urged Annette, his companion, to take his Pontiac, even though Marsh knew she didn't drive. Why'd he do that? Maybe, in his agitation, he forgot. Campbell's description didn't sound like a man in a panic, just somebody in a hurry. So I was going on the assumption that Marsh had a good reason for not taking his car and giving the keys to non-driver Annette Campbell. Now I was trying to find that reason, if it existed.

I'd searched the trunk and the passenger compartment with painstaking care, lifting floor mats and prying at possibly loose pieces of molding. Now I was lying on the cool concrete floor of the parking garage, peering at the frame, the tires, axles, the power train and such. It was obvious that the underside of this vehicle had not been cleaned in many miles. Without knowing exactly what I was looking for, my search was difficult, but I had convinced myself that the reason Marsh gave the car keys to Campbell, was that in said automobile was something of importance and value. I have occasionally in the past made erroneous assumptions. Still, I'm quite good at my business so I was now lying on the concrete floor of Catherine's garage, wishing I had a blanket to lie on, minutely searching Mordy's vehicle, stopping just short of the disassembly you often see in those films about drug smuggling.

I'd jacked the car up on one side and had crawled completely underneath, making it to a position directly below the front seats, thinking these thoughts and was now peering at the greasy mess of the transmission housing. Looking closely, I saw that a small section of the undercoating was grayer than the rest. It looked like a patch. I scraped away some of the grease. Pay dirt. Am I good or what? Something protruded from the thick undercoating that was not part of the transmission housing. Somebody'd sliced into the sprayed-on coating and then inserted something into an indentation up near the hump in the floor between the housing and the floor panel. I reached for my pocket knife.

I widened the slice in the undercoating and pried out a small piece of silver duct tape. It was wrapped around what felt like a small key. I lay there on my back for a moment, eyeing my find. Now, a lot of people would figure this was the prize and quit searching. Not me. I try to be more thorough, even if the only place left to search was the engine compartment, which search would leave me even dirtier and smelling of grease, engine oil and similar petroleum unpleasantness. I tore the tape off the key which appeared to be gold-colored just like the ones for numerous apartment and house front doors. There were no identifying marks on the key, other than that of the manufacturer, Schlage. A good, solid, lock maker. Thousands of 'em around, if not millions.

I heard the overhead garage doors open and a car that sounded like my Taurus rolled past. The driver stopped and then reversed into an empty spot close by. Catherine knew I liked to have the car pointed out whenever possible. I heard someone alight and a brief squeak from a remote locking device. Then the footsteps crossed slowly toward the Pontiac under which I was lying, with no part of me exposed.

"If that's you, Sean, come out here. Something else has happened."

Catherine's voice was flat and calm. It was late and she sounded tired. I noticed she stopped far enough away that I could not have grabbed her ankles from my position under the Pontiac. I wriggled out and saw she was holding the little .25 caliber semi-auto she usually had in the apartment. I hadn't known she'd been carrying when we went to Marsh's. When my head appeared, she slipped the gun into her purse.

"Hey, babe, what's up? Did you expect to find somebody else under this car?"

"Just being cautious. When we got to Annette's we found it had been ransacked. At first it looked like a vandal had broken in and just trashed her place, but I decided it was too calculated. Whoever came in didn't do a whole lot of damage, but they were thorough. They searched everywhere."

I sat up and nodded, stretching my back muscles. "That probably means they didn't find whatever they were looking for. Where's Annette now?"

"I took her to a motel over by the Art Institute. It's pretty obscure so I doubt anyone will find her before tomorrow."

I nodded. "I know the one you mean. Excellent decision. We'll have to help her find a new place to stay. Meanwhile, I've been busy and have found this." I held up the key.

"Ah, so now we have to figure out what the key unlocks. Are you finished here?"

I hesitated. "Probably so, but just in case, I'm gonna go over the rest of the car."

Catherine smiled. "You ought to change into old clothes—older clothes. And please be careful. I don't wish to come back down here to find you smashed flat under Mordy's Pontiac."

I grunted and slid back under the car. All my older—rattier—clothes were fifteen miles away in Roseville. Since I'd started at the back of the Pontiac, the engine had mostly cooled off I wasn't expecting any singed skin from hot headers or exhaust pipes. Unfortunately, Mordy has a small oil leak somewhere around the filter. When the car was moving, the dripping oil sprayed over the rear of the engine block and the clutch housing. When the car was standing still, as now, the oil tended to drip straight down, on me. Hot and burned oil stinks.

After an hour and a half, I had grease and oil on my clothes, on my nose, under my fingernails, and in one ear. I also had a small magnetic key case that had been attached to the wishbone frame of the car beside the engine. In it I found another key, this one of unusual design which I immediately identified as a key to a safety deposit box. At a bank. Also inside was a tiny wad of notepaper stuffed under the key. The only writing on the paper was some numbers. 243698.

My efforts had been worthwhile. Now all I had to do was avoid any residents or the security guy on my ride up to Catherine's apartment. It wasn't easy, even when I opted for the rear elevator, the one less elegantly appointed. Twice I started around the corner at the back of the building from the garage door to the elevator, but even at this late hour someone had to be wandering in from somewhere. I ducked

The Case of the Stolen Case

back into the garage both times. Finally I made it into the elevator unseen. I remembered to use my clean elbow to punch the elevator buttons and just crossed my fingers, hoping no resident would appear at one of the floors, but I made it to her floor and found the hall empty. I used my clean elbow to rap on Catherine's door.

When she opened up I saw her wrinkle her nose at the odor wafting about me and grin at what she saw. "I hope it was worthwhile. Hit the shower, bud. I've already hung your robe in there."

"Here's the other thing I found," I said and put the key case on a tissue. Then I went off to shower. It took a while, but I emerged clean, and pink from the hot water and scrubbing. Catherine was looking at the key, a brass thing, thicker than most keys. There weren't any grooves, but it had a pimple at the end opposite where you normally hold it and there were four square notches in one of the long edges. There was a round hole in the fat end, and numbers incised in the fat end, different from the numbers on the tiny piece of paper.

"Looks like a safe deposit box key," Catherine said when she saw it.

"A lockbox key."

"Sure. Don't you have one at your bank? Look at this." She delved into her purse and extracted her key case. On one hook was a key that looked very much like the second one I'd found in Marsh's car.

"No, I don't have a safety deposit box. You know I hardly have a bank account most times."

"Safe deposit box," she said. "There's no 'ty' on the end. It's a common mistake. Look how similar these keys are in design. They aren't all the same, of course, but I've seen some that are. All you have to do is figure out which bank, get a court order, and get the box opened."

"That's all, huh. Pretty time consuming. Why couldn't it have just been an extra ignition key so I could forget about it?"

"What about the other key? The first one you found in the car?"

"It looks like a door key, doesn't it?"

"Correct, but to what door? It isn't to Mordecai's apartment. I already checked"

"I don't think your cousin needed to hide an extra key to his apartment under the transmission housing of his car. I might be able to get a line on the lock through the manufacturer, but it won't be an easy search either."

"I'm worried about Mordecai." Catherine frowned. "Given everything that's happened the last few hours, I think he must be on the run, hiding out. But who from?"

"It's almost two a.m. I'm wiped out and I bet you are too. Lying on that concrete floor has done me in. Let's get some sleep and we'll deal with all this tomorrow."

11

"Glad to learn you're on the job early, saving our city from the bad guys, Lieutenant Brooks. Do you always bellow like that into the telephone?" It was only eight-thirty in the morning and I was on my first cup of caffeine.

"Sean? Why are you bothering me again? For that matter, why are you even awake? I thought all you private eyes led dissolute lives, sleeping late and all that."

"You know me, pure in mind and body. I need some information."

"Don't you always?"

"I have some names. They came up while I've been looking into the real estate scam for Sally."

"And?"

"And I wondered if you can tell me, or find out, if any of them have been in trouble in Saint Paul."

"Jesus, Sean, you have more gall than anyone I know."

"Mac, you know what I want is all in the public records. I can eventually find out what I need, but, in the interests of time and efficiency, I just thought ... I mean, what are friends for?"

"In a pig's eye. Give me the names. But know this. If any of them are part of an ongoing investigation, you get nothing."

"I understand. The names I'm looking for are, Annette Campbell, Mordecai Marsh, Jake Larson, Eddie Talbot and Henry Talbot."

Brooks was silent for a few moments. "Nothing comes to mind. I'll get back to you." He hung up the phone.

I called the Ramsey County prosecutor's office. Yes, the woman on the telephone said, Mr. Ford was available. Jerry and I shot the breeze for a couple of minutes and I made the same request, and provided the same list of names. Lastly, I called my friend Ricardo Simon, a detective in the Minneapolis police department. He and I went back a long way, to even before I got into the P.I. biz. There was always the chance that either Hennepin county or the Minneapolis PD had contact with my happy band of thugs. Ricardo would find out for me. I knew, as did all my contacts that I could search through court, arrest and other public records on my own, but that would take a lot of time. By segmenting the searches and calling on my contacts, I hoped to save hours, if not days. Of course, I had no proof the people on my short list were all thugs, happy or otherwise, but I had strong suspicions. Having started things in motion, I turned my thoughts to Mordy Armstrong's inamorata, Ms. Annette Campbell.

Catherine went off to her day job, overseeing her massage therapy school and conferring with some of the businesses with whom she had massage contracts. I went to the motel and took Ms. Campbell to lunch in the attached restaurant. We went over her story again, which didn't change significantly. Then I laid the two keys on the table between us.

"Does either of these look familiar?"

She poked at the keys. "This 'un looks like a door key, doesn't it?" I agreed that it did. "An' this other is funny." Annette picked up the key and turned it around in her fingers. I watched her carefully. Either she was a really good actress, which someone in her former profession often was, or she'd never seen a safe deposit box key before. I was prepared to believe the latter. I decided not to tell her about the paper and the numbers.

"Annette, do you have any idea where Mordy was going when he left last night?"

She shook her heard. "No, man. I thought about it a lot last night, an' even today. He didn't say anything about where he was goin." We both stopped talking for a minute, thinking about Mordecai, I suppose. Then she glanced up from the table and said, "What am I gonna do, Mr. Sean? I don't have no job. I don't wanna go back on the street. What if Mordy never comes back?"

A lot of questions, none of which I could answer for the moment. I certainly didn't have any long-term solutions. I patted her hand with a disagreeable sort of paternal reassurance. Then without thinking about it, I took out my wallet and laid two twenties on the table. "Here, Annette. Here's a little walking around money. Until we think of something."

She glanced at me out of red-rimmed eyes and slid one hand over the bills, but not before a couple at the next table looked at our transaction with a certain air of disapproval.

Annette ignored them. "What do you want me to do?"

I leaned toward her and lowered my voice. "Just stay here. Go to a movie. Get a book and go read in the park across the street, if you want. But stay away from anyplace you and Mordecai have been. Don't go to your apartment and call either me or Catherine if anything unusual happens, all right?" We left the restaurant. At my car, just outside, Annette reached up and gave me a quick peck on the cheek. "Thanks," she whispered. When I got into the Taurus, I could see the silhouette of the couple still seated in the restaurant, watching us.

When I arrived at my office there was a message from Jerome Ford on my answering machine to the effect that a man named Eddie Talbot was currently in Stillwater Prison, after having been convicted of assault with a deadly weapon, namely a vehicle which he had used to permanently damage another man after a falling out. Talbot, according to Ford, had relatives in South Carolina. A tenuous link, but one I'd better follow up on. Meanwhile there was another way I could possible narrow things down.

I'm no computer whiz. In fact, I've only recently come to accept the computer as a necessary tool. But the Revulon cousins fill me in whenever necessary, as does Catherine, of course. After I listened to my messages, I went down the hall with my short list of names and hired the Revulon team to do some computer searches to see what might be learned.

Belinda smiled at me from the keyboard where her long fingers danced over the keyboard like things possessed. Their rhythm changed not at all when raised her eyebrows in interrogation. "Hey, Sean, master detective. How be ya, friend? What brings you to this end of the hall?"

"I need to find out about some people. I thought maybe you could help." Belinda nodded, never ceasing the rapid tattoo of her fingers. I explained the task, provided her the names on my list, omitting Eddie Talbot, and went back to my office.

Jerome Ford had given me with the name of Talbot's public defender, an attorney I had never met named Burl Barrer. When I reached him by phone, he was accommodating. His client had been convicted four years earlier and was serving his term without any apparent problems. If Talbot agreed, he'd have my name added to the visitor list. Two relatively unproductive days later, I was driving east toward Wisconsin on Highway 36, a four lane ribbon of asphalt that took me to Oak Park Heights on the bluffs overlooking the Saint Croix River valley. The Saint Croix River is the eastern border between Wisconsin and Minnesota. Oak Park Heights is the location of Minnesota's newest, high security prison, where they shut away the nastiest, most dangerous, most violent felons. I don't like it. Even from the outside, with the surveillance cameras, the chain link fence topped with razor wire, just standing in the parking lot outside the entrance, the atmosphere is chilling.

Inside, it was worse. You have to step through a metal detector and they relieve you of anything that could remotely be considered a weapon, including mechanical pens and pencils. They stamp your hand with fluorescent dye which they examine periodically at check points if you are moving from place to place while inside, and they give civilians like me a wide black belt with a box attached. On the box is a big red button. Press the panic button, a guard told me and we'll be there in ten seconds. Ten seconds! Yeah. Any longer and it won't matter, he said. Great.

That was the Minnesota State Prison at Oak Park Heights. Today I wasn't going to that prison, I was going to one of the other warehouses for miscreants. the big gloomy first prison among state prisons in Minnesota, Stillwater State Prison.

12

Just over the lip of the hill, Highway 36 bends north past some spectacular rock formations and then drifts on down past the Bayport turnoff to Stillwater. Bayport, a small river town, is home to Stillwater State Prison. It's called Stillwater Prison most of the time, because the original prison was built by the Territorial Legislature in Stillwater, in 1851. The prison was located in a kind of swampy place called Battle Hollow, where Indians fought a skirmish years earlier. It was never a good place for a prison, and was probably some kind of political payoff. But that prison lasted until 1914 when a new one opened a few miles south of Stillwater, in Bayport. People still call it Stillwater Prison though. Go figure.

The prison is surrounded by high grimy stone walls with guard towers at regular intervals. The town of Bayport has grown up around the prison so there isn't any real separation between the good and the bad, except the stone walls and the guard towers. I parked on the street, right in front of the main entrance. I looked but didn't see any guards in the towers. It was very quiet in Bayport that day. Only the passing of an occasional car disturbed the serenity of the place.

Inside was not much different from any correctional institution in Minnesota, or elsewhere, I suppose. Not that I've been in more than one or two. I mean I wouldn't want you to get the wrong idea. The thing that struck me the first time I was inside this particular prison, even in the entrance area was the noise. I suppose because of the hard brick and concrete every sound was magnified. It wasn't like Oak Park Heights which was unnaturally quiet. Subsequently I found that almost everywhere in Stillwater Prison was big and loud.

I went inside, out of the morning heat and started through the routine. I identified myself and my mission to a guard sitting behind a thick glass partition, submitted to a search and passed through the outer, glass partition, where I acquired an escort. Directly in front of me was a tall gate constructed of steel bars that ran from the painted concrete floor to the painted concrete ceiling. The bars were set into a brick and stone wall. In the middle of this huge grate was a rectangle on wheels. The bars were painted the same color as the walls, pale, institutional green. It was not a pleasant color, especially in such immense amounts.

At a signal from my escort, the locking mechanism released with a clank and the gate rolled back and allowed us entry. We walked two steps forward and the gate rolled to its original position. I had the same though I have every time I came to this place, an unreasonable fear that they, the unnamed, faceless, 'they' who control all our destinies, would forget me and I wouldn't be let out. And if there was no paperwork on me, would anybody ever penetrate the bureaucracy and come for me?

It felt colder inside and probably was. Certainly nosier. Even the white rubber soles on my red Keds sent squeaks caroming off the hard walls. The farther into the interior of the prison we went, the noisier it became. "This way," gestured my escort. She was unarmed and seemed at ease among the entirely male population. I intercepted almost constant leering glances from dungaree-clad inmates, most of whom seemed to have nothing much to do except stand around. I naturally assumed they weren't leering at me.

"It's not regular visiting hours. Some of the guys are on break before lunch, some don't have jobs. A job to earn a little money is a privilege, you know." She spoke in a conversational manner, but her tone suggested she was answering questions that had been asked a thousand times before. "Usually, visitors go to one of the rooms over there." She pointed to her right. I looked over at a group of glass-partitioned cubicles each with a small table and a couple of chairs. I assumed prisoners came to this location to see their lawyers or family members.

"We'll be meeting Mr. Talbot in a separate office in C Block."

As we approached Cellblock C, we headed toward an ordinary doorway set into another brick wall. As we approached, a small group of men gathered in the doorway, blocking our path. It seemed casual enough, but the men weren't moving aside to let us through. I noticed they all had their arms crossed on their chests.

"Just keep moving, Mr. Sean. It's a power thing some groups do every so often. They want us to stop or hesitate. That way, they send a message to other groups of cons in here" My escort moved a half-stride ahead and raised one hand about chest high, palm out. I scanned the men confronting us. They were all taller than me and each one outweighed me by forty or fifty pounds. I fixed my eyes on my escort's hand and we plowed through them. It was like a ballet, except for the adrenaline rush I felt. As we went forward through the door, the men silently shuffled aside just enough so we could pass into the cell block beyond. Nobody touched me. When we passed into the cell block proper, I felt their eyes on my back, but I didn't look around.

"These kinds of confrontations occur frequently between individuals and groups of the men. When one gets large enough, we call it a riot." She said this in a matter-of-fact tone of voice.

The cell block was four stories high, a brick and steel rectangular column with barred cells on each level. At three upper stories an open steel walkway passed across the front of each cell so the men could move about. At each end of the cell block, a steel stairway allowed access from the floor to each level and to ground level where we were. I saw only three doors out of the cellblock. It's strange, the odd thoughts I sometimes have. I wondered how all the men in the place would get out if there was a fire. I didn't see much of anything that could burn.

The whole block was inside a huge windowed building, the walls of which were about thirty or forty feet away from the cell tier. A lot of sunlight streamed through the windows, but I had the impression the rays of sunlight didn't penetrate very far into the cellblock so there were a lot of murky, dim corners. It was depressing. And loud.

All those hard surfaces bounced around voices and the sounds of hard heels on the tile floor, and multiplied them into an indecipherable babble of sound. On one side opposite the door, a large television on a strong metal stand with wheels was playing a soap opera to a gaggle of mostly empty folding chairs. How the few men watching could understand the sound track, I didn't know.

We walked to a cell partway down the tier at ground level and went in. Unlike other cells, this one had no toilet and was equipped with a small desk and a couple of side chairs. It was separated from the cells on either side by big thick blankets that reminded me of the blankets movers use to protect nice elevators in upscale apartment buildings.

"This is my office. Mr. Talbot will be here in a minute." She still hadn't introduced herself. We stood around and I watched her shuffle some files on the desktop. After a few minutes of silence, a tall slender man with a tiny mustache banged his hand on the frame of the cell. The woman nodded him to one chair beside her desk. She said, "I'll be back in about fifteen minutes. This is Mr. Sean, Eddie. You don't have to answer any questions you don't wish to." Then she went out with only a glance in my direction. Talbot looked at me and crossed his arms over his chest. He planted both feet squarely on the concrete floor in front of him.

"I'm a private investigator, Mr. Talbot. I'm looking into a real estate deal. You may be able to help me with some of the details." No reaction.

"When did you arrive in Minnesota?"

Knowing the information was available elsewhere, Talbot said, "I got busted about three years after I came here."

"From California?"

"Gnaw, North Carolina."

Since Talbot was in prison for five years on an aggravated robbery bust, I had nothing to offer him in return for the answers I sought. We both knew that. I decided to play it pretty low key. Maybe I could entice him into telling me something useful. So we talked about the weather, the Twins and how he was getting along in prison for a few minutes.

Talbot's answers got shorter and more abrupt. Finally he stirred in his chair and looked directly at me. "You're a private cop. What are you doing here? What is it you want?"

"Well, Mr. Talbot, that's my question. Your name keeps turning up linked to a real estate deal in North Carolina and maybe here in Minnesota. What I hear is there was a lot of money involved. So why try to take down that corner store in Minneapolis?"

His mouth turned down and he snorted. "Lotto money, yeah. Who knows? I never saw any. I was broke, see? Needed cash."

"So you were involved in the real estate deals?"

"I didn't say that, did I. What I heard is the money was being collected. The people involved were going to get their cut later. Then somebody ripped off the cash."

"What else have you heard?"

"The money was in a suitcase and was being held for us."

"Suppose I give you some names and you tell me if they're involved."

"What's in it for me?"

"I can't offer you a thing. If you do good time in here, you'll be out sooner than later. Maybe I can talk to somebody. If you cooperate, things might go easier while you're in here."

"Fat chance."

"All right. Let me tell you a story."

"It's your time." Talbot settled back in his chair.

I leaned forward and watched his eyes. "A man named Armond Anderson set up the real estate operations in North Carolina and later on the West Coast. The profits were collected and then transferred to St. Paul. Six years ago, the money that was stored in an aluminum suitcase or valise got stolen. This was right before you got busted.

"I figure that after the money was handed over to a man named George Beechy things went sour and somebody ripped of the money in that pharmacy murder. I figure you did the robbery that got you in here because you ran out of ready cash, which means, either you weren't part of the pharmacy deal, or the money went someplace you couldn't reach. Or there wasn't any money in the aluminum case.

Whatever, word on the street is that the contents of that aluminum case never has turned up."

I leaned back and stretched out my legs, still watching his face. Talbot was probably a bad poker player. "Oh yes, then a couple of weeks ago, George Beechy was beaten to death in his front yard and his house burned down. You're in here and the rest of the guys you did the deals with are all out there somewhere."

"Beechy's dead? Son of a bitch!" Talbot threw himself up out of his chair and whirled around. He was angry. I'd brought him unexpected news. A guard who had been standing out of earshot across the tiled corridor appeared in the doorway. I raised a hand toward the guard. Talbot glanced at the guard and then at me and said, "I'm through here. We got nothin' more to talk about."

He walked out with the guard and my escort appeared, eyebrows raised in a question. On my way out, yes, they opened the bars so I could walk through the door into the sunshine, I thought about what I had learned. Talbot participated in the pharmacy robbery and his partners were staying away from him, presumably to avoid coming under police scrutiny after he got busted for the 7-Eleven robbery. The aluminum case was an important factor. If I could find it, a lot of questions would be answered.

13

When I got back to my office from the prison, I found an urgent message on my machine from Mike the Mole. Besides being my main electronic sweeper guy, Mike was an occasional client. Turned out his current urgency was an apparent stalker. MtM was a little paranoid. Sometimes when he reported to his clients the offices he swept were clean of electronic ears, he wasn't believed. Some of his customers were also a little paranoid. Hence, from time to time the mole became convinced he was being stalked and possibly set up by one or more of his occasional employers. So he would call me. Then I would spend a couple of days discreetly following Mike the Mole around and watching his electronic repair place on Lyndale. After that I'd give Mike a log that showed where I'd been and when, which tallied with his movements. That way he was convinced when I reported there were no other followers. At least until the next time.

I called the Mole and learned he was going to spend an evening visiting a few strip joints in town. Great.

That's how I ended up at eleven thirty in the night sitting in an evil-smelling booth of cracked vinyl in some Minneapolis dive near the river. The place was loud and smoky and I was tired. I can't avoid drinking a little when I'm on this kind of a tail job, but I try to keep it to a minimum. Right now, I would have been happy with a nice shot of Crown Royal from my own bar.

I glanced at the Mole who was sitting stage-side staring open-mouthed at whatever dancer was currently cavorting about the stage. According to my watch and my recollection of similar evenings, I thought he'd soon give it up for the night and I could knock off.

Then this stripper arrived at my booth. The light was behind her so all I could see was this female form standing over me, swaying slightly. I knew it was a stripper because of her odor, a peculiar blend of deodorant, stage makeup and sweat. I tried to wave her away but she ignored my gesture. One of the current crop of dances at Happy Buns, I supposed.

"Heyyy, sweets," she said, or hollered over the booming sound system. "You look like you could use a little company."

"I'm sorry," I said. "I really don't want any company right now."

She leaned over and pressed her hand on my wrist, fingers tapping out some kind of urgent message. When I tried to draw my hand away she pressed harder. Listen fellow. You need some company right now." Something in the voice alerted me. I looked hard and realized I knew her. It was Dusty Larson, the stripper who'd been a guest at my home a couple of nights earlier. I was surprised to see her there because she almost never worked in Minneapolis. Dusty turned slightly and the light from the stage washed over her features.

I shrugged and pointed at the seat opposite, but she wasn't having any. Instead she bent over and shoved her way onto my bench so we were sitting haunch to haunch. Her right hand dropped below the table top and her nails lanced into my thigh.

"Now, isn't this comfy? So, what's your name, sweetie?"

"Sean," I said. "You wanna drink Miss....?" I let the question trail off so Dusty registered that I knew she was playing some kind of game. I looked at her face. Usually when she was in an intimate conversation, her gaze remained fixed on you. Now, her eyes darter here and there. She seemed to be watching everybody in the place at once.

We started a little verbal dance. "C'mon little man, show a girl a good time and get us a small bottle of Champagne."

"Good things come in small packages," I simpered. "I guess it wouldn't hurt none."

The server handling our part of the club was already leaning over to get a drink order. She sensed a mark, because she brought what appeared to be an unopened bottle of champagne to the table in record time. Twisting the cork off with relative ease, she slammed a pair of glasses on the table and filled them before I could even think to take the bottle from her. She set the bottle on the table and wobbled off with nary a word, just a little wave of her fingers.

I gave Dusty a glass and raised it in a little salute. "I don't suppose this is spiked, is it."

She laughed louder than necessary and took a quick gulp. So did I. While she refilled our, glasses spilling a fair share, she whispered, "We need to get out of here."

I glanced across the room at the Mole who hadn't moved and was still staring at the nearly naked dancer on stage. Then I leaned toward Dusty as if I was propositioning her and whispered in her right ear, "Okay, I'll play along. This is a proposition."

I was in a quandary. It was late and if he followed his usual pattern, Mike the Mole was about done for the night. Still, I was on a job. On the other hand, Mike didn't know I was on him so how would he know if I left? The answer seemed obvious, and since I was ninety-nine and nine-tenths percent sure (like the old Ivory Soap ads) that no one other than moi was following him, I could break off the surveillance with no harm done.

Dusty threw back her head and guzzled down her Champagne. I signaled the waitress who hadn't gone far and handed her some bills. Dusty grabbed my arm and we swayed together as we sashayed out of the place. I couldn't see anyone paying any more than ordinary attention. We turned left out of the door and walked toward the parking lot. With her long legs, and her apparent desire to put a lot of distance between herself and the club, I had to hustle to keep up. We got to the end of the building and I grabbed her arm.

"Wait a minute. Where's the fire?"

"There are people in there I needed to get away from."

"Yeah, the long arm of coincidence." I glanced back toward the entrance just in time to see my man, Mike the Mole leave the club and turn away from us. Two more men followed him out, loosing a blast of babble and music to the night air. Mike turned left, the two men turned right. "Well, my car is around the corner the other way," I said.

"Shit."

"Come on, we'll go down here a little way." I took her arm to keep her from tearing off again and we strolled to the next corner and around it. I looked back again. The sidewalk was empty.

"Here," Dusty said. "I'll wait here while you get the car."

She sidled into a dark doorway and I heard the scratching of cardboard then the brief flare of a lighter as she lit up.

I left her there and went back around the corner. I eeled through the night club's parking lot. There were a lot of vehicles but I didn't encounter anyone acting suspicious or normal, for that matter. There was a low board fence at the back of the lot that separated it from an alley. I hopped over and trotted down the alley, startling a feral cat and some other critters rustling among the dumpsters and assorted detritus of the downtown urban scene.

I slowed down and looked both ways like a good citizen when I emerged from the ally, just a few feet from my Taurus. I still didn't see anybody. When I turned slowly up the street, staying as close to the cars parked along the curb as I dare. The streets seemed ominously empty. I realized then Dusty's fear has infected me and I was looking for kidnappers, assassins or other bad guys where there weren't any. A shadow flickered at the edge of my vision and I snapped my head around. Nothing.

When I got to the doorway where I'd left Dusty, I didn't see her. After a minute, I got out of the car and stood by the driver's side. "Dusty," I called.

"Shhh," she hissed at me.

When she slid into the car, I drove off at a sedate pace, turned left away from Happy Buns and we drifted through the dark, nearly deserted streets of Minneapolis. Dusty twisted around and looked over her shoulder until the club disappeared from view.

"Okay," I said. "You want to tell me what's going on? I was on a job, you know."

"I'm sorry, Sean, but I hadda get out of there. I ran into a situation."

"A what?"

"A situation. While I was changing after my last show, I overheard some stuff. These guys were standing in the hall outside the dressing rooms."

"How many guys?"

"Two. Three. I don't know. What difference does it make how many there were?"

"I don't know yet."

Dusty grabbed a cigarette and lit it up, drawing in a huge lungful of smoke. I hit the window control on her side and opened the window halfway. I don't smoke anymore and I don't like the smell of it in my car. "So these two or three guys are standing outside the dressing room talking," I prompted.

"Yeah. They were talking about some robbery and then they mentioned having to off some guy who wouldn't tell them where the case had been stashed."

"Uh-huh," I said. I was starting to get a tingle behind my eyes. "Did you get any names?"

"Well one of them mentioned somebody named Talbot."

Now the tingle was stronger. By this time I'd found a stretch of empty curb and pulled over. It was yellow but I wasn't planning to stay there very long. I wanted to concentrate fully on Dusty and what she was saying.

"What else?" I said

"Only two of them talked. The other voice said they might have to 'do' some local yokel."

"Do? Did they name the local?"

"No, Sean. I didn't want to hear any more so I banged a cupboard door at the other end of the room and started to make other noises. Then I grabbed my stuff and beat it out of there. I just walked right by them and out into the club. I was afraid they'd think I overheard them and come after me."

"And when did you know I was in the club?"

"When I came out." Dusty stirred in her seat and threw the butt out onto the sidewalk.

"You'll be arrested for littering," I said. "And you really didn't know I was in the place until you saw me when you came out of the hall back there."

"No, Sean, I just told you." She jerked up her head and stared at me. "Why? When I saw you I thought you could help me get away from the club. It's my last night and I got my money an' I'm goin' out of town tomorrow morning. I'll be gone for a month. I was just glad you were there."

"Okay, Dusty. I'll drive you home. But I think you can forget about what you heard. Don't worry about it, but I wouldn't go around telling people about this little incident."

It was a short drive to her apartment and we were short on conversation the whole way. I let her out with a quick kiss on the cheek and started back across town toward my favorite 'burb. I had a good deal to think about. I don't believe a whole lot in coincidence, even though I know it happens all the time in real life. I have a very close friend who's fond of saying that there are really only four hundred people in the world and if you stand on one street corner long enough, they'll all walk by. She also says a good wood fire is nice, but that's for another story.

Anyway, I figured there were two possibilities, setting aside a whopping coincidence. One was that Talbot and the others had found out that Dusty and I are acquainted and that eventually, she'd relay to me the message from Talbot. But that was fraught with all kind of problematic delays. The other possibility, and the more insidious one, was that they knew I was coming to that club and they knew Dusty was a friend and they set up the whole thing in order to remind me to stop meddling. If that was a possibility, I had to talk to Mike the Mole and very soon.

***

The summer breeze from the river lifted Catherine's hair off her ears. We were walking hand in hand along an unpaved path in the Hidden Falls park of St. Paul, along the bank of the Mississippi. In spite of the constant rushing rumble of the city which formed a background to birds twittering in the trees and the rustle of grass and leaves, we could have been in the country. It was a rural patch in the midst of an urban population of nearly three million people. Catherine was carrying an honest-to-God picnic hamper. I hadn't been on a real picnic since high school. That one time I got bitten by a wasp, tossed in a cold lake with all my clothes on, and stuck my hands into some poison ivy. I'm not a big fan of picnics. In fact, even though I live in a small urban forest, I'm not a big fan of intruding into rural outdoors for any reason. Concrete and asphalt pavement, that's my scene. It's not like fires which both attract and repel me. I prefer that nature go about its business without any interference from me. In turn, I stay as far out of nature's reach as I can. It had taken weeks of persuasion to get me on this picnic. But it was a nice contrast from the smoky bar-crawl of the night before.

In sharp contrast to my mood, Catherine, was smiling broadly. I even thought I detected a giggle or two. CM was actually reveling in the event. She turned her face to the sun and breathed deeply. I admired the way the front of her baggy sweater pushed out when she did that. Her long skirt swirled around her. I admired her trim ankles. "You'll love it," she burbled. "I know a private spot down here on the other side of the bridge. No one goes there." Undesirables? Did they go there? The bridge she was talking about, the concrete structure overhead, carried Highway Five across the river to the airport and then merged with which separated a long strip of hotels, restaurants and nightclubs. My urban scene. My hunting grounds. We walked down the path a while longer, not talking. I was cogitating about my conversation with Eddie Talbot and the night before at Happy Buns. I was also watching where I put my feet. I don't know what Catherine was thinking about. After stumbling down the dusty path that wound through the waist high weeds, we came to a small grassy patch right on the river bank. It was surrounded by brush, nodding Golden Rod and other growth, unremarkable bushes and a few scrubby trees I didn't recognize. What could be nicer than this, a cool wine, some good looking sandwiches accompanied by my most favorite lady? Plus a bag of fruit."

CM looked sideways at me while she placed the sandwiches on two small plastic plates. "You have a stable of lesser favorite ladies?"

"Well, there is that stripper I told you about,"

"Of course." She nodded wisely. "Not to change subjects, what else can you tell me about Eddie Talbot?" I'd repeated the gist of my conversation with prisoner Talbot in the car on our way to Hidden Falls.

"I think he's angry because he's in jail and his fellow felons in the real estate deal are outside and apparently ignoring him. He's had no visitors, according to the prison records. I think he knew about the pharmacy robbery and that George Beechy was supposed to hold the money for the gang. It upset him a lot when I told him Beechy had been killed."

"It's a gang within a gang."

"I think so."

"What does it mean? Here, pour me some more wine, lover." I became aware of the rising sound of a heavy engine and I looked up to see a river tugboat pushing a load of empty barges along the water in front of us. They were heading upriver, presumably toward the lock and dam half-a mile away and from there to the upper harbor.

I watched the traffic slide ponderously by on the river and set thought about CM's question. Privately I admitted to myself I was having an enjoyable experience in this bucolic setting. Companionship was certainly a large part of the ambiance. And so far I hadn't seen a single snake. "I guess I think there really was money in that aluminum case carried off from the Grand Pharmacy, and I think lots of people besides Sal Belassario are looking for it. And Talbot is one of the three who ripped off the pharmacy. I suspect that he recruited some locals to help him. The violence bothers me. There hasn't been any linked to the real estate games."

"If you don't count the fires."

We polished off the sandwiches and a good bit of the wine. I was reclining on one elbow, staring at the opposite river bank when I felt a warm breath on my face. Catherine planted a lengthy, warm kiss on the corner of my mouth. "I have a little secret," she breathed.

"Yeah? And are you going to share this secret?"

"I'm undecided. But I might let you put your powers of deduction to work."

I ran one hand up her back under the sweater and felt the warm play of muscle under her smooth skin. I started to pull her closer but she put both hands on my chest and pushed me down so I was flat on the blanket. Swinging one booted foot over me, she settled on my hips.

Oof."

"Oof, indeed."

We listened to leaves slithering together from a nearby Birch tree and birds twittering. Then, in the background, intruded the thrashing and thrumming of one of the paddle-wheeler excursion boats that operated out of the St. Paul marina down river a mile or so. The boats ran tourists up to the mouth of the Minnesota River or the base of Lock and Dam No. 1, locally known as the Ford Dam. Not because some guy named Ford built it, but because the dam is right across the street from the big Ford truck plant. During summer days like this one, the excursion boats were usually crowded with binocular-wielding folks examine the river-bank scenery.

Catherine was smiling more widely down at me from her perch. "You still haven't divined my secret, lover." With that she took my right hand and placed it on her thigh, her bare thigh, under the edge of her skirt. When I slid my hand upward, as she knew I would, I discovered her secret. She leaned down and we kissed, thoroughly and most satisfactorily. While I was detecting her secret, her hands were busy with my belt and my fly. In the near background, I heard the sound of the paddle wheeler full of tourists with binoculars, drawing inexorably closer.

14

Sal Belassario looked across the table at me, his jaws moving slowly over the last of his meal. We'd finished an excellent luncheon of middle-eastern pita bread, stuffed grape leaves, hummus and garlic-heavy tabuli. It was great. We were shoehorned into a tiny corner upstairs at Emily's out on University Avenue in Northeast. It was just after twelve, their heaviest time, but situated where we were, in a corner of the upstairs dining room, conversation was relatively effortless and the other conversations going on around us reduced any chance of being overheard. That possibility was something Sal was always concerned about whenever we met. I wondered if it was me or if it was his naturally cautious nature. We were meeting so I could report on my progress, or lack of it. One of Sal's quirks was that he occasionally got paranoid about the telephone being tapped. This was one of those occasions so we were having face time. After I explained what little I knew so far we were just chatting while we finished lunch.

"What do you do about bugs and telephone taps?" he asked abruptly.

"I hire a guy to sweep the office periodically."

"Isn't that expensive?"

"Yes, so I don't do it very often."

"Anything every turn up?"

"Not in the last year. I hear you turned up at the service for Beechy out in Willmar," I changed the subject.

"Rumors," Sal grunted. He didn't want to be labeled a softy or a concerned citizen, even though it was well known that made guys in the mobs on the coasts considered appearances at members' funerals to be part of the job description.

"I don't think so," I said. "You better be careful, Sal, people will think you're getting soft."

Sal's lips twitched in what I though could be a smile and shrugged. The cookie he was eating crumbled and slid down his massive front. He brushed ineffectually at the crumbs and came back to the reason for our meeting. "Where's the woman? Annette Campbell?"

"I don't think you need to know that, Sal. It's not exactly a trust thing, but if anything should happen to her, I don't want to have to look at you, or even think about you. I can produce her whenever she's needed. Let's just say she's perfectly safe."

"Yeah, sure. Safe. I mean, why wouldn't she be?" He looked at me sharply. "You figure she's in danger because of the other night?"

"Because of the break-in at Mordecai's, that's right. Which reminds me. What do you know about that? You hear things. What do you hear on the street?"

Sal laughed. "On the street? Where do you think we are? Look out there. It's University Avenue in Northeast Minneapolis. Empty, wouldn't you say?"

I looked. He was right. A few cars passed. No gangbangers, no gunners. Across the street an old man was being pulled along behind a small white poodle-like dog straining against his leash. It was definitely quiet. No mean streets anywhere in sight. We liked our city that way and sometimes I felt like I was one of those who helped keep it that way. But that was only in my dreams.

Sal and I parted on the sidewalk. I was still nervous about some of his reputed connections, but he was a likable, personable, fellow in spite of that, and once in a while his connections, including the political ones, were useful. I drove to the south side to visit once again with Annette Campbell. Even though I'd been relaxed and sure during lunch, I decided dropping in on la Campbell would be worth my while, even if I didn't have a whole lot to talk to her about. Our lunch time conversation had got me thinking that I didn't know about a lot of Sal's connections. There was a lot of scuttlebutt, conjecture but I had no proof and I decided if I wasn't really worried about Sal, it still wouldn't hurt to be alert.

When Annette Campbell let me in the security conscious high-rise apartment where we'd stashed her up on the fifth floor, at an outrageous monthly rent, she was wearing a short robe and, it appeared, very little else. Apparently my discomfort showed, because she started flirting.

I went straight to business.

"Annette, you said Eddie Talbot brought a small leather suitcase to the airport for you to bring to Minneapolis. Right?"

She nodded, caught her lower lip between her teeth.

"Do you know what was in it?"

"I already told you, you know? I didn't ever get curious about that stuff. It was the same as other times. Eddie just tol' me just to bring the bag."

"So, you were the bag lady for the gang and—"

"Do I look like a bag lady to you?" Annette sat up straighter and stuck out her chest at me.

"Well, what would you call it?" I tried to keep from dropping my eyes to her considerable cleavage.

"Well, mostly, I was a courier. I, um, took files and stuff from office to office."

"In North Carolina."

"Yeah."

"Did they have a lot of offices?"

"What's a lot? They had several. In different places, you know? Once I went to Atlanta and brought back a big valise."

"What's a valise? What was in it?"

"What's a valise? She sighed in exasperation. "A valise, a medium size suitcase. It was old and scuffed up leather. Are you sure you're a detective?"

"Do you know what was in the valise?"

"Sure. Money. That one time I was still in the room when they opened it. Just before they shooed me out." She stopped then and looked at me, batted her eyelashes. Just an old fashioned girl, I guess. "Look, Sean. These guys have been all over. Florida, Georgia, Louisiana. It's been goin' on a long time, gettin' bigger and better."

"And they moved cash from place to place, instead of divvying up after each job was over, right?"

"I guess. The way I heard it, everybody drew a fixed amount of money, depending on whatever has been set up."

"Like a salary," I said.

"I guess. I don't know from salaries. I always got paid up front. In cash. We were supposed to all get together and split up the cash sometime later down the road."

"Sounds really odd," I said. "How'd they get everybody to go along?"

"Most of the time we had more money and less worries than ever before. But some of the guys didn' go along, you know? A couple of guys dropped out earlier. Eddie Talbot hadda go and try to rob some store. He's in jail," she said in what sounded to me like a virtuous tone. "I guess he wanted more money. Mainly though, we was—were—told that some of the money from the early jobs would finance later things which needed a lot more front money."

"But didn't some of the money for the St. Paul jobs come from people here, like Mordecai?"

"I guess. But they didn't tell me everything that was going on, you know? Until I met Mordy, I was supposed to be available to keep some of the guys happy, run errands and that was all. Like I told you all ready."

"But when you and Mordecai got together, he took you out of the gang, is that what happened?" She nodded and looked away. "Then something happened and the cache of money got ripped off and the pharmacist and his clerk were killed."

She licked her lips and squinted at me. "Look, I don't know nothin' about that. I was in California when that happened."

I drummed my fingers on the arm of my chair. Right then, I changed my mind. I'd planned to get more background on my short list of names before asking Ms. Campbell about them, but now I decided to go ahead with what I had.

"Eddie Talbot and his brother, Henry, were in the group, right? Eddie's the one in jail." She nodded. I didn't see any reason to tell her I'd already had a talk with Eddie in Stillwater Prison.

"All right, besides you and Mordecai, and the Talbot brothers, there's Jake Larson and Armond Anderson?" She nodded again. "Describe the Talbots and Larson for me."

Annette described Henry Talbot as looking very much like his brother whom I'd met. Jake Larson was apparently a dark little weasely person, with a sharp pointed nose that twitched, little dark, beady eyes, and a long hairless tail. No, no, that last was just my invention. But Campbell did tell me Larson had prominent teeth. She said he was a sharp dresser, but I couldn't decide just what that meant.

"Tell me about Armond Anderson."

"I can't," she responded. "I never met the guy. Henry Talbot talked to him, carried messages back and forth, you know?"

"So even though Anderson was the head of the whole enterprise, only one of the group, this Henry Talbot, ever met the man or talked to him, right?"

Annette nodded. "Yeah, I guess. You see, Henry Talbot was the guy who told us what to do, where to go, when to do it, stuff like that. He called himself the foreman of the crew."

"How did you all get together?" I was getting an unsettling sensation that A. Anderson was slipping away right under my fingers. I didn't like the sensation.

"Well, it was all Henry Talbot. He got Eddie, of course, and between them they knew the rest of us."

"If the Talbots were never in the Twin Cities before, how did they get Mordy involved?"

She shrugged her shoulders elaborately, another mannerism. I noticed she often did that when she didn't have an answer, or didn't want to tell. The mannerism jiggled her noticeable bosoms. It was mildly distracting, which, I suppose, was the point.

"I can't say. You better ask Mordy."

I would certainly do that, as soon as I could find the man.

I had more questions but Annette was becoming a little surly and her answers were becoming shorter and shorter. I decided to cut the questions and took my leave, once again admonishing the lady to keep a low profile.

"Sure," she said. "You be careful, too. And tell Mordy to call me real soon."

15

Catherine and I were due for a dinner out that evening so I went home after my interview with Annette Campbell to shower and change into something more suitable for dinner. I wore an expensive sports jacket over a colored shirt, nice pressed slacks and my usual red high-top tennis shoes with the white soles. It was my usual uniform. Except for the expensive jacket. I was so comfortable in the tennies that I had several pair and wore them almost all the time. In fact, it was because the red tennis shoes were on my feet at an elegant Symphony Ball a few years ago that Catherine introduced herself to me, intrigued as she was by the reasonable-looking, if short, fella in the nice threads with, as she murmured a moment after floating across the floor and introducing herself, the intriguing bulge over my left hip.

"What do you mean?" I had responded.

"If you stand hip-shot like that, anyone looking at you will see the handgun on your belt."

"I'd looked at her in mild astonishment and said, "How do you know it's a weapon instead of a fat wallet?"

"I can smell it," she'd said and floated away.

When I arrived at her apartment, Catherine was standing at the small bar in a corner of her living room mixing us a drink. We had our drinks and went off to dinner at the recently refurbished Lindy's Steak House. It was a very un-PC dinner. Over coffee, Catherine reached into her purse and handed me a heavy cream-colored envelope. I took it and raised one eyebrow at her.

"The people who support the Twin Cities Foundation are holding a benefit for the social services fund of the foundation. That's my invitation. You probably don't remember, but I did mention it several weeks ago."

I took out the embossed card and read it. I said, "Thursday night at the Hilton. I see you're invited to bring a companion."

"Yes, and I choose you to be my escort. It'll be a high-toned affair. Dress-up, you know."

"You mean I can't wear my tennis shoes?"

She smiled. "Correct. There'll be lawyers, some politicians, wealthy people and business leaders there. Many board members of important social agencies. Like that."

"The sort of boring event where people stand around and try to impress other people, maybe make deals and contacts? The kind of gathering where you're likely to be more noticeable by your absence than your attendance?"

"Exactly."

"Do we get fed?"

"Indubitably."

"Will there be a program?"

"Inevitably. For one thing, they'll want to remind everyone that the cost of the affair doesn't cost the foundation anything."

I bowed toward her over my coffee. "It would be my honor to escort you."

Early Thursday evening, I arrived at Catherine's in my best dark suit, white shirt, conservative dark tie, and my red tennies. When I walked in the door, she was wearing a slinky dark gray affair with spaghetti straps, a deep décolletage, and a long skirt that just kissed her ankles. I bounded across the room for a welcoming kiss at the head end and discovered she was wearing heels which gave her two more inches of height advantage than she normally enjoyed.

"I hope you don't mind," she murmured, drawing back slightly from the embrace. "I just felt like really dressing up tonight."

"Have I ever? You do me proud. Every eye in the place will be on us."

"I'll say," she said, glancing down in disapproval at my feet.

I grinned. "Couldn't resist. My black dress shoes are in the car."

The lobby was filling up and when we entered the ballroom at the hotel, there was already a sizable crowd. Along the wall at the back of the room was a long table covered with white table cloths, crowded with trays and dishes of bite-sized crackers with caviar, mounds of shrimp in ice-laden crystal bowls, nuts a selection of cheeses and other assorted goodies.

"I'm curious," I said, bowing Catherine through the huge double doors to the ballroom. "You accepted this invitation months ago, right? So you must have indicated then that you'd be bringing a companion. What if I'd been unavailable?"

CM looked at me an allowed a tiny smile to flicker about her lips. "You think you're the only suitable male in my escort stable, sailor?"

"Ah," I said. Best response I could come up with at the moment.

A few of the men were in dinner jackets and bow ties, others in dark business suits. Most of the women were wearing long dresses and the rest wore dressy cocktail outfits with a few elegant pantsuits also in evidence.

Two portable bars on either side of the ballroom bookstopped long lines of people getting drinks from a wide assortment of choices. "Wow," I murmured. "You could feed a whole town full of the homeless with what this spread cost."

"All donated by the hotel," Catherine replied, "or paid for by big donors."

We sashayed smiling and nodding across the floor, heading for another table where three young women sat accepting donations to the cause and handing out pledge cards for those who weren't carrying enough cash. CM placed her donation in an envelope, accepted a receipt, and we turned toward the bar. Across the room I spotted Sal Belassario. He'd encased his bulk in a tuxedo over shiny patent leather shoes. He was engaged in close conversation with a man I didn't recognize.

On our way to the bar, Lawrence St. Martin, senior partner of St. Martin, St. Martin, et cetera law firm, crossed our path and stopped in front of us. "Well, Sean. I'm surprised to see you here." His close-set eyes switched to my companion. "My my. I insist you introduce me to your lovely companion." He was eyeing my gorgeous companion in a rather indiscreet manner. I introduced Catherine. He took her hand and bowed low over it. It gave him an opportunity to examine her cleavage more closely. "Mckerney, Mckerney." His brow furrowed.

"I'm the CEO of MPMT," she said retrieving her hand.

"Indeed?"

"Mckerney Professional Massage Therapy. I believe you are acquainted with my attorney, Robert Peschl."

"Oh, Bob Pestle. Of course. Of course."

I could almost see the synapses firing in his brain. How could a massage therapist afford the high priced talent of one of the top corporate lawyers in town? Since he wasn't indiscreet enough to ask the question, he left us.

We moved on, and after snagging a couple of glasses of a pretty good white Chardonnay, stopped to talk to Jerome Ford. He introduced his wife, Ella, a petite brunette with a quick smile who said, "I was so sorry to miss your party, Sean, but we'll have you and Catherine to dinner soon."

The four of us stood chatting about the Vikings and the hopes of the Gopher football team and the new coach, and I felt the crowd growing around us. I intercepted a number of admiring glances which I knew were focused on my stunning companion. I was pretty sure they weren't asking themselves what kind of studmuffin I was. Glancing around, I satisfied myself that Catherine was the best looking woman in the hall.

When the group shifted, John and Dianne turned to move on. Gerry stopped and shifted his cane to his other hand. His action brought him closer to my side and he murmured, "Games, Sean. Games. See the man next to Sal?"

I nodded.

"That's Jake Logan. He represents a new developer in Bloomington. He's on your list."

I didn't wonder for a second what list he was referring to. I smiled and touched Catherine's arm. "I'm going to have a brief chat with Sal. I'll find you later." She nodded and veered off toward the buffet table. When I ambled up to Sal Belassario and his companion, they stopped talking as I got within earshot and Sal smiled at me. Lots of smiling going on at this affair.

"Ah, Sean Sean. Meet Mr. Jake Logan."

Logan stuck out a hard, callused hand and squeezed mine. He appeared to be comparing hand strength so I left my fingers limp. A lot of small men feel they have to do that, demonstrate a macho handshake. I never got it. He had big shoulders and was obviously in good shape under his dark, expensively tailored, suit. He wasn't more than an inch taller than me. Of course, he could have been wearing lifts on his shoes.

"Sean Sean, is it? How ya doin'? I'm in real estate development and construction. Commercial real estate," he said. His eyes never left my face. He was very good. At the mention of my name, there'd been nary a flicker from his dark, close-set eyes. The adjective beady came to mind. If I hadn't known better, I'd have been sure he'd never heard of me.

"Real estate development," I said. "Don't know much about it myself. I'm a private detective and I don't get many clients involved in that game."

"Just what kind of clientele do you attract," Mr. ... Sean?" He twitched his nose.

See, that often happens. With identical first and last names, people never can decide if they are addressing me formally or not. I use that to my advantage, sometimes. "Oh, I do a little investigation work for some of the law firms in town. Find lost people. Root out industrial espionage, shoplifting. That sort of thing." I smiled at him.

"Well, that must be very interesting."

"Sometimes it is, Mr. Logan. But most of the time it's boring, tedious slogging through dusty records and interviewing people." I shrugged elaborately. "Once in a while I happen on some insurance fraud and that can be more of a challenge."

Not a scintilla of a reaction from Logan. Sal smiled and nodded. Logan pulled back his sleeve and consulted a heavy gold wrist watch.

"Gentlemen, I fear the press of business calls. It's been most interesting meeting you both, but I better get on."

The Case of the Stolen Case

After Logan left, sidling though the press of bodies, I looked up at Sal and said, "How do you suppose he got an invitation?"

Belassario shrugged and leaned closer so I could hear. "I'm glad I ran into you, Sean. A little bird at Onyx John's palace tells me the neighbors in Frogtown are pressuring the city to tear down that burned out house."

"Do we care?"

"I have no idea, just thought I'd mention it." He tapped me on the shoulder with his soft hand and strolled away. Time wore on and the crowd in the ballroom increased and thinned, but there were always around a hundred people present. It was a fine turnout and I could see from the activity around the pledge table that they must be doing very well.

At the end of the ballroom opposite the main doors was a low platform on which a trio of performers entertained us with soft-rock and melodious ballads. A tall lean man in a tuxedo stepped up to the single microphone and tapped on it, then called for attention. After several tries, he had most of crowd faced his way.

"Good evening friends," he said quietly in a strong baritone voice. He glanced around the room, nodding at important people he recognized. "My name is Phillip St. Martin, and I'm chairman of the board of the Twin Cities Foundation.

"As some of you know, this is the third such annual affair. Now I have some very good news. But first, let me salute the management of the Hilton Hotel, and the following corporations which have contributed so handsomely to tonight's success. I'm very pleased to report that no costs for this event will be borne by the Twin Cities Foundation." He was interrupted at that point by a round of applause from the audience.

"I want to encourage all of you to patronize the firms that have contributed so generously to the foundation and to this evening. Their names are included in the pamphlet you each received when you arrived.

"Now, let me introduce the director of the Twin Cities Foundation, Ms. Adrianne Wolfe." More applause.

Ms Wolfe, a slightly anorexic blond of indeterminate years, appeared at the microphone. She positively beamed at her audience. "I'll keep this short," she said. "I know you want to get back to socializing, but I am just so excited, I need to give you the news the minute. For the third year in a row, the foundation has exceeded its target, this year by a much higher percentage than expected."

Since the goal had been announced in the Strib as $1 million, this was good news.

"And one of the reasons is a very generous pledge of $50,000 from Mr. Armond Anderson and his firm. The first payment was received this evening and we are just thrilled to publicly acknowledge Mr. Anderson's generosity. I wish he could have been here this evening to accept our public thanks. Well, that's all. Thank you for coming. I hope you're having a wonderful time and thanks again to each and every one of you for your generosity." Ms. Wolf waved happily and stepped away from the microphone. The band struck up a soft tune I didn't recognize.

Now I knew the why and how of Jake Logan's appearance at this affair.

As the crowd dispersed from in front of the platform, three couples began to dance and I looked around the room, searching for Catherine. When I sighted her, there was a crowd of men around her. As I walked up she turned on me such a bright, welcoming smile, I tell you I felt ten feet tall.

Again the crowd shifted and we found ourselves in semi-isolation. I pulled back my sleeve and consulted my steel cased Timex wrist watch. "Had enough, darling?"

Catherine nodded and we strolled toward the ballroom doors.

16

I was changing into a pair of tennis shoes below my black jeans. Catherine came into the bedroom holding the Star Tribune. She was in her big velour bathrobe, the one I like to snuggle in, when she's in it, of course. "I still think you should talk to Jack about it," she said.

"Babe, we've been over this. The place is scheduled for demolition tomorrow or the next day and there's a very good chance whatever's in there will be destroyed. I have to go look."

"What are you looking for?"

"A clue or clues to this case. Possibly even an aluminum case."

She sighed and gestured with the folded newspaper. "The Almanac says there's a new moon tonight, just right for skulking about."

"Good. No need to wait up, sweetie. I'll just take a look around and be back in a couple of hours."

"Unh huh. Watch yourself out there, sailor. I wouldn't like having to get out of bed for a trip to the hospital." She turned back the duvet and slid under the covers, dropping the robe as she did. I noticed she wasn't wearing anything else.

I leaned over, kissed her on the nose and left, adding my big Maglight to the small carryall. The carryall already contained my B & E tools, a small crowbar, a tool belt, pliers, a screwdriver and an expensive set of lock picks.

I hoped I'd carried it off. Catherine didn't know how I detested fires. And at the same time how attracted I was by them. I guess I am drawn to firemen and fires when they are happening. From a safe distance. But I hated the aftermath, the smelly, reeking odors of burned wood and melted plastic. I've been known to cross the street to avoid walking right by a burned out building. Now I was going into one. My gut told me I was being a very bad boy.

At two a.m. I parked the Taurus around the corner from George Beechy's Frogtown address and walked silently down the alley. The house had been boarded up and a fence erected around the property, but I had no doubt I'd find someplace where the fence had been breached.

There was no wind and as I reached the back side of the property I could smell the soot and charcoal of partially burned wood. I detected the smell of burned paint or varnish. Conflicting emotions skittered through my gut. I was both repelled and fascinated. Maybe I should have been a fireman. Maybe not.

I went through the fence and made a quick and almost soundless circuit of the three story house. The smell was intense. No attempt had been made to clean up the yard and I picked my way carefully around piles of debris including scorched bedding, insulation and a lot of stuff I didn't try to identify. I started consciously breathing through my mouth.

After my exploratory circuit, which revealed very little except to intensify my feeling that I didn't want to be here, I approached the back door. It was covered with a big rough sheet of plywood and my questing fingers discovered it had been thoroughly nailed. Entry would have been time consuming hard work and noisy. When I peered to my right, I discovered an unbroken window which was not covered. I went back to the side yard and retrieved a partially burned single mattress. I stuffed the mattress over the window to muffle the sound of breaking glass. Then I slammed a long 2x4 against the mattress. The piece of wood cracked with what seemed to be a loud crack, and the window collapsed inward. So far, so good. In the distance a dog barked, but close by there was no sound, no light in yonder windows, not even the whisper of a summer breeze.

I exchanged leather work gloves for latex and slid inside the house. I paused and listened again. My heart was hammering.

There was no hope of searching the entire house. Too time consuming and much too dangerous. But if my theory of the case was correct, I wouldn't have to. If I found something, I'd know I was right. If I didn't, I might never know.

Beechy had been beaten in the yard. With broken bones, he'd crawled around the house, already aflame, through the back door and across the kitchen floor to the basement door. Why?

I stood where Beechy's life had expired and touched the door to the basement stairs with one hand. Broken glass and other things I couldn't identify crackled underfoot. In the shaded light of my flash, I could see my fingers were trembling slightly. Somewhere above me, something creaked. I took a deep breath through my mouth and pulled the door open.

If anything, it was darker in the stair well than where I was standing. A miasma of fetid odors, a mixture of burned wood and other substances, water and, in the background, eau de basement greeted me as I inched my way to the top step. The linoleum on the kitchen floor had lifted and cracked under the two pronged assault of heat and cold water from the fire hoses. I tried not to stumble over the random cracks and edges.

I unhooked my Maglight from my belt and aimed its narrow beam down the cellar steps. The stairs were a straight shot, no landing, no turns. The steps were dirty and tracked with charcoal and mud, but I couldn't see any evidence of burn. That probably meant they were safe. I stepped forward and carefully placed my weight on the top step. It held. So far ... as the saying goes. Moving slowly and cautiously, I went down into the cellar. My brain entertained thoughts of what could happen if any part of the upper stories abruptly gave way and found me skulking about in the basement. My stomach jumped and I took another deep breath. Mistake. The smell of the place filled my nostrils and caused a choking sensation at the base of my throat. I swallowed rapidly several times and peered around, still moving forward. Except for random pieces of rafter and flooring which had fallen through holes in the main floor, the basement appeared to be mostly undisturbed. Everything was covered with a layer of dust and dirt, a lot of it from the fire, but much of it due to years of little or no traffic.

Standing in the middle of the basement, I pushed away my fear of being trapped in this stinking hole and faced the furnace. It remained still and silent in response to the probing beam of my flash. Behind me there was the sudden sound of scurrying feet. I dropped to one knee and whirled around.

Nothing. But directly ahead of me was an old brick wall. I heard the scurrying sound again. This time, marginally calmer, I was able to identify the sound as some kind of critter, apparently of the four-legged kind. Apparently behind the wall. Outside?

It didn't sound like it. I looked at all the walls of the basement from where I crouched. Quite ordinary. Just old brick. Brick. That was interesting, because I recalled that in my nocturnal creep around the outside of the place, I'd noted that the foundation walls above ground were the usual stone one expected to find in houses of this vintage and in this part of the city. So, why didn't I see the stone walls, or whitewash, or plaster instead of this old brick? Odd. Then there was that scurrying sound.

Perhaps whoever built the place didn't like the look of the stone. Did I care why the brick wall was there? No, because the brick was unbroken. It reached from concrete floor to rafters and there were no opening or panels, obvious or secret. I know because I looked. Quite carefully. My search took the better part of an hour and served only to make me grimier than before.

Now what? If I was going to break down a brick wall, I wanted some assurance that I was going in the right direction. My theory that the deceased George Beechy had been trying to get to the basement, even after his grievous injuries, before succumbing finally to the fire, still made sense to me. I further assumed that if he would risk his life to get down here, a place likely to be a trap, there was something almighty important down here. That police and fire fighters hadn't found it meant it must be hidden. Okay, so good so far.

But, what was it and where was it?

I decided to leave the basement, if only to clear my lungs of the foul odors. Outside, it was no lighter, but the air was cleaner. Quietly

The Case of the Stolen Case

I ambled around the house again, thinking furiously. I approached the last corner, toward the back of the house and my hand touched the cool steel pipe protruding from the wall. I recognized it as the vent pipe for what had once been an oil fired furnace used to heat the place. I'd looked at the furnace and seen the more recent modification including a connection to the natural gas pipe. So what?

Wait a minute. At the court house I'd looked at the property abstract. This particular house was built before oil heat had become a normal state of affairs and way before natural gas arrived. So what, I again asked myself.

So, self silently replied, what heated the house before oil came?

Indeed, I said in my internal dialogue. Recall the look of the furnace area. There was a pattern or stain on the floor near where the old furnace squatted that could have been a box to contain coal.

I turned the rear corner of the house and sure enough, my questing fingers encountered a large metal door set into the foundation stones. It was the cover for a coal chute. Of course it was cemented shut, but at least it was an opening through both stone and brick walls and worth investigating further.

Sure enough, in the basement, partially concealed behind some heating pipes, I found the semi collapsed open end of the coal chute. It angled downward and emerged through a notch in the brick wall just below the first floor rafters. The chute itself was long gone. But the notch was easily wide enough to accommodate my slender body.

I was a little too young for Viet Nam. Had I been in the service, I would undoubtedly have been one of those sent in to ferret out the tunnels installed by the Cong. A tunnel rat. I scrambled up until my shoulders and head were through the brick. Just as I had begun to suspect, there was a two-foot wide gap between the granite foundation and the interior brick wall. I aimed my flash along the gap. The space was mostly filled with the trash of construction and accumulated dirt, not the least of which was numerous mouse droppings.

But directly below me, resting on that accumulated dirt gleamed a smooth rounded case, handle uppermost. Jackpot! Perhaps.

I withdrew from the chute and located a straightened wire coat hanger in my carryall. After I straightened out the hanger, I figured its hook end would reach the handle of the case. Somewhere above me I heard a muffled whump. After listening for a minute and hearing nothing further, I crawled back into the chute and hung over as far as I dared. The handle of the case was down and resting against the inside brick wall so I had to jockey the wire hook around to get a hold of it. Concentrating, with my flash in one hand and the coat hanger in the other, I was largely oblivious to anything else. Except the smell. While I was hanging in the gap the burned smells seemed to concentrate in the space.

Finally, I snagged the case and hauled it carefully up. After that it was only a moment's work to climb down out of the ruined chute and set the case on the basement floor. In the light of my flash it appeared to be in good condition. Except for a few scratches which must have come from the brick wall, it looked good as new and undisturbed. The latches were heavy duty and the locking mechanism was designed to protect the contents. Opening it was a job for later. I turned to repacking my tools in the carryall. That's when I heard a crackle, and the sound of something shifting. Then a bang and a huge crash overhead that shook the rafters and send dust sifting down on my head. Creaking sounds of stressed wood followed. What the Hell?

I went to the single basement window and glanced out. It was still dark, but reflecting in the windows of the house next door, I could see first a flicker, then a glow and then flames. The damn house was on fire again.

I grabbed the case and the carryall and ran for the stairs. I started up and realized the basement door was now shut. My stomach clenched in my gut. I was sure I'd left the damn door open when I descended the second time. Not only was it shut, something had wedged against it and it was stuck tight. Damn, this was serious. If I didn't want to end up barbecued beside the big clue, I had to find a different way out. Smoke and heat began to slink into the basement. Sweat popped out on my body and my breathing got short and sharp, all signs of incipient panic on my part.

I wheeled and dropped back to the basement. The single window appeared to be the only available exit from this tomb. It was a typical small basement window, not easily reached from the floor by an average-height person. For me, a ladder was a necessity. I didn't see one. I dragged some boxes over to the wall and stacked them haphazardly below the window. There was a terrific bang somewhere over my head and the rafters shook, sending more dust into an already thickening atmosphere.

It was obvious, even in my panic, that the pile of boxes was a seriously uncertain escape route. I took two deep breaths to try to calm myself and get a little more oxygen to my brain. Then I took a long, slow look around the whole basement again. Over in once corner I spied some furniture. Aha! I pulled and tugged and dragged an old sofa out of the pile and when I got it close to the window, I upended it, leaning it against the wall so it made an incline. By jamming my feet through the fabric under the pillows, I figured I could make some steps.

I grabbed the handle of the aluminum case—forget about possible fingerprints—and threw it with all my might at the window. It sailed through, exploding the window out of its frame. I threw my carryall after the case and made like a frightened rabbit, crawling up the sofa, jammed my body through the window and sprawled onto the side lawn. Even beaten down, the grass was sweet and the air was cleaner.

From outside the perimeter of the yard, I could hear people calling and in the background, sirens. Bending low, I collected the case and my carryall and scuttled toward the farthest back corner. This time, it was easier to see where I was going. The flames clawing skyward from the second floor windows lit up the yard all too well. Smoke swirled through the heavy summer air and sweat poured down my sides. There were a few neighbors in the alley when I scooted through the fence but they were far more interested in the fire than in me.

I straightened and started down the alley toward my car, forcing myself to walk slowly, and glancing back from time to time at the now-raging fire. Behind me there was a terrific crunch and the back half of the house collapsed into the basement.

17

I unlocked my car and sank into the driver's seat until my nose was just below the level of the steering wheel center. A cloud of dust and smoke and flames rose high in the air over Beechy's former house. Down the street rolled a pumper, red lights flashing, siren growling down to silence. Its big, side-mounted arc lamps crackled on. They flooded the house with bright, blue-white light and made the flames that were eating away at the remainder of the second story, seemed puny and insubstantial.

My clothing gave off a powerful stink of basement and burned wood. I dropped the aluminum case on the floor beside me and shoved a blanket over it along with my carry-all of tools. My fingers trembled, jangling the keys against the steering column as I tried to fit the key into the ignition slot. The euphoria I felt over recovery of what must be the aluminum case that figured in the Grand Pharmacy murder and robbery, was tempered by my narrow escape. I don't mind admitting that I was close to total panic in that basement, before I found the window and crawled out onto the grass.

I checked the increasing traffic around me and drove out, heading for Roseville and home. I decided to call Catherine when I got to Roseville instead of following my original plan which was to return to her Kenwood apartment. I smelled too bad to inflict that on her. The streets were mostly quiet at this early hour so I must have been particularly inattentive. North of the city I turned off Dale and headed west on County Road C into Roseville. That was when the lights in my rearview mirror became glaring and intrusive. The SUV was right on my rear bumper and the brown car in front of me was braking rapidly to a halt. I was sandwiched. I screwed up my face in irritation at myself and looked for a way out. I thought briefly of gunning the Taurus into the yard on my right. But it was over a curb, uphill and I knew it was a bad idea. Both the vehicles crowding me had stopped a little to the street side of the Taurus so there was no chance of just making a sharp left. All of that went through my mind in a flash and then I saw the shotgun aimed at my face through the windshield from the driver's seat of the car in front. It's not the first time I've had a long gun pointed at me, but the visceral reaction never goes away. My fingers slid to the vinyl pouch I'd built under the dash beside the steering column. The cool touch of my big .45 caliber Colt automatic resting in its rig was reassuring, but I didn't think I could draw it and shoot before the shotgun rearranged the Taurus and quite possibly my physiognomy. The radio continued to play soft jazz as if nothing at all was the matter.

In my rearview mirror I saw a large figure slowly exit the driver's seat of the SUV. He looked up and down the street. Interesting. He must have been alone or they should have left the driver behind the wheel. I couldn't tell for sure but he appeared to be wearing a stocking cap mask which must have been hot and uncomfortable. I know I was hot and uncomfortable. The guy seemed jumpy. I carefully drew my gat and placed it in my lap, aimed at the door and thumbed off the safety.

The large thug came up alongside and pointed his gun at me. With his other hand he yanked on the car door. It was locked and didn't open. "Open the damn door, he yelled."

I nodded at him and pivoted my hips and upper body in his direction. There was just enough slack in the seatbelt to allow me to slide a few inches to the right. My left arm traveled across the steering wheel toward the seatbelt latch, drawing the eyes of both my assailants, which I knew it would. Given all the evidence before me, I was pretty sure these guys weren't on the side of the angels so when my fingers reached the button, I shot through the door. Twice. At the same time, having neglected to take the car out of drive, I floored the accelerator. The Taurus jumped forward and slammed into the back of the car in front of me. Naturally the shotgun went off. I saw the muzzle flash. I didn't hear it through the windshield. The sound of my own weapon discharging had given me a serious case of ringing in my ears.

Fortunately, the guy in the car ahead wasn't braced so when I smacked his vehicle, he fell forward, bringing his aim down. Shotgun slugs from his weapon pretty well destroyed the back seat and trunk of his car. A few stray shot caromed off the trunk lid and made stars on my windshield. Meantime, the other dude was rolling around in the street clutching one leg and screaming he'd been shot. He yelled that several times, interspersing his facts with an amazing string of epithets.

I yanked the wheel to the right and slammed into reverse, just clipping the right front of the SUV. My rear fender crumpled at the impact. I shifted into forward and hauled the wheel all the way to the left. Tires screeching, I bounced off the brown car ahead of me and roared into the opposite lane. Did I worry I might run over the thug I'd already shot? Not a lot. I fishtailed out of there. Nobody followed me home, although after I'd nursed a damaged Taurus into the garage and collected my very own shotgun, I was kind of hoping they'd make another try.

After the adrenaline high leaked away, I admitted to myself I was glad they hadn't made another run at me. I wasn't feeling exactly up to fighting snuff at the moment. My professional pride had been sorely wounded. It had taken several minutes to get both vehicles close enough to sandwich me. It was especially upsetting because there was hardly any other traffic on the streets at that hour. Ruefully I admitted that if I had taken the most direct route home and stayed on the main multi-lane drags, these guys would have never have had the opportunity to try the heist.

The car was damaged on both ends, but seemed drivable. I did have to pull one side out a little to keep the body off the front tire. I hauled my tools and the damn case to the basement. Under my bright workbench lights, the aluminum case looked pretty much like it had when I found it in the Frogtown basement. I picked it up and shook it. Hard. Now there might have been a motion trigger attached to a bomb or

The Case of the Stolen Case

something but after what we'd been through in the last several hours, I didn't think so. It had the weight that indicated it wasn't empty.

I examined the case carefully. It was a serious case of heavy-duty construction with rounded corners and a very tight-fitting cover. I couldn't get a fingernail in the seam between cover and body. I hadn't heard anything when I shook it, but from the heft I decided it wasn't empty and was strongly made. There were three recessed slots next to the handle, one on either side and the third under the handle. They looked a little like key slots, but not ordinary ones. I pulled out a magnifier and a strong hands-free lamp I affixed to my head. Then I peered very closely at the slots. Inserting various things like lock picks, a small screwdriver, the end of an Allen wrench taught me nothing of interest. Each of the items I stuck in the slots met resistance after only a few millimeters. I sat back on my stool and pondered. I noted my fingers were still shaking a little, cumulative effects of the house fire and the attempted theft of case from my possession. I decided to abandon my effort to get into the case, in spite of my almost overwhelming curiosity.

I knew I could open it, but not without damaging the case. Sure, I could do that and then tell Sal that's how I found it, but he knew me well enough to know I wouldn't do that. So, in the end, I locked the thing in my basement safe, the one concealed in my basement wall and went upstairs.

With a glass of brandy and a dry cigarette from an old pack I still have lying around, I sat on my rear deck, oblivious to the mosquitoes. Several questions rattled around in my head; who were those guys? How had they made me? Were they watching from when I entered Beechy's? Were they the ones who firebombed the house? There was no question my pride was bent.

* * *

The next morning, washed, combed, and a more alert, I was talking by telephone to my friendly Lieutenant of Police, Dan Brooks. "Maybe you'll tell me what you were doing hanging around Frogtown early this morning," he barked at me.

"Excuse me?"

"You heard me. That house where George Beechy died was firebombed again, a fact I'm sure you already know. One of the patrols responding called in your license number. A lot of guys on the force know you on sight, which might be unfortunate, Sean. It could indicate you're not as anonymous as you'd like to be. What were you doing there?"

I wasn't about to tell him what really happened, so I made up a little story which had a lot of truth in it, like all good lies. "Sometimes I like to revisit scenes important to my cases, you know? I get ideas, vibes, sometimes."

"Yeah, right."

"What's the status of the place now?"

"As we speak, the bulldozers and backhoes are being assembled to pull the structure down and cart off the trash. The foundation will be filled in before dark tonight. Tomorrow they'll remove the fences and it'll be just another vacant lot in Frogtown."

"How come it's coming down so fast? Isn't that unusual? What about an arson investigation?"

"There's no fixed time frame. The arson inspectors have released the site. Once a house is declared uninhabitable or a hazard, owner responsibility kicks in. It could be weeks or months before the owner gets around to fixing or clearing a place. But when you get another fire and, as in this case, lots of complaints from the neighbors, the city responds. So the city fired up the 'dozers when the owner apparently declined to do an immediate teardown."

"Who owns the place?" I heard a rustle of paper.

"Double A Realty."

"Do you know anything else about the company?"

"Such as what? Are you asking if they figure in some investigation? Nothing I'm aware of."

I called Jerome Ford at the County Attorney's office.

"Sean, I have nothing to say about Double A Realty."

Really, I thought, hanging up the phone. Ford was pretty emphatic which could mean I was intruding on an open investigation. Or maybe he was just having a bad morning.

18

I called Sal Belassario. He wasn't in.
"Do you expect him later?" A pause.
"No sir. Not today."
"Do you know where I might reach him?"
There was another pause. I wondered what was going on. These weren't hard questions. Was she being coached by somebody, possibly Sal himself?
"His schedule indicates he'll be at the real estate office later. You might reach him there, sir."
"And do you have that number?" Another pause. Finally she gave me the number. I hung up the phone and then, even though it wasn't any later, I dialed the number she'd given me.
"AA Realty. Leave a message and we'll call back. Thank you."
Terse and to the point. Not very welcoming, though. I left my name, requesting a call from Sal. I didn't leave a number, Sal already knew mine and I didn't want one of his over eager agents, assuming he had any, cluttering up my life. After I hung up it occurred to me that I hadn't known Sal was in a real estate firm. I wondered if he'd had his license all along. It was also a little odd he never mentioned he owned the house in question when I first met him and this whole mess got started.

I called city services and they confirmed Brooks' statement that crews were scheduled to clean up the site. I drove my battered Taurus back to the scene of the crime. In my mind, that's how I thought of the house where George Beechy had been killed—scene of the crime. Of course it was the scene of several crimes I now knew of: Beechy's beating, the fire bombings of the house and before that, Beechy's receipt of stolen property, namely the missing aluminum case now residing in my basement safe. Although I'd never prove it, I was sure Beechy had hidden the aluminum case stolen from the Grand Avenue Pharmacy six years earlier. He'd died in the fire after being beaten almost to death. I was positive he'd been trying to reach the case. I was also sure there were several people who knew or thought they knew that Beechy had the case. The interesting question was, if some of those people had known all along, why was there all this hue and cry now? Maybe Beechy's probable possession of the case had only recently started circulating. If so, Beechy was one unusual fellow, sitting on a large chuck of possibly untraceable cash for six years. Or, maybe he thought the case was empty. Or maybe he opened the case, extracted the cash and substituted something else. Or maybe, like me, he was an honorable fellow who just did what he was told, took possession of the case and held on until ordered to do something else with it. Or ... nuts.

Sal Belassario was my client. I was going to deliver the case to him. But first I had to find him. I still wanted to have a look inside so maybe I could prevail on Sal to open it in my presence. But Sal was only one player in this little drama. Obviously others wanted the case.

At least one other team was probably led by that paragon of community philanthropy, Armond Anderson. And then there was Mordecai Marsh, Catherine's third cousin. I still didn't know how he fit, except that his primary link appeared to be through Armond Anderson, Jake Logan and Annette Campbell. But where was he? For that matter, now three hours later, noon had come and gone, where was Sal, and why hadn't he returned my calls.

All these gossamer threads came together or lead away from the burned out hulk on Raney. I decided to drive down there. Since Sal owned the property, maybe he'd show up to watch the final destruction. My feelings toward the place were much different today, compared to the other night. No fire this time. I found a parking spot half-a block away. There was a bigger crowd than there had been the first time I'd seen the place. No flashing lights, no cops, and only a single pumper to wet down the dust. Sorenson Construction had the place surrounded and the issue was no longer in doubt. Two bulldozers and a Bobcat danced around the property doing their destructive thing. From the look of it, the fire truck probably wouldn't be needed. The place still reeked of wet and burned substances.

There were lots of people on the sidewalks watching the 'dozers and the Bobcat. As I walked up to the edge of the crowd, the backhoe took out the one wall still standing and the small remaining section of the second floor imploded into the basement. The growling, ratcheting noise of the big yellow and black machines masked the soggy crump of falling plaster and shingles from the roof. Around the edges, the Bobcat started busily scooping up trash and depositing it in one of two dump trucks that sat on the boulevard at the edge of the property.

I scanned the crowd and eventually I spotted him, so I walked over and put my hand on his arm. He flinched and turned his head so I was looking into the jowly, shiny face of Salvatore Belassario. "Sean? What are you doing here?"

I said, "Sal, we have to stop meeting like this, people are starting to talk."

"I'm surprised. You've never struck me as the sidewalk superintendent type. Or is it that you're just late arriving?"

"Neither late, nor early," I said. "There's an old law enforcement axiom, Sal. Criminals often return to the scene of their crime. So, I thought I'd come on down and see who might turn up. "I've been here a few minutes and then I look around and who should I spy but yer own fine self. Begorra."

"Don't pull that Irish shit on me, Sean. I know you better."

"The plain fact remains, Mr. Belassario," I poked him in the chest. "You are here. Why?"

He shrugged, "So are several others, Sean. Look around."

I did, noting one very large fellow who stood leaning against a boulevard Elm tree across the way. His large arms were crossed on his chest. I tried to imagine him in a dark ski mask with a dark handgun in his fist. The image fit, but there wasn't what you'd call a bolt of recognition from the blue. Besides, he didn't stand as if he'd recently been shot in one leg. At that moment, the object of my scrutiny turned his head and looked back at us. I didn't see any meaningful streams of intelligence passing between Sal and the man, but that didn't mean there weren't any.

"Sal," I said. "You haven't answered my question."

He shrugged. "I have nothing to say on the subject. I knew George Beechy, as I've already told you, and I think he may have had some information relating to a certain brushed aluminum case."

"When we met at Dunkin' Donuts the other night you might have mentioned that you own this property. But never mind that, as my client of record, I owe you a report which I shall happily make verbally right now if that's of interest."

"What do you mean, 'client of record' or is that just your obscure way of speaking?"

"Nothing obscure about it. Sal, you hired me to attempt to locate a certain aluminum case which you say contains or perhaps contained is a better word, a large sum of cash." I glanced around. One of the large dump trucks was trundling down the street, carrying away some of the remains. The backhoe and the small 'dozer were busily ripping down the brick and granite foundation of the house.

"Look at that. There was a false basement under that sucker."

"Sal," I said.

"Sorry, Sean, you were saying?"

"I'm trying to give you a progress report." I shifted so I was between Sal and the street. He had to turn so he had his back to the man by the tree across the street. I leaned closer. There wasn't anyone standing close enough to overhear us, but I wasn't taking any chances. "I'm aware of the false wall. I suspect you knew of it before today. In the space between that brick and the granite wall I found a case. An aluminum case."

That may sound overly dramatic as a way to report something this important to a client, but I was getting all kinds of alarms. Sal looked over my shoulder, glanced at my face and then down the street.

"I'm lead-pipe certain it's the same case that was removed from the Grand Pharmacy six years ago."

Sal fixed his eyes on me. I could see a whiteness around his fleshy lips from the tension he was trying to conceal. "So you have this case, is that right? Have you opened it? Actually, that's one of the reasons I'm here. I was hoping you'd show up and we could have a chat."

Momentarily stopped by this obvious canard, I waited and Belassario hurried on, his gaze now fixed over my shoulder.

"Yes, you see, I've lost interest in the case, in the aluminum case and the question of who actually robbed the Grand Pharmacy."

"You are dismissing me?"

"Yes, I'm afraid, Sean, that my priorities have changed. I've decided that with Beechy dead and the house destroyed, there's no longer any hope of recovery. I can't afford to spend any more cash on a fruitless search."

"I guess you didn't hear me, Sal. I found the case."

He glanced up and then back. "I see. Well, that is good news. I admire your abilities. I guess I should thank you." He backed up a step. "But you see, I no longer care. Do you have the uhh item in question with you?"

"Sal, what's the matter with you?"

"No, no." He backed up a step. "Nothing's the matter. Uhh I have a new place, by the way. The address is on this card. Here." He whipped a business card out of his shirt pocket and thrust it at me; pointed one fat finger at the pasteboard. "Call me sometime. Oh, yes, we'll have to talk about your bill of course. Now I really must...." He stepped back again, stumbled over the edge of the boulevard turf and turned on one heel.

I watched him hurry away. It would serve him right if I took him at his literal word and turned the case over to the cops. Why was he acting like this? I glanced around at the thinning crowd. Now that trucks were dumping fill dirt on the site, interest waned. The tall person by the Elm tree across the street was no longer there.

I looked back at Sal's blocky figure wobbling up the street. If I didn't know better, I'd think Mr. Belassario knew or thought he knew I'd been robbed of the case shortly after it came into my possession. If

I didn't know any better, I'd think he no longer cared about Beechy or the case. Maybe I didn't know any better. Maybe Sal had discovered that the elusive Mr. Anderson and his cohorts carried bigger hammers than Sal wanted to know about.

19

At five-thirty the following afternoon I was sitting in a cool dark bar on the east side of St. Paul, about two miles from the Metropolitan State University campus. I'd never heard of this place, which is not to suggest I know every bar in the Twin Cities. Far from it. But I do know the names of a lot of them.

I was in this unfamiliar place because I was waiting for Jerome Ford. He'd picked this particular bar on East Seventh because nobody other than the regulars could ever find it, and because it was between City Hall where Jerry had his office, and his home on the western edge of Lake Phalen. The bar was called Finns. I knew that because there was a neat, discreet sign on the front of the brick-faced one-story building that said so. And it was the right address. I'd missed it on my first pass up East Seventh.

Finns was dark and cool with wooden floors, a polished wooden bar and no stools or hanging plants. In one corner was an old-fashioned juke box; the big round kind with the fat colored lights that curved over the top and ran down each side. There weren't any satellite stations, so you had to get up and walk over to the thing and insert your coins to make a selection. It cost a quarter for each selection. I stuffed a coin in the slot. The juke box was quiet for the moment. Then metal things inside began to move and it made whirring noises.

There weren't any booths, either. Just that long polished bar and a bunch of tables. It was an old-fashioned, tin-ceilinged, neighborhood kind of bar. They probably had a tiny kitchen tucked in back somewhere, from which you could get a sandwich. If you weren't terribly picky.

I shut off my pager and sat down. The record I'd selected, an old piece by the original Brubeck trio, filled the room and suppressed the routine sounds of any barroom. The blend reminded me of the first time I'd heard "Take The A Train" by this jazz trio, in a smoky night club in Washington, D. C. But, that's another story.

I'd picked a table toward the rear of the place. There were lots of choices; only two others were occupied. "I'm meeting a friend," I said to the dark-haired waitress. She was wearing faded jeans and an oversized gray sweatshirt that said Property of Michigan State University Athletic Department across the chest. "While I wait, I'll have a Sam Adams ale if you stock it."

"No problem," she said and turned away.

I was tempted to ask her if the legend on her chest referred to her or the shirt, but thought better of it. Catherine wouldn't have approved. When she brought me my beer I asked, "You have sandwiches here?"

"Yeah, sure. Do you want a menu?"

"No, thanks. I was just confirming something." She smiled and walked away. The place was starting to fill up. Ten minutes later, Jerome Ford walked in, hesitated and found me. I ordered him a Sam Adams and waited while he loosened his tie.

"Very obscure and very nice little bar you have here, J. I had to go around the block because I missed it the first time. No parking lot, either."

Jerry smiled. "That's the way we like it. Finns has been in the same family for generations and they own the building outright. When I was starting out as a lawyer, I did a few legal errands for them. So," he smiled after a long draught from his glass, "to what do I owe the pleasure?"

I opened my mouth to reply and then paused to watch a tall woman in a business suit step to the juke box and punch in some coins. What came out, to my pleasure and surprise, was Peggy Lee singing "Hot Coffee." I looked at Jerome. He smiled a little smile at

The Case of the Stolen Case

me. "This place is a real anachronism, Jerry. I'm surprised you let me in on the secret."

"I figure you and Finn's are compatible and you won't be telling all your yuppie friends about it. What can I do for you?"

"It appears to me there is a roving band of jolly scam artists running a pretty sophisticated operation. They've probably worked on both coasts. They run various scams, including some white-collar crime. I don't know all the players yet, but I'm working on that."

"So far it sounds pretty ordinary. What's your interest?"

"This seems to be an organized group that's been together a while. It looks like they haven't been splitting the take. Instead, they're stockpiling some of it to finance later deals."

Jerome's eyebrows went up. He took a slug of Mr. Adams' finest ale.

"Another thing they are doing. They find local investors, people who will pony up some money for a cut of the results. Then the out-of-towners move in and start churning the real estate market, buying and selling quickly to inflate their profits, mostly distressed properties or homes in less than affluent neighborhoods. They work with willing inspectors, real estate salespeople and an S&L or bank or two. They also do an occasional armed robbery and some petty stuff."

"What for? Walking around money?"

"I guess. They appear to have run up against some local competition here. At least, that's how I interpret what's been going on."

Jerome nodded and I could see he was not unfamiliar with the situation. "That's right," he said. "There happen to be some people already operating a real estate scam., mainly in Hennepin County, but here in Ramsey County, too. They didn't take kindly to out-of-town competition. In addition to which they figured, rightly it happens, that if things got too active, it'd call down the heat quicker."

I said, "The guy running the local deal is unknown to me, but I think I know the name of the head honcho for the outside gang. Armond Anderson. Other people involved with him appear to be the brothers Talbot, a new contractor operating in Bloomington named Jake Logan, and one or two other bad sorts. How'm I doing?"

Ford smiled. "Very good so far, Sean. We have lots of suspicions but few facts. Yours tally with what we know. I assume the Jake Logan you're mentioning is the same one who turned up at that Foundation fund-raiser and offered a big chunk of cash from Mr. Anderson. The one we met there. Am I right? It would be entirely too coincidental if there were two Jake Logans. I don't get why Anderson did that, though"

I nodded and swigged from my own beer. "Such a coincidence would never be possible in a detective novel. Of course, in real life things like that happen almost every day. Howsomever, it is indeed, the very same J. Logan. It sort of turns my stomach, but the money will be useful to the foundation. Maybe we should not take these people down until the pledge is fully paid."

Ford laughed. "You have an evil mind, Sean, a very evil mind. One of the factors that bothers us is this." He paused to consider his words. "Some of these mutts have been in and out of town before. We have some intelligence--"

"As different from facts," I interrupted.

"As different from verifiable facts," Ford went on, "that this roving gang planned something here around six years ago. For unknown reasons, they never went ahead with it."

I thought about that. I wondered if Ford and his cohorts in the courthouse had a link from the money presumably in the aluminum case, to this Anderson. I owed Jerry Ford a lot and I both needed and wanted to keep him as a friend. At the same time, I wasn't eager to reveal that I'd been suckered into retrieving the money stolen in the Grand Pharmacy murder case. Even if I was almost certain now that the money was tied to Armond Anderson and his gang. I thought I had the money and that Anderson would come after me. I was going to use the case as bait to try to extricate Catherine's cousin Mordecai. If I could.

20

I decided to pin down my understanding of the real estate scam. I'm kind of an action guy myself. I'm Paul Drake, not the old guy, whatsisname, who sits at the desk and makes erudite if sometimes confusing statements. Not the one who directs his secretary and others to find out the facts until the trial, where he makes those incredible leaps of logic that force the right person to confess in open court without benefit of lawyerly advice. So I called a banker I know who works in the loan department of my very own personal bank.

He was no help. His name is Andy and he acted like a CEO, a boss. You know, deep denial. He told me bank people are honest and don't do the kind of things I was asking about. I knew better. Of course, I spend more time dealing with the dark side, the thieves, the con artists, the people who'd smile in your face, slap you on the back with a loan offer and pick your pocket when you weren't paying attention. I knew there were banks involved. Or, to be more precise, a few bankers. And an S&L or two. There had to be because they were making the loans. But I discovered bankers are like doctors. They protect each other until things get so bad nobody can stand the smell any more. I didn't want to waste a lot of time breaking down that stone wall, so I called my friend Ricardo Simon, the cop? He gave me the name of a woman who had been scammed. I went to see her. It pays to have friends in the right places.

She lived with her two children, both in school, in a large public housing place in North Minneapolis. It was an okay place, but it smelled like a lot of those places do, that is, as if there hasn't been any fresh air in the place since they built it. In this case in the early sixties.

Her name was Clarissa and she worked nights so I could talk to her in the afternoon. I did that.

After we got the amenities out of the way and she'd scrutinized my driver's license and my PI license, we sat down and she offered me some tea. Tea! Imagine that. She was a tall thin woman with dark circles around her black eyes. That was their color. Nobody had beat her up.

"So, Clarissa," I said by way of starting with an easy one. "How are the kids?"

"The kids are fine and they'll be home from school in about half an hour so that's all the time you got."

I nodded. I could smell the tea. "I understand you got ripped off in a real estate scam a few months ago."

"That's right. A man I met at a party, said he was a friend of my cousin, Teddy. He offered me a deal."

"Which was?"

Clarissa poured us each some tea. "You want milk?" she asked.

"No, this is fine. Thanks."

"This man, he said he had a sure fire way for me to make some serious money. Not a fortune, but some serious money." She nodded. "Yes, that's what he said. I said I might be interested, but I wasn't going to do something to get into trouble. I had the kids to think about, you know?"

I nodded and sipped my tea. It was ordinary tea but it was hot and tasted good. "So what did he tell you?"

"Oh, he wanted me to meet some other people. Two of his friends, he said. But they weren't at the party so he wanted my telephone number and address. He said he'd bring his friends over."

"Is that what happened? When was that?"

"I didn't like the sound of that. I got the kids, you know. I don't invite just anybody over here. This was three, four, months ago. I told him he could meet me at the K-Mart over on Broadway. They got-- have a coffee shop next door. So that's what we did. Him and his two friends came and we talked."

"What did they want you to do?" I already knew the answer from talking to Simon and reading the newspaper, but I wanted her to tell me in her words.

"They told me they wanted me to buy a house. Well, I'd sure like to move the kids to a house, but I don't make enough to qualify for a loan. So I laughed and said sure, I'd do that in a second, if I won the lottery. Then they explained that all I had to do was bid on a house they had in mind and go through the application process. They'd pay any expenses and tell me how much to offer for the house and everything."

"How were you supposed to make any money?"

"They said I wouldn't actually buy the house. What I'd do is help them to get some other loans arranged by signing some documents and then after everything was done, they'd pay me a couple of thousand dollars. For my trouble, they said."

I was beginning to wonder how Clarissa had gotten out of the deal. "What happened next?"

"I said I had to think about it for a day or so and I'd be at the same coffee shop in two days with my answer. I thought the whole thing sounded fishy. 'Never look a gift horse in the eye.' That's what my daddy always said. But momma always said 'if it's too good to be true, it ain't.' So I talked to my friend Hilary and she said to call the cops. This cop came and asked me to continue to meet with them, always in public places, and to try to get the names of others if there were any."

"How long did this go one?"

"A couple of weeks, I guess. Maybe a month. I got a few names and after while I signed the papers to buy the house. One of them took me to see it. It was an okay place, but I didn't like the neighborhood a whole lot. It was too close to Broadway." Clarissa paused to take a drink of her tea. "Then we went to the bank and I signed the loan papers. A couple of days later, I met with these guys again and they had me sign some more stuff they said was a sale of the house. When I saw the price they were asking, I figured out what they were doing."

"It was significantly higher?"

"Well," she said, "I don't know from significant, but I know that no house in that neighborhood is gonna go up over ten grand in value in two weeks."

"Do you have copies of the loan papers? The mortgage and documents, like that?" I asked.

"Naw, they tole me I didn't need to worry about that. They said they'd take care of it all 'cause I wasn't going to have the house very long anyway."

"And you kept the police informed every step of the way?"

"Sure I did. I didn't want to do any of it in the first place. They kept selling the place over and over again, each time raising the price of the house so they were makin' a lot of money."

"Can you remember any of the names of the men you met?"

"Sure, but I only got first names. I never asked. I just remembered. I was a little scared. I was pretty sure they had figured out where I lived and I didn't want any trouble. On account of the kids, you know?"

"So, can you tell me the names?"

"Yep. One was George and the other was Alvin." Clarissa screwed up her face in thought. "There was a Bob and I think a Mike, too. Alvin did most of the talking."

She described them and I knew for sure these were not the people I was dealing with. For one thing, they were black. Clarissa told me all the people she talked with, including the two cops and the man at the bank were black. Two of them talked with accents, like they were from somewhere else. But one of them, she said, could have passed. He was very light skinned and very tall, over six feet. A big dude, she said.

"So, how did it all end up?"

"They must have found out about the cops because they quit meeting with me. I went to that coffee place three times and they never showed up. I never saw any of them again. I don't care if I never do."

"What happed to the house? Do you know?"

"I wanted to know if they'd arrested the guys, but the cops didn't say. That house has got my name on the loan papers, but since I can't get the loan, the cops say they'll wipe out the whole thing. I'm supposed to get a paper. If I don't I'll have to sue somebody, I guess."

"I was told you got scammed too. How did that happen?"

"Well, those guys never paid me the two thousand they promised."

21

As the sun sank into the western horizon, I was sitting in Catherine's Kenwood living room, holding a brass key, the one I'd extracted from Mordecai's car, and thinking about the aluminum case in my basement.

I should have gone home and blown the thing open. What was I waiting for? I hadn't told Catherine Mckerney that I had the case, nor about the thwarted heist. What I was waiting for was some insight. I know a lot of people would have opened the case first thing. It even made some sense to do so. But me, I'm made of sterner stuff. As long as I didn't open the case, I could deny. I could even, if it came to that, dispose of it in a surreptitious manner and deny ever having seen it or laid a hand on it. Sal of course knew I had it, but I doubted he'd tell the authorities. The question was who else might he tell?

I blew out my breath, stood up and began to roam around the spacious living room. I looked at the key in my hand and set the problem of the case aside. As I have already mentioned, I have a few contacts in various banks around town. It's the result of doing a favor here and there and some discreet business I don't talk about. That's one of the things P.I.s need to be, discreet. Most of us try not to get our names in the paper either. But none of my contacts had been able to tell me anything useful about the safe deposit key. Except that it wasn't one of theirs. That helped a little, but not much. What I needed was a break. Usually by this time something had happened to point me in a new direction. This time, no breaks, nothing. I hoped the damn case would be bait by which I would snare a perp who'd give me some leverage.

Of course, if I opened it, I might find information that would lead me where I wanted to go. On the other hand, if I never opened it, I might yet be able to extricate Mordy from this thing. I picked up the latest criminous novel I was reading and sank onto the sofa. "Lullaby Town" by Robert Crais. Cole hasn't needed any breaks so far. He and Pike are slogging through the landscape, touching pressure points and getting the bad guys to make mistakes in reaction. Some of the good guys, too.

After a couple of chapters, I dropped the novel and began to think about my case again. Since I hadn't made any progress with the clues I found hidden in Marsh's car, perhaps I could find something in his apartment. By now it had got to full dark. Catherine wasn't due home for a couple more hours and she'd have eaten. I left a short note for her so she wouldn't worry too much. Gone burgling, my note said. Back after midnight. I didn't stop to reflect that not so long ago I'd left her place on a similar mission, one that almost got me killed. Twice. Well, one learns from experience, I guess, but not by hand-wringing or dwelling at length.

I found a small neighborhood restaurant, one of the few left in the city, where I had a more than passable supper of meat loaf, mashed potatoes with gravy and green beans. Then I drove south to Marsh's apartment building.

This time several of the sixteen apartments in Mordecai's building showed lights behind drawn drapes or blinds. When I went in I heard voices in the hall a floor or two above me, but they'd gone doggo and all was quiet by the time I made it up the stairs to Mordecai's floor. Since I had a key there was no need for stealth. When I got to Mordy's door I bent my keen detective's eye to the handle and lock in an attempt to discern whether anyone had done a B&E since I was last there. Just being careful. No such evidence.

The key snicked in and I eased open the door into a dark cavern. Mordecai's drapes were pulled tight and only tiny slivers of light reached inside. I recalled that the light switch was somewhere in the normal place on my right. I stepped inside and quietly pushed the door almost closed. When I snapped the wall switch, the big lamp in one corner came on. I glanced around.

Oh, shit!

I was looking at the round black hole in the end of the barrel of a pistol. The pistol was being competently held in the pudgy hand of a largish fellow sitting on the sofa. It was a small pistol, but the hole in the end of the barrel looked enormous. It was clearly a pistol up to the job.

"Who th' fuck are you?" largish fellow queried.

"Since I have the key to my front door," I bluffed, waggling the key at him meanwhile keeping my hands well away from my body, "and since I've never seen you before, maybe I should be asking the question."

"I've got the pistol, so tha' gives me trump. Wha's your name?"

"Sean Sean."

"Oh yeah, the hick P.I. from Roseville."

There was something in his voice. "You have the advantage of me, Mr.—"

"Let's not waste time wit' formalities and don't make any sudden moves." He moved his free hand and ponderously scratched the other arm through his short sleeve.

Aha! I had him. My keen detective's ear had come through again. The last time I'd heard that voice, its owner was standing close behind me next to a basswood tree on a very dark night in a dark grove of trees. He'd had a gat on me then, too.

"We been patient up to now, ya know? In spite of warning you, you still poking your nose in where it ain't wanted. What are you doin' here?

"Looking for clues."

"Clues? To what?"

"Mordecai Marsh is a friend. His cousin is a friend of mine. Marsh may have gone missing and I'm looking for him. Who are you?"

"Where is George Beechy's stuff?"

"Beechy? Stuff? What's this in reference to?" I wondered if I looked as stupid as I sounded. I hoped so.

The man with the gun waggled it and nodded at a chair beside the door. "Go sit over there while I figure what to do next." Something that might have been annoyance flitted across his face. Since I couldn't see any ready alternatives, I did what the fellow ordered. We sat there for a few minutes. His eyes never left my face. And while he rested his hand holding the pistol on his knee, his aim never wavered.

The building was quiet. The door to Mordy's apartment was slightly ajar, but if anyone came down the hall, I didn't hear them. Once I shifted slightly in my seat and the pudgy fellow came immediately alert. Then a little while later I sensed an alteration in the atmosphere. I didn't know what it was, just that something had changed. My captor didn't seem to notice anything. I carefully turned my head and glanced at the door beside me. Was it my imagination? Or was the door open a bit more? I couldn't tell for sure because I was sitting on the hinged side.

The telephone rang. Not the soft, irritating electronic pseudo-ring of some modern phones. This was the old-fashioned bell-and-clapper ring. A loud ring. The man with the gun turned toward the sound. He twisted his big body away from me and lost his aiming point. Like a suddenly released spring and without conscious thought, I launched myself through the air at him. We went ass over teakettle with the sofa and thumped onto the floor. My impetuous leap had enough momentum so when the sofa went over, largish fellow hit the back of his head on the floor with a satisfying thump. He was stunned.

I saw his pistol slide across the floor, just out of his reach, and I snatched my own .45 semi-auto out of its hip holster. There was a sharp bang behind me. The door to the hall slammed open and whacked the chair I had been sitting in a moment earlier. I rolled to one side and snarled something wordless at the pudgy guy who was still sprawled face down on the floor. I risked a quick glance around the end of the sofa.

Mordecai Marsh filled the door frame. "Have ya got 'im?"

I grabbed a big lungful of air and wheezed, "Mordy! Where did you come from?" I turned my attention back to pudgy and his gun. I grabbed it up and shoved it in my pants pocket.

"Never mind that now. Who's this guy?" Mordecai came into the apartment, swinging the door closed behind him. He leaned over the sofa and peered down at the fallen thug.

"I think that's Henry Talbot," I said. "One of the crowd lookin' for George Beechy's satchel. I've encountered this one on at least one earlier occasion." I checked the guy again, but I didn't frisk him. Mordy seemed nervous, but it didn't seem to be associated with the pudgy guy on his living room floor. I fixed Mordy with my best steely P.I. glare. "You're telling me you don't know him? I thought you were tight with the Beechy bunch."

"Who, me? You must be kiddin', Sean."

"I've been talking with Ms. Campbell, Mordy. At length. She's been quite forthcoming and she tells me you're invested in this real estate game now playing at selected local real estate firms and banks. Is that true?"

"Who me? I wouldn't do nothin' like that. I don't know nothing about no real estate game."

"That makes Ms. Campbell a liar, I guess."

"Listen, Sean? I don't have time for conversation. I gotta get what I came for and go back to hiding for a while. How's Catherine doin'?" He turned and headed toward the bedrooms. I tagged along.

"Don't come in here, Sean. You don't need to see anything in here." Mordy went into the dark bedroom and snapped on a small table lamp beside the bed that barely illuminated the corners of the small room. I stood in the doorway and watched. Behind me I heard a scraping sound and turned around to see Talbot, or whoever he was, rising groggily on his hands and knees from the floor behind the sofa. He'd found another gat because I could see it in his hand.

When he saw me looking, his fingers twitched and he fired off a shot that went into the wall somewhere. The noise wasn't very loud.

It was a small semi-auto. Smaller than the one I'd just relieved him of. Looked like a Beretta. I cursed myself for not patting him down and waved my big .45 at him. I snarled in my most menacing voice, "Drop that, you jerk!"

Behind me, Mordy suddenly banged a drawer and Talbot tried to get up. He slipped on the crumpled edge of the rug and fell over again, out of sight. He squeezed off another shot. I yelled and ran back toward the living room. Talbot crabbed around the sofa which put him closer to the door. The smell of burned powder tweaked my nose.

Behind me, Mordecai hollered something I didn't catch. I saw the top of Talbot's head swivel toward the sound of Mordy's voice and then back in my direction. He was mostly hidden. I probably could have shot him through the bottom of the sofa. A .45 packs a lot of power.

I didn't fire.

I saw his hand come up. The one with the second gun. I ducked again and he squeezed off two quick ones into the wall over my head. While I was ducking, he slid out the door and I heard him thundering down the stairs. For a big man he ran pretty well. I decided not to go after him.

Mordy came running out of the bedroom with a small cloth duffel bag in one hand, the kind you see people carrying into exercise gyms. It was dark blue and had two cloth loops for handles.

"Jeeze, Sean, why din't you shoot 'im?"

"Forget it, Mordy. I didn't want to mess up your sofa, and I'm not in the habit of shooting at people if I can help it, even people shooting at me. Never mind about him. What's in the bag?

"Nothin' Sean. Just some stuff I need, an' some socks and underwear. C'mon, I gotta get out of here before the cops show up."

I stared at him and at the bag in his hand. I decided he was right for once.

"All right. Shut off the lights and we'll take it on the lam. I'll drive you somewhere." I knew some neighbor had to have called the cops by now, even if they hadn't heard the shots. I wanted to talk with Mordecai in a calmer setting and I wanted to keep a leash on him as long as possible. So we shut off the lights, locked up and beat it out of there.

Mordy said he'd come in a cab. It wasn't at the curb when we ran out, but I didn't care. I was driving him wherever he needed to go. We hopped in my car and cruised serenely down the dark street. Sure enough, we barely made it to the end of the block before a squad car, blue and red lights flashing, squealed around the corner and drew up at the curb in front of Mordy's building.

"Where to, Mordy?"

He opened his mouth to say something, then slid a glance at me and closed his mouth. Mordy was doomed to show every emotion and nearly every thought on his face. He'd never make it as a card player. I saw indecision, irritation and probably a little fear, all mixed together. He and I had never really got along. Mostly we tolerated each other whenever we'd run into each other after I started going with Catherine. I had no idea how much he trusted me, if at all.

"Well, how about a general direction. Downtown? St. Paul? Mall of America? Where?"

"Take me downtown. I can grab a cab. What'd you do with my car?"

"It's in the garage at Catherine's. You can get it anytime. Do you want to give me a few hints as to what's going on?" I wasn't going to tell him I'd found the keys hidden on the chassis of his car.

Mordy grunted. "Never mind what's going on. You just stay out of it and I'll be fine. And don't be hassling Annie neither. She's good people and is trying to get straight, got it?"

"Any time you want to talk, or you need something, you know I'm around. The more I know, the better I can help. You okay for money? Should we drop by your bank?"

It was pretty transparent. I knew the banks weren't open at that hour, but lots of people drive out of their way to use their own ATMs to avoid those ridiculous fees. If I knew Mordy's bank, I might find the lock for that safe deposit key. Of course, he could have a box in a different bank from his regular accounts. There was no response. When I looked over, Mordy was staring through the windshield and chewing his lower lip—not one of his more attractive habits.

"Well?" I prodded. "You want to hit your bank?" An unfortunate choice of verbs, given the circumstances. Still no response.

We stopped for a red light at Hennepin and Franklin. Abruptly, Mordy threw open the door and stepped out.

"Hey!" I said, reaching for him. "What?"

He slammed the door and then immediately opened it again to reach in and grab his duffel. "Forget it, man?"

"Mordy!" I yelled.

He threw out his hand in a despairing gesture and dodged across the traffic. By the time I got my car across two lanes of the busy street to the curb so I could park, and got out of the car, he was out of sight. I forced my way back into the nearest lane of traffic amid black looks and blasting horns and hung a right in the next alley. I was desperately trying to recall what I knew about streets and alleys in this part of Minneapolis. I bounced into the next street over and screeched right. It was dark and there were lots of places to hide. I went back up to Franklin at the next block and made a couple of more casts, circling around nearby blocks. Nothing. By now, Mordecai could be almost anywhere.

22

The next morning I woke up with a bad feeling about the whole mess. Somebody had told somebody else that Mordecai was returning to his apartment last night. That's why Talbot was there and why he was surprised when I walked in. So who would know? It could have been several people. Hell, it could have been thousands—almost anyone in the city who knew Mordy. I guess thousands was too many. I knew it wasn't me and it wasn't Catherine. I was betting it was somebody else close to the case. Logical, wouldn't you say? My money was on Annette Campbell. I'd bought her story for a while, but she seemed prepared to come on to me at the drop of a strap. Or maybe it was just her automatic reaction to any male who got within a city block of her charms. Too eager. That made me suspicious of her professed feelings for Mordecai.

I drove south through the morning to the small apartment in the out-of-the-way building on a dead-end street at the edge of Richfield, another Minneapolis suburb. It was a place Catherine had found some years ago. She knew the owners of the building and when she and I had hooked up, she'd asked me if I ever needed a bolt-hole.

Now, a bolt hole, as anyone knows, is a place where the detective can stash people he, or she, doesn't want found. In some novels, there always seems to be a place where the said detective can stash somebody, but in more recent times, the housing shortage, at least in Minneapolis, is so severe, empty apartments are hard to come by.

Anyway, it was a boon to discover that Mary knew this couple who had an out of the way place and that there were almost always one or more small studio apartments unoccupied. The deal was I paid for any furnished place in the building, just not a specific apartment.

It was there in Richfield, where we'd stashed Annie Campbell. I drove out to the address. When I rang the bell there was no answer. I leaned on the bell for a couple of minutes in case she was asleep but still there was no answer.

Sandy Bacon showed up and cocked an eyebrow at me. She's the co-owner of the place, a trim, good-looking redhead who works out a lot. Like now, she was dressed in her running gear, a sports bra and tight shorts that showed off her excellent legs. Were she not married and were I not involved with Catherine, here was a woman I would definitely have pursued, although I'd bet she could run faster than me.

"She's not here," Sandy said, pushing through the door into the lobby. Her key ring jangled.

"Any idea when she'll be back?" I assumed Ms. Campbell had just gone to a nearby convenience store. She knew it could be dangerous for her to wander around the city.

"She went out sometime yesterday morning and I don't think she was here last night. I'm gonna run. I'll be back in an hour if you want me. Jeb's doing some work at our other place." She wiggled her fingers at me and jogged down the street. I had a key to the apartment so there wasn't a problem. I went through the security door and up the stairs to the top floor. This place was a far cry from Catherine's luxurious suite. No carpeting on the floor, but the paint on the walls was reasonably clean and there wasn't any trash in the corners, but give me a break. I wasn't in the business of stashing high-priced fugitives in nice places. Something clean and functional, thank you very much.

I opened the door to our current bolt hole and immediately felt the emptiness. Since there are only two rooms, including the bathroom, it took me only a moment to decide that Ms. Campbell had become a missing person. Oh, her stuff was still there, pantyhose drying on the shower rail, for example, a lacy red bra on the rumpled bed and her suitcase in the corner. But I knew.

There weren't any signs that she'd been forcibly taken, either. I couldn't decide if she had, but she was definitely gone, and it looked like she hadn't been there in a while. I calculated she'd probably been gone since mid-morning yesterday, the time Sandy said she'd seen Campbell in the hall.

I tossed the place. Neatly, but I didn't waste time, either. Didn't help. Her purse and the billfold I knew she owned were not there. What else might be missing I couldn't say. There weren't any frantically scrawled lipstick messages on the bathroom vanity mirror; no little scrap of paper with an impenetrable message in smudged ballpoint ink. And there weren't any muddy tracks left by her kidnapper. Always assuming there was a kidnapper. I couldn't check for foreign fingerprints or DNA so I left.

I again encountered Sandy Bacon. She was coming in, a fine sheen of sweat on her face and arms, breathing rapidly. "Anything?" she said.

"What time was it you saw her yesterday?"

"Ten, ten-thirty, about." Sandy drew a big gulp of air, expanding her chest under the sleeveless tee she wore.

I nodded and went down the step. "We'll leave everything as it is for now. I'll call you," I said and went away, thinking hard. What I was thinking about was why Campbell'd decamped and where she might have gone. I also was beginning to feel she could be the linch-pin that could break this thing open. I just needed to find the right button to push. Talk about mixed metaphors.

To push the right buttons, I needed to lay my hands on the lady, in a manner of speaking. I did what all the good private eyes did in such circumstances, they asked around. Specifically, they made contact with their contacts. Not only the cops, but the people who lived on the fringes. What we used to call finks, weasels, informants. So I did that.

Over the years, I'd cultivated a fair number of individuals who had their ears to the ground in matters criminal. Most of them were people you wouldn't want to encounter in a dark alley after midnight. You probably wouldn't want to join them for a meal at a nice restaurant. Come to think of it, barrooms were where I mostly found them, seedy smoky barrooms. A lot of them were people you wouldn't turn your back on, either. There was one exception. She was a woman of the streets. Not a working girl, but someone who seemed to have no permanent address. She hung around. Tall, slender, blond, willowy, even. Every time I encountered her I was reminded of a seeker, someone looking for answers. At times I thought she was hanging around to do research, you know, soaking up authentic atmosphere for her next dissertation, or maybe a novel.

People on the street agreed, she was Mysterious. That was about all they agreed, on when it came to Laura. We didn't know where she lived or where she came from. Sometimes she accompanied a purloined shopping cart filled with cans and other stuff I never looked at too closely. The carts were easier to come by in downtown Minneapolis now, ever since Target opened a store on Nicollet. Laura might be my best bet.

I parked and sauntered into a tiny bar down on First, a block off Minneapolis's great white way, otherwise known as Hennepin Avenue. Several years ago the City Fathers had decided to make a few blocks in downtown Minneapolis the centerpiece of Showbiz. So they moved an ancient Shubert Theater onto the street, wiped out a bunch of interesting looking buildings that housed a few bad-rep bars and some theaters that showed porno films, in the process scattering night people into other parts of the city. Now they were at long last building an entertainment complex on a plot labeled Block E. Long a street-level parking lot, a concrete tower was now rising. The concrete would house movie theaters, a hotel and some eateries. Hopefully, planners would remember that parking was already crowded in downtown.

This bar I went to was nothing special. It was old, been around for years. The sign out front didn't celebrate anyone. The sign said Bar. That's all. The people inside were working stiffs and hangers on. The place, deep and narrow and dark, was also the favorite hangout for the contact I sought, Laura Lipp. Or Laura the lip as some dubbed her. She had a few enemies, small-time scufflers whose incautious peccadilloes had come to Laura's attention. She had no apparent qualms about ratting out people who were doing harm. She had a keen eye for ripples in the urban pool. She could have been a reporter.

For all we knew, maybe she was. Anyway, she'd been around off and of for a couple of years and she'd made a lot of contacts and several friends.

George Ort was tending bar. I think he's the manager or perhaps the owner. I never bothered to find out. I snagged a stool and asked for a draft. When Ort brought the glass I said, "Laura been in today?"

He shrugged and said, "The Lip? Man, I'll say. She was in here 'bout an hour ago. Just cruisin' I guess. But you shoulda seen her."

"Why is that?"

"She was on one of her cleanup pitches. All dressed up she was. Long dress, clean hair. She musta took a bath 'cause she smelled real nice."

"What do you think it means?"

Ort shrugged. "How would I know? But she fixes up real good, you know? You want another?"

I nodded yes and slid a fin across the bar top. "She say anything about where she was going?"

"Naw," Ort said, palming the bill. "But she did say she'd be back later. Seemed like she was looking for somebody."

I sipped my second glass and swept the place with my gaze. There were only five or six other people in there, none of whom I recognized. Annette's disappearance hung at the back of my neck. I itched to do something to find her, even as I knew waiting for Laura was probably the best thing I could do right now. Still.

I fished a couple of quarters out of my pocket and went to the telephone hanging on the wall by the johns. The smell of disinfectant hit me like a rabbit punch when the door swung open and somebody slipped out of the men's room. I didn't know him either.

I plugged the coin slot and called my office. I don't have voice mail. I have a cutting edge answering machine that I can access from any telephone. My machine did tricks. By punching in a numerical password and some other codes, I could retrieve my messages. It was a lot cheaper than a secretary or an answering service. It was also cheaper than voice mail. It worked really well, except when I forgot the codes. Or when I made a mistake and erased messages before I heard them.

There was only one message. From my homicide friend, Ricardo. He wanted me to call. So I did. He wasn't in, or he wasn't answering his page. I went back to the bar, thinking. One of the traditions in this

PI business is that people have a couple of principal reasons for engaging the services of a PI, a peeper, a gumshoe. First they want their business with the detective to be private, which, even in Minnesota with its privacy laws is harder to retain when you're involved with the authorities. Second, they may harbor grave suspicions about the incorruptibility of the cops. Moreover, they often wanted someone who could deliver the goods, the booty, the info, sometimes with less regard for a few of the niceties of the law. Travis McGee, Lew Archer and Sam Spade, to name a couple, all did things which someone of high moral standards would object to. They got results, however. Me too.

In this case, Sal Belassario needed someone to locate a purloined aluminum case with a minimum of fuss and below the law enforcement radar. Enter Sean Sean. Sal's problem was he knew that I would object to helping the murderer of the two people in the pharmacy, so he was doing some fancy maneuvering, hence refusing to admit interest in the case once I had it. There was also the possibility that he'd become aware of other players with more firepower.

My contacts in the cops we saw as mutually helpful from time to time. On rare occasions, they assisted me out of sticky situations which helped me to preserve my stellar reputation. But it was a little unusual for Simon to be calling me on the blower. I didn't exactly advertise my contacts, and the cops I knew didn't either. If they wanted to talk to me, they sent a car. So, as I made my way back to my stool I wondered.

Ort was right where I had left him. So was my beer. I hopped up on my bar stool, munched a handful of over-salted popcorn—they always over salt it in bars to make you thirsty—and drained my glass. Now what? Since Ort had nothing more to add to my store of knowledge, and Laura-the-lip was not in evidence, I split, suggesting to Mr. Ort that he pass along to the said Laura a message from me to call. He would. She probably wouldn't.

Then I went home. I was in a sour mood, having no leads on the whereabouts of Marsh and still debating myself over opening or not opening the mysterious aluminum case. I went to my place in Roseville, rather than inflict my mood on Catherine.

23

Home. Home is on a pleasant street roughly equidistant from downtown St. Paul and Minneapolis, on the north side of the cities. It's only a few blocks from a freeway, far enough away so the traffic noise is only a murmur, but close enough so I can get places fairly fast. Also convenient. I make no big secret about where I live. It's a split level on a nicely wooded lot. Has a deep back yard, a deck, an indoor hot tub—mosquitoes, you know, and very little grass to mow. I have some retired neighbors who keep an eye out and a pretty elaborate alarm system.

My neighbors don't know exactly what I do for a living. They guess I'm some kind of consultant which accounts for my erratic hours. One guy down the street accused me of being a writer. I just laughed.

I also have a slightly modified shotgun on a special bracket next to the front door. After letting myself in and resetting the intruder alarms, I watered my cats and my house plants, some of which were looking a little peaked. Then I took the shotguns (yes I have another stowed elsewhere in the house) to my tiny workshop in the basement and broke them down, checked and cleaned them and reloaded with fresh ammunition. I rarely needed either one, but I wanted to be damn sure they would fire when required. Cleaning my weapons, doing all the little home-minding steps, relaxes me, lets my mind loose to wander. Sometimes it wanders into a clue to my present dilemma. Other times it just wanders. My workbench is right next to the door that leads to my built-in safe, the one where that damned sealed case was now resting.

I went back upstairs and paid some attention to the cats. They let me know they felt neglected. After they got bored with me again, I cranked up my sound system. For months the turntable had been inoperative. Then I found this service place over on Lyndale where they said they could repair just about anything in the electronic field. Apparently they can. They cleaned, adjusted, balanced and replaced the drive belt on the thing. At long last I could listen to my favorite vinyls. Oh, sure, I have a CD player, and a tape machine and several other state-of-the-art gizmos. I have several big band recordings from the thirties and forties and a lot of original cast musicals. Then there's my jazz collection. A lot of the stuff I have on LPs hasn't been re-released on CD. I like the art and the great liner notes on the big albums. I put on some Les Paul. He was a pioneer in multi-track recording back in the forties and fifties and created an electric guitar style that is still unsuccessfully emulated by a lot of today's musicians. Paul was a huge influence on the popular music culture and I understand that Gibson still markets a Les Paul guitar.

Several years ago, I inherited a big LP collection from my dad. Our tastes are dissimilar, to say the least. I haven't listened to ninety percent of his LPs and I never will. But I haven't gotten rid of them, either. Once in a while I paw through them to see if anything rings my chime. Nothing ever does.

So, with little else to do, I went through them again, looking at the illustrations, the titles. Like Dutch Sax with the seductive strings and orchestra of Dolf van der Linden. Right. Dutch Sax? Is their sex, er sax different from ours? Then I laid my hands on an album I knew I had, but had misplaced for years. Frances Faye: Caught In The Act. Recorded by GNP Crescendo records which also issued an album with Helen Gurley Brown called Lessons In Love.

I put F. Faye on the turntable, cranked up the volume and built myself a drink. Several hours later, at about two a.m. with images of those albums in my head I came mostly awake in my chair. On my stumbling way to bed, I began to get the glimmer of an idea as to what my next move should be.

* * *

When real morning, the kind with light in the sky and birds twittering in the trees, came around, I got out of bed and did all the usual morning stuff. Then I headed out to my office, bristling with energy and ambition. Everything was normal in my building. I could hear my neighbors, the big blond Revulon cousins down the third floor hall, bustling about their high-tech computer systems and calling back and forth to each other. Their voices retained faint accents from their Swedish heritage. Their two-room office was crammed with computers, printers, modems and I-have-no-idea-whatall. Most of that electronic stuff is noisier than you'd expect, what with the fans and other mechanical parts.

I waved at Betsy and went inside. When I checked my answering machine there was only one call, from Ricardo Simon, made about the same time as the call I'd picked up at Ort's yesterday. The detective was leaving messages for me all over town but every time I responded, he hadn't been available. I called the cop shop and true to form, he wasn't available then either, so I left another message. At least he'd know I was trying. It was too early to find Ort in his bar, but I knew of a couple of other places where Laura the Lip might be so I called Al's in Dinkytown where she sometimes showed up for breakfast. From the sound of things, Al was having a busy morning. He told me that Laura had indeed been in, but earlier, and he thought she was headed uptown, that is downtown, that is, into the loop. The center of town. That's what we call it here. The loop. I figured she was likely to show up somewhere on Nicollet or Hennepin by noon.

I went through my telephone list. I was making a serious effort to find Mordecai. Last night I'd decided that Mordy had some answers and I was going to get them from him. He had to have information, I needed. He might even have knowledge that he was unaware of. I should have made a greater effort to round him up last night when he'd bolted out of my car. If anybody in town knew where Ms. Campbell had got to, it was going to be Mordy. After all, she was his frail, his skirt, his woman. With the phone squeezed between my jaw and my shoulder I waited for the next person to pick up. Unconsciously I fished in my desk drawer for a cigarette. When I realized what I was doing, I stopped. There haven't been any cigs in my desk for months, anyway.

The line rang and rang and nobody picked up. Damn. That was the third non-answer. I set the handset back in the cradle and just as I let go, it rang. I jumped and then I answered it. It was my police buddy Ricardo Simon. Finally.

"Yeah, Ricardo. What's shakin'? Wuzzup?"

"Will you get off that shit? I don't like you when you're trying to sound like Sam Spade, either. Do normal. Normal is better."

"Okay. So normal. We've been playing telephone tag for a while."

"Yeah. This may be nothing, Sean, but one of my CIs told me he saw Mordy early yesterday down at the Shelton."

"The Shelton? Isn't that a fleabag hotel on Goodroad downtown?"

"That's the one. My CI tells me he thought Mordecai was probably staying there."

"Thanks, Rick. I'll check it out." Finally, I thought, things are starting to turn my way. I was going to have a sit-down with Mordecai and in the process get him back together with Ms. Campbell. That in turn would make Catherine happier.

24

To say the Shelton was a hotel was stretching it. To call it a fleabag rooming house would have been more accurate. It was one of those places that's been in Minneapolis for a century. Maybe longer. It was built of some kind of stone, granite, probably, since there is a lot of that rock around the state. The stone face was so dark with the accumulated grime of the city it was hard to say just what the material was. The building was seven stories high and narrow. It had a date chiseled into the stone up toward the top but I couldn't read it from the street. Anyway, why would I care?

The door from the street led into a lobby with no casual seating. My red Keds squeaked across the cracked linoleum floor. At least the floor wasn't sticky. It wasn't a large lobby. It took me eight strides to get to the desk. You expect to see an old, wizened-up senior citizen working in this kind of establishment, someone who didn't hear too well. He'd have almost the only light in the gloomy place, an overhead socket with a shade swinging on a long cord and throwing the clerk's face into harsh shadows. Influence of the movies, I guess. In fact, the kid behind the desk was younger than me by a lot of years.

"Help you?" No accent. No inflection. No interest.

"Yeah," I said. "Is this man a guest here? I laid two items on the linoleum counter between us. One was a copy of a portrait of Mordy, that I got from Catherine, taken a couple of years ago, back when he was flush. The other item was a worn sawbuck. The kid raised

The Case of the Stolen Case

one eyebrow and slid the picture closer. He left the bill where it was. Either he was incorruptible or he wanted a bigger payoff. While he looked at the picture I laid another sawbuck on top of the first.

"Yeah, I think so. This gentleman has been a guest here the last couple of nights." He reached out and picked up the two bills. There was no need to be discreet. We were the only living beings in the place. Overhead I spied what appeared to be a surveillance camera pointing at me. It was probably inoperative. More likely it was just a cheap fake or an empty shell. Some places did that to discourage thugs, but they didn't want to pop for a real security camera.

The clerk put the folding money in his shirt pocket and repeated himself. "Yeah, this guy is staying here. I haven't seen him go out this morning so he could still be upstairs." He turned without any prompting from me and looked at a smudged sheet of paper tacked to the pasteboard wall of his cubicle. "He's in 410." He pointed at the stairs.

"Elevator?" I asked hopefully.

"Nope," smirked my source. I wondered if he was Simon's confidential informant.

I shrugged and squeaked over to the uncarpeted stairs. They weren't what you'd call bright and well-lighted. I started climbing. The building was old enough the stairs were wooden, heavy stained planks. They were worn, but not too badly. After the first floor, they got narrower but they seemed solid enough, except for the grimy railings which looked fra gile. I didn't touch them. Who knew what you might catch? The railings obviously hadn't been cleaned in this century. But the stairs squeaked hardly at all so I felt safe enough and kept climbing steadily upward. I arrived at the fourth floor only slightly out of breath.

The place was quiet and dim. Management didn't believe in spending money on hall lighting. Like the gloomy stairs above the first floor, the hall was narrow, but not very long, because the building wasn't very deep. Like the other floors, there wasn't any carpeting on the floor. I didn't meet anyone on the way up and I hadn't even heard any noises except for the occasional faint creak of a stair tread. The numbers on the doors had been painted over a few times so I had to peer closely to find the one I wanted. Leaning close to 402—there weren't any odd numbered doors—I faintly heard some music that might have been a radio. Signs of life at last. 410 was the last door down the hall.

I knocked. No response. I pounded and said in a loud voice, "Marsh. It's me, Sean." No response. The doorknob didn't turn, although it rattled. I rattled it. I glanced along the hallway toward the stairs. Then I went to work on the lock with a piece of stiff plastic I usually carry. It only took me a few minutes of jiggling and prying before I was able to separate the bolt far enough from the strike plate to open the door. I didn't even have to mess up the wood frame.

I stepped to one side and pushed the door open a little way. As usual, I wasn't heeled, and I had no idea how revved up Mordecai might be. Or if he was armed. There still wasn't anybody else around so I took my time and nudged the door open a little further. Still no response.

"Mordy," I called. "It's me, Sean. You in there?" Silence.

The door stopped its swing against the side of the bed. This was a small room. It seemed to be empty. I exhaled and went in. I found a sagging single bed with one dingy blanket and a sheet thrown back, a solid-looking three drawer bureau, and a soiled side chair. On the wall over the bed a small lamp was fastened to the wall. Opposite me was another door. Closed. I listened for a minute and then shut the door to the hall. I didn't latch it.

When I walked to the bureau I saw a tote bag on the floor beside the interior door. It looked like the same one Mordy had been carrying when he jumped out of my car three days earlier.

I sidled to the wall beside the bureau and listened. Nothing. I tapped on the door to what I presumed was a bathroom. More nothing. I took a couple of breaths to settle myself and twisted the knob. As I pushed the door open I saw a tiny sink and the edge of a shower stall. There was some resistance, something that gave but seemed to push back. I sidestepped into the bathroom and discovered that the door was obstructed by an untidy bundle of clothes piled on the floor beside the toilet. Otherwise the room appeared to be uninhabited. I assumed the pants and shirt and the underwear were Mordy's but I had no way to prove it.

The Case of the Stolen Case

I backed out of the bathroom and stood there a minute. There was a table lamp on the bureau and light coming from a grimy window, but the room wasn't what you'd call brightly lit. I bent down to grab the gym bag on the floor by the bathroom door and that's when I found him. He was under the bed, lying on his side fully clothed, facing away from me. It was immediately obvious he was dead when I touched his neck under the collar of his shirt. I could see he'd been helped along because there was a pool of almost dried blood under his head.

Shit.

I stared at him for several seconds. It wasn't that I hadn't seen a dead body before. Death comes with the job, sometimes. Up close and personal, sometimes. But this was somebody I had known. Sorta. Knew in a non-professional way, if not well. More importantly, this was somebody related to a woman I cared about. There were entanglements here that I knew instinctively would make it more difficult for me to remain objective.

I got myself back up and stepped away from the bed and the body. Went to the grimy smeared window and stared out at the rooftops across the alley.

Then I bent over the other side of the bed and peered at the body, and got another shock. It wasn't Mordecai after all. It was somebody else. Somebody I didn't recognize.

Double shit.

I stood up again and walked to the window where I stared out at the roof of the next door building for a moment. Even in my business human death wasn't a routine happening. I considered my options.

I decided not to move him. I'm not particularly squeamish, and I wanted to poke around, but I didn't want to have to spend a lot of time dancing with the cops over messing up a crime scene. To get at his pockets I'd have to drag him out from under the bed and there was no way I could do that and not leave traces of my presence. I couldn't figure why he was under the bed anyway. I was pretty certain he'd died quickly. The body was cool to my touch, but there was no odor, so he hadn't been dead very long. His eyes were shut and he had a peaceful look on his face. I looked more closely at where he lay in the dust. Then I went around the bed again and looked at the floor. He must have fallen here, in the narrow space between bed and wall of the bathroom. Then he'd been shoved under the bed. I could see the shiny path where the dust had been pushed aside. Looking over my shoulder I constructed a possible scenario.

This dude had entered Mordy's room without permission while Mordy was in the bathroom. The intruder must have seen the gym bag and stopped by the door. Mordy then yanked open the door and shot the guy. After that, he shoved the body under the bed and lit out. Mordy was getting good at splitting the scene.

I thought a moment and decided Mordy had the right idea, although for different reasons. I would remove myself from this scene forthwith. I looked more closely at the db and saw the slight bulge where his wallet must have been carried on his hip. I could see it wasn't there anymore, so I left the guy in peace. I smudged the places I'd touched. No polishing. That's a quick giveaway, but I ran my palms over the places I thought I'd touched. The forensic folks could pick up enough to get a DNA sample, but then they'd have to match it with someone. If I wasn't linked to the scene some other way, the cops wouldn't have any reason to check my DNA. I looked into the bureau drawers and carefully around the room. There was almost nothing visible to indicate Mordy had ever lived in that room, except for the pile of clothes in the bathroom and the gym bag. I did open the bag, but whatever papers Mordy'd carried off from the apartment were no longer there. I was breathing rapidly through my mouth and my pulse rate was up. I could feel sweat collecting in my armpits. It was time to boogie. As I went out and closed the door, making sure it locked, I wondered if that unknown body would still be alive if I'd been more diligent and located Mordy the night he bolted from my car. Downstairs I crouched on the stairs until I saw the clerk leave his chair. Then I slipped out the rear entrance. Across the street from the hotel was a tiny bar I'd never visited before. I plugged a quarter into the telephone hanging askew on the wall by the bathrooms and called the cop shop.

It didn't take long for a patrol car to arrive. While I watched from the doorway of the bar, two big cops got out and swaggered into the hotel. A little later, about as long as it took the uniforms to get up to Mordy's room, an unmarked unit pulled up and out hopped my friend, detective Ricardo Simon. He straightened his jacket and spent a couple of minutes looking up and down the block. Then he swiveled his head and looked right at the door I was standing behind. I knew he couldn't see me, but it was like he knew I was there. When Simon went into the hotel I split.

25

When I walked into the Kenwood place, Catherine immediately tasked me about Annette Campbell's whereabouts.

"I think you better find her," she said, pacing slowly up and down the living room. "And what about Mordy? I know we hardly knew each other and I haven't actually seen Mordy for probably a year. But he is family, and he did call. You shouldn't have let him get away."

"Yeah, you're right, the people connected to this case seem to be disappearing faster than I can round them up. I need a corral with a twenty-four-hour guard." I had withheld the news about the db in Mordy's hotel room. I was assuming Mordy had shot the man but with no proof either way, I didn't see any upside to telling her right then.

"I'm gonna change," Catherine said abruptly. "I'm going to the health club to work out. Can you get dinner on your own? There's plenty of stuff in the 'fridge."

I went to the kitchen and built myself a drink while I examined the larder for whatever might come to hand. We'd long ago decided that hanging on to leftovers until they came back to life was not productive. So the refrigerator was not well stocked. Nevertheless I located the makings of a decent Caesar salad, and plunked myself down to nosh away.

Catherine skipped in and planted a big sloppy kiss on my cheek just before she whisked out the door. After my healthy supper salad, I

The Case of the Stolen Case

scribbled a quick note to the lady and left. My objective was Ort's bar. Catherine's question about Annette Campbell's whereabouts nettled me. I was going to find her. Ort's was a place to start. As I went out the telephone rang but I didn't stop.

Downtown, things were pretty lively for the middle of the week. I had to park in a ramp three blocks away from the bar. Unlike what happens to most detectives in the mysteries I read, I often can't find a convenient parking space. Unless I want to pay a lot of parking tickets, and the job doesn't pay that well. When I got to Ort's, there were more barflies and assorted hangers on than I could ever remember seeing in the place at one time. Most of them were better dressed than Ort's usual clientele. After my eyes adjusted, I could see the main attraction.

At the curve of the bar, right next to the wait station, the tall blond I hoped to encounter was holding court in the midst of a thick group of admirers. Ort was right. Laura was tricked out in some sort of long, low-cut dress that left her arms and upper chest bare. Her bright blond hair was clean and carefully coifed, highlights reflecting the lights from the back bar.

She saw me when I was half-way across the room and waved me over with a grand and imperious gesture. After I forced my way through the bodies surrounding her, she smiled and extended one long shapely arm in my direction. I took her hand and brushed my lips over her fingers.

"Ah, Sean Sean," she said and waggled her tiny cell phone at me. "I just tried to reach out to you."

At her mention of my name, I sensed rather than saw a shifting in the group of men around Laura Lipp. When I glanced around, the press of bodies had diminished considerably. Interesting. Mention of my name in bars usually didn't provoke such a negative reaction. I could see that Laura had also noticed.

"I can't remember such a negative reaction, my dear. Are you stepping in something?"

"Possibly. Let's take a table."

Somehow a table toward the back of the place opened up almost as if the occupants had anticipated our need. Like lots of tables in bars, this one was small so we sat knee to knee and nose to bosom. Mine to hers, given the disparity in our heights. Our lowered voices were unintelligible to anyone else in the place. Ort, still on duty, brought me a beer and a fresh drink for Laura. I hadn't asked what she was drinking.

"So," I said, staring up into her deep blue eyes. "You called me, did you not? Wuzzup?"

She wrinkled her nose in the delicate manner she has and sipped her drink. "I heard on the street you were looking for me so I thought I'd make it easy. And here you are. I suppose you are aware of some of Mordecai's recent associations?"

"Yes, but that isn' why I wanted to talk to you." I raised an interrogatory eyebrow, still waiting.

"I've also heard you're looking for his friend. Annette Campbell?"

"You know where she is?"

"First tell me about this real estate business you're involved in."

I wasn't really surprised that Laura knew about the scam. Secrets are harder to keep in this town than snow in April. "It's called flipping. You get a group of people together who have little or no previous contact with the law but who are not averse to making some extra cash. Especially cash off the books. They also have to be a little shy of straight-ahead ethics. You need a friendly banker or two and a real estate evaluator, plus a building inspector to round things out and touch all the bases."

Laura raised her eyebrows "Sean."

"What? Too many clichés?"

"It sounds complicated."

I nodded. "You buy a property. Then you get it appraised. The idea is to get a document stating the value of the place is higher than real. On the basis of the appraisal, your bank guy okays a loan for someone who isn't quite up to snuff. Then you sell and resell the property in quick succession, each time jacking up the assessed value of the property, paying off people as you go with the proceeds of the latest loan. Assessors and inspectors on your payroll go along for a piece of the action. After a while, when the value of the property gets ridiculously high, you quietly walk away with a chunk of cash, leaving the latest bank and whoever signed the loan papers on the hook."

Laura nodded. "I get it. Replicate that with a bunch of different properties at the same time, especially with a small business or two thrown into the mix and you could be talking about a fair amount of money."

"Right. What's more, I think the people here who have been flipping real estate, have some other thievery going at the same time." I had to remind myself that Laura was not exactly a confidant. There was something about her attitude I'd never been able to pin down, but she was so easy to talk with that she collected more information than you might expect. I wasn't going to tell her about Beechy, the Grand Pharmacy robbery or Sal Belassario in connection with this real estate scam. "Again, why were you calling me?"

"Flipping, hey? Who's involved?" She ignored my question but I knew we'd get back to it in a minute.

I gave her the names of the people I knew. We weren't talking proof for the courts here. This was street knowledge and I figured it couldn't hurt if word got around I was zeroing in on the Talbots and their buddies. I left Armond Anderson out of it. Being the big time developer he apparently was, I wanted more proof before I'd slander his name. Besides, there was that incident on the path in Roseville.

"Then there's the woman who's apparently been cozying up to Mordy."

"Annette Campbell. She's staying with a friend of mine in Dinky Town."

Laura dropped that bomblet with nary a flicker. "Excuse me, she's staying with a friend of yours?"

She nodded, sucked on her cigarette and flicked a glance over my shoulder. "Right. I know you set up that pad for her in Richfield. She got lonely. Nothing to read apparently and she didn't care for the TV."

I was nonplused, to say the least. "So how did you two connect?"

"Now, Sean, you don't have to know everything. When I talked with her we hit it off right away." She patted my hand in a condescending way. At least that's how I took it. "I'm not going to give you the address or the name of my friend. But if you want to talk with Annette I'll set it up." Laura raised one perfect eyebrow and smiled across her glass. She wasn't exactly looking down her nose at me—she wouldn't do that. But it was close.

I figured Annette probably got in touch with Mordy who put her in touch with Laura. I already knew Laura and Mordy were acquainted. Hell, Laura knew practically everybody. That's what made her so useful—and so irritating at times. That she knew about the Richfield pad meant I'd have to find a new place next time I needed a hideaway.

"Okayyy, sweetheart," I mumbled. "Convey to Miss Campbell we need to have a sit down as soon as it can be arranged. I'm relieved to know she's safe for the moment. By the way, I don't suppose you can give me a lead on Mordecai's immediate whereabouts can you?"

Laura smiled and shook her head. "No, but I'll I nose around if you wish. Now," she leaned forward until her cleavage pretty well filled my view, "what can you tell me about that little altercation over on Goodroad?"

I had no doubt what she was asking about but I didn't want to be too easy. I had a feeling serious negotiations with Laura would be an interesting experience. "I'm not sure what you mean."

She leaned back in her chair, removing her bosom from my immediate range. "Oh, c'mon now, Sean. At the Shelton? The cops got a tip and very quickly your pal Simon showed up. Detective Simon."

I shrugged. "I understand somebody phoned in a tip about a dead body in one of the rooms. But that's all I know," I said.

Laura smiled. "Really. That db wouldn't have been in the same room where Mordy was staying, would it?"

I shrugged again. "I never visited Mordy at the Shelton and I only have your word that he was living there.

It became clear Laura wasn't offering any more information about how she'd hooked up with the Campbell woman. I finished my beer, paid for the round with a generous tip to both Ort and the lady and split.

When I got home, the light on my answering machine was blinking furiously.

26

I was in no mood to listen to sales calls and a bunch of silent hang-ups so I ignored the imperiously blinking red signal on the machine and went to get ready for bed. But the image of that imperiously blinking light stayed with me. So I went downstairs and looked at the answering machine's readout. There was only one message.

I pressed the button. After the greeting, the single message was very short. "Call me," the voice said. Then there was a long, quiet pause and I imagined the caller's shapely arm as she slowly lowered the telephone to its bedside cradle. Catherine's voice was quiet, almost sad. So I called her. While the telephone rang I looked at the desk clock. Nearing midnight.

"Hey," the voice said, a little muzzy with sleep.

"Hey," I said back. I heard her breathe.

"You home?"

"Uh huh. Just got in." I waited.

"Hang on, sweetie." I listened to rustlings as she must have moved pillows and sheets around to get more comfortable.

"I wish you were here, babe." She breathed into the telephone then said in a brisker voice. "Laura Lipp called. She seems to want to talk."

"I had a little verbal dance with her tonight at Ort's. I gave her my case, at least the outlines and some of the players."

"Did she have anything for you?"

"Yeah, seems she's connected up with the Campbell woman. She's going to put us in contact."

"Not surprising she'd have something already. Do you think she knows anything about Mordy?"

"Apparently not. I'm hoping Annette Campbell does. I'll try to find out when Laura takes me to her. What are you up to tomorrow?"

"Clinic in Mankato, then to my lawyers. Dinner?"

"You bet. I'll call you."

"Night, love." We broke the connection and I smiled my way upstairs and into bed.

* * *

The next morning dawned bright and sunny with the heavy promise of another hot day. It was still early and I poured a tall glass of chilled orange juice from the refrigerator. I strolled out on my deck at the back of the house.

I'd already checked the intruder alarms so I knew there hadn't been any unusual activity around the place. I sat down in a plastic chair and stretched out my legs. There was a little movement toward the back of the lot. Since there wasn't even a light breeze, I figured one of the local cats or dogs was making a foray through the underbrush. I was wrong.

After a minute, while I just sipped orange juice and listened to the birds, from just to the left of the big caged pile of rotting leaf and grass clippings, known in the suburbs as a compost pile, appeared a furry gray-brown rabbit. He was a big fellow. His questing eyes ears and nose surveyed the place and he hopped a little farther into the open. I didn't move. This particular rabbit has been a feature of this block for a long time. I had no idea how long, but I'd been seeing him around for years, ever since I inherited the place, a gift from a grateful client. I knew it was the same rabbit I saw half a dozen times every year because he had a big flashy diamond stud in one ear.

Now I know I'd never been close enough to the hare to examine the stud, but why not? It should be a zircon? Or glass? Nah, it had to be a diamond. Anyway, Benny the rabbit, or whatever his name was, coolly looked me over, flapped his long ears, flashed his stud at me, and loped casually across the back of the lot and disappeared into the neighbor's yard.

I opened the shed and hauled out the lawnmower and the hoe. I spent a sweaty, intense, ninety minutes killing, clipping, trimming and such like. Meanwhile I went over what I knew and considered possible moves. At the moment it seemed I was a prisoner of circumstance. I needed to get some answers from the Campbell woman.

I finished my yard work and went inside to shower and begin another day in my role as Sean Sean, master detective, seeker of truth, justice, and the right way, righter of wrongs, and so on. I also figured I'd better get to the office and send out some bills or I'd be spending time in the welfare office.

There were more messages on the damn machine. The first, third and fourth were from Ricardo Simon urging me to call him at my earliest convenience. He sounded more insistent as we progressed from first to last. The second was one of those ubiquitous hang-ups. Some damn auto-dialer that didn't get the expected response so it didn't know what to do.

The fourth was from Laura the Lip and the last was from Catherine. It was terse and it worried me. "Sean," she said. "Call me. Something's going on." The tone of her voice was totally different from last night.

I speed dialed her apartment and got her answering service. Either she'd left right after she'd called or she wasn't picking up. I grabbed a frozen bagel and jammed it in the toaster while I ran upstairs and took a quick shower. I ate the warm bagel with cream cheese and grape jelly standing at the kitchen counter. From my built-in safe in the basement I took my hip holster and a gat. I opted for the .38 Chief's Special light-weight I'd recently acquired. It didn't have quite the firepower of my old .45 caliber Colt semi-auto, but I figured I might be gone a while. The colt weighed a ton and wore me down after a day toting it around. Its bulk was hard to conceal in the bargain. So, the .38. In this day of heightened security, it was likely I'd have to stash it before entering some places, but at least it wouldn't be too obvious I was carrying. The damn aluminum case was still there. Unopened. Staring at me accusingly.

In the car, racing down 35W, I fished out my cell phone and dialed Catherine again. It was a little tricky. My small motor skills were just barely up to the task of punching the tiny buttons while trying to keep the Taurus in the right lane, but I managed. Still only the machine. How disturbed was I? Should I go to Kenwood? If she wasn't home I wouldn't know anything more. On the other hand… I went to Kenwood. The apartment was silent, no note, no signs of disturbance. I tried her cell phone. No response. I left a note on the kitchen counter with a big black question mark on it, the time, and my initials.

My office was a peaceful haven of quiet. No break-in, no hassles, and the glass in the door was still there. I called CM's office. Yes, they confirmed that she was driving to Mankato to visit the clinic there. That relieved my mind. I called her Mankato clinic and left a message to call me at my office. Then I did some necessary scut work.

I pulled some files, laboriously typed out some bills and prepped them for the mail slot at the front of my building. I tried the cop shop and R. Simon, but he was out. The phone didn't ring. I reviewed a couple of low priority jobs I was working on. Read the mail. Nothing of any interest. Damn. Drummed my fingers on my desktop.

It got on to one in the p.m. and my stomach growled. I left my .38 in the safe and went downstairs and up the block to a little hole in the wall lunch counter. The food wasn't particularly good, but there wasn't much traffic and the place was convenient. I had an overcooked fried egg sandwich and a cup of burned coffee.

When I got back to the office there was just one message, from Catherine. I called the strange number. A strange female voice said, "Wild, Korth, Manchee and Knopf. How may we be of assistance?"

"A friend of mine gave me this number. Catherine Mckerney. She asked me to call."

"And you are?"

"Sean Sean." There was silence for a moment. My name does that sometimes.

"Oh, yes, of course. I'll ring through."

She did and CM came on the horn.

"It's me, babe. What's going on?"

"Oh, good. I'm here with my lawyer. Charles Wild. It's just routine business, but there is something else."

Her voiced was normal in tone, but I detected a faint tremor. "You want me to come over?" I said.

"No. No, that's not necessary. It's not why I called."

I waited, and heard her blow out her breath. I waited.

"It's the calls. This morning I'm all of a sudden getting a rash of heavy breathers and hang-ups. Sometimes there's just nobody there. Other times I can hear or sense someone on the line. You understand what I mean?"

"Yeah."

"Five this morning before I left the apartment. And I haven't checked since."

"I get quite a few from those damn automatic dialers."

"I know. That accounts for some of them, I guess. But, Sean. I can't say why, but there's something threatening about them. It's like they're trying to keep track of me, pin me down. I don't—"

"Do you think you were followed when you left the apartment?"

"No. And I looked. But I don't really know what to look for. And now—gosh, it sounds like I'm losing it, doesn't it? Maybe I'm just imagining things. When I talk about it out loud, it sounds a little silly."

"Not to me it doesn't." Alarm bells were going off in my head. "Tell you what. You stay there for a while, okay? I'll run by my place and pick up some fresh clothes and some equipment I need. Then I'll meet you at your lawyer's office. Take me about three-quarters of an hour, maybe a little longer." I tried to sound as casual as I could. I didn't want to alarm her unnecessarily. I was alarmed. "You just hang out there until I arrive."

"That would be good, I think." I could hear relief in her voice. She gave me an address in St. Louis Park, a southwestern suburb of Minneapolis.

"Okay, hon. I'll be there quick as I can."

I dropped the telephone back in its cradle, grabbed my weapon and beat it out of there. As I rattled the hall door to make sure it was locked, I heard the telephone ring.

27

I stayed at or near the speed limit all the way to Roseville. Inside I raced around and checked the feed tower for the cats. I also gave them fresh water. Then I stuffed some clothes in a duffel bag and threw it in the car. The mail had arrived and I whipped through the envelopes. There was nothing of any importance. I dropped the mail on the table and trotted to the basement to my safe built into the wall behind the furnace. I took a box of bullets for the Chief's lightweight on my belt and ran out of the house. Yeah, I set the alarm system as I went out.

Back on the freeway, I threaded my way through Minneapolis' gut and into that affluent suburb called St. Louis Park. My destination was a ten story newish office building a couple of blocks off Highway 12 in an area of offices and small businesses. The building was surrounded by a big parking lot. Half a block away I dropped my speed to a crawl and turned in to the lot. It was a very quiet business location. There was no traffic, which made things a lot easier. I began a slow drift down the rows of cars. There were reserved spaces close to the building entrances. Some were empty, but there were plenty of cars in the lot. After a couple of turns down the rows, I spotted Catherine's bright red Miata. There were empty spots a couple of cars away, but I didn't slow down. I kept driving, looking for occupied vehicles, possibly someone parked where they'd have an easy line of sight to her car. I went around the whole lot. I didn't see anything suspicious, so

I parked a quarter block away from the entrance in a corner of the lot and locked my bag and bullets in the trunk. My ordinary-looking Taurus has been modified just a little. It has a more powerful engine and a trunk that can't be easily popped.

I strolled into the quiet lobby of the building and glanced around. Nobody. So I took the elevator to the eighth floor and the officers of Wild, Korth, Manchee and Knopf. I gave my name to the pretty receptionist and she nodded, then pointed me toward an office door with a discreet brass label that said C. Wild. I rapped and went in. Catherine gave me a big smile, the one that always made me feel ten feet tall and as if I could leap tall buildings in a single bound.

She turned and introduced me to Chuck Wild, a trim, older, fellow with a weathered face and a firm handshake. I noticed his eyes. They were watchful. I liked that.

"What's happened?"

"I'm embarrassed I even mentioned it, now you've come all this way. Mostly it's just a feeling. There were several telephone hang-ups this morning and then another just when I left to go to work. I've had this feeling of unease all day. But nothing specific. I guess it's making me paranoid."

"What about at the clinic in Mankato?"

"My sense of being watched was still there."

"Have you seen anyone watching?"

"No, I said that, Sean." She put her hands on my shoulders. We were standing beside her lawyer's desk. Charles Wild watched us with a frown.

"Yeah, I know," I said. "What about being followed?"

"You mean in the car? A car following me?"

"Exactly."

"Gosh, Sean, I don't know. I don't pay that much attention. Even after the calls I looked, but I'm usually thinking about other stuff, like the people or the meeting I'm going to. Whatever we're going to talk about. Sometimes I think about you." She smiled a little smile.

"Anybody looking for you wouldn't have too much trouble finding you, would they? I mean we haven't exactly tried to keep you secret."

Catherine nodded. "That's right."

"Maybe you ought to consider hiring some protection," suggested Wild.

"A bodyguard?" said CM. "Oh, I don't think so. There's no real evidence of anything, is there?"

I shook my head. Catherine and Mr. Wild concluded her business and we said goodbye and went out. In the lobby of the building, I put a hand on CM's arm and stopped her near the door. "I don't want to make a big thing of this."

"Me neither."

"Just to be on the safe side, I'm gonna follow you home."

She frowned. "Okay."

"It isn't the easiest thing in the world, following another vehicle. Yeah, I know, in the movies the detective or the cops jump in the car and follow the suspect through town making all the right turns and hitting all the lights just right until they get to his secret pad. It's harder than that."

"Okay," she said doubtfully.

"Point is, make it easy. Don't jump any yellow lights. Drive at a steady speed within the speed limit. Keep checking to be sure I'm still behind you. If we get separated by a red light or traffic, pull over to the curb and wait for me."

CM sighed and nodded. "Okay. If you think—"

"I do. I most definitely do." I went out the door and scanned the lot. She walked to her car and got in, waiting while I went to my own vehicle. Red Miata and gray Taurus made a short caravan out of the lot.

The plan was to go up Highway 7 to where it linked with France, then jog north around the west side of Cedar Lake. Then we'd go back into Kenwood to the apartment.

That was the plan.

Traffic wasn't bad so the trip was going smoothly. Then we hit the intersection at France and turned north. Traffic grew heavier and we got separated by some hot-dog in one of those big SUVs who think they're immune to vehicle laws. He squeezed in behind CM and rode her bumper for a couple of blocks. She slowed until he got impatient and blasted his horn at her and swerved around the Miata. I was distracted but it probably wouldn't have made any difference. When the SUV cleared out, I was two car lengths behind her and in the right lane. CM was in the left hand lane still heading north. Why? I wondered.

In the block after the intersection of Cedar and France a big green and white truck, one of those delivery vehicles with high straight sides, blasted out of an alley, ignored oncoming cars and slammed right across France. The truck caught Catherine's car in the left rear quarter, a few inches behind the door. That Miata doesn't weigh much and the momentum of the truck threw the roadster across my lane in front of me and up on the sidewalk. It smashed into the light pole there on the corner and partially wrapped around it. It made a helluva noise.

I screamed her name and mashed the brake pedal, slewed sideways partially across both traffic lanes. I was out the door and running toward the accident almost before my car stopped.

The truck driver shifted into reverse and floored it. The big engine and the rear duals screamed. I vaguely heard horns blasting, but I was concentrating on that little red car crumpled against the light pole. Spinning tires sent up clouds of steam and smoke from burning rubber. The truck slewed backward, ripping the Miata's rear fender apart. The driver of the truck ground it into forward gear and rabbited out of there. I remember that the truck had a big steel grating welded over the front of the engine compartment. I didn't look for a license plate, I was grabbing for the Miata's door, still yelling Catherine's name. Pedestrians, scattered by the crashing vehicles, now returned to the scene, some to offer help others to just gawk or give useless advice.

I yanked on the door handle. Other than rocking the car a little, the door didn't open. It was jammed tight. One glance at the other side made me realize that she was trapped in the thing until the Jaws of Life or some heavy crowbars arrived. I could smell the peculiar mixture of oil, anti-freeze and gas that often attends automobile accidents. My stomach was in knots. I couldn't get my breath. I peered into the interior. Catherine didn't seem to be moving. I figured out that she was slumped in her seat belt leaning toward the passenger side.

Dimly in the background I heard a siren approaching. I continued to yank ineffectually on the door handle, repeating her name over and over, interspersed with several choice epithets. A heavy hand grabbed my shoulder and I whirled around.

"What?" I snarled. The man who had grabbed me was holding a fire extinguisher.

"You won't get it open without help. We have to keep it from catching fire." I looked at him wordlessly and he stepped around me and began to spray the foam over the street under the back of the car where the gas was dripping. Somebody else came forward with another extinguisher and began to spray under the hood and on the right side. A cop came up to me and said. "You do this?"

"No," I said. "She's my friend. I was following her home. A truck hit us—her."

"Damn truck almost hit me," said another voice. "He shot right out of that alley and crossed in front of me."

The cop took us both by the arm and tried to move us away. I resisted. Just then a fire truck rumbled up making all kinds of noise, followed by an ambulance. Three big firemen shoved through the crowd carrying a big tool I recognized as the Jaws of Life. With efficiency born of lots of practice, they sliced open the side and top of the Miata. The paramedics crawled into the opened body of the car and began to work on Catherine's inert body. She still wasn't moving and I still didn't seem to be able to take a deep breath. The cop was asking me questions, which I guess I was answering. A hand came up from somewhere and gave me a white handkerchief. I realized there were tears mixed with sweat running down my face.

Equipment from the ambulance and the fire truck was piling up in the street around us. We were in the way but I was stuck to the spot, staring at the crumpled red Miata and the unmoving figure inside. There was no fire, but I still couldn't tell how Catherine was. The paramedic backed out of the car and called for a backboard. His eyes met mine and he said, "She's alive. Unconscious and there's a lot of blood, but her heartbeat's strong."

With infinite care, firemen and the EMTs extricated CM's limp body from the car after they pretty much peeled away everything on the left side. When I finally had a clear view, she looked really bad. There was a lot of blood on her face and upper chest, and her head was swathed in a huge bandage. Blood was already starting to leak through the white. Trembling, I started toward her, but the cop held me back. I knew I had to let the professionals do their job unhindered by a concerned lover who was falling apart in front of them.

I turned around as they placed the stretcher in the ambulance and saw the cop had stepped back a few paces and was looking at me strangely. Behind him, his partner was also staring at me with a very tense expression.

"Excuse me sir," said the nearest cop. "Are you carrying a weapon?"

"Yes. Officer, I am armed." It didn't sound like my voice that came out. The cop'd apparently seen the holstered weapon on my hip. I stood very still and said, "My name is Sean Sean. I'm a licensed private investigator and I have a permit. I'll show you my identification if you'll let me. But I want to get to the hospital as quickly as possible."

The cops both seemed to relax minutely and the one furthest away spoke into his shoulder mike.

"Are you working here?" asked the cop who had been taking down my statement.

"I was escorting the lady home. To our place. That's all. She's not involved in anything."

"But you said this thing was deliberate."

"Yes officer, but I think whoever did this is after me, not Catherine."

The second officer stepped forward and spoke in his partner's ear. He nodded once and said, "All right Mr. Sean. You better get down to the ER at HCMC. We'll be in touch later. I hope the woman will be all right."

"Thanks, guys," I said and beat it through the crowd toward my car. It was right where I'd left it and the keys were still in it. My briefcase, on the other hand, which had been lying on the front seat, was gone. I wiped my face with the borrowed handkerchief and cranked the engine. Then I leaned on my horn and maneuvered through the crowd to the side street. I still didn't know how badly Catherine had been hurt. Her eyes were closed when they put her in the ambulance. I could see her lips moving but there was just so much blood.

My vision kept blurring as I drove to the hospital. I was on auto pilot. I couldn't ever have told anyone what streets I took or how many pedestrians had to jump for their lives. Or how many red lights I ran.

I slammed through the doors into the ER right into the arms of a big blond nurse who must have outweighed me by sixty pounds. "You're Sean Sean," she growled, refusing to move out of my way. When I feinted left and tried to scuttle around her right flank she grabbed me by the shoulders and lifted me onto my toes. "Come with me," she said.

I went. What choice did I have?

She hustled me down a short corridor past some curtained alcoves and around some corners. She corralled me in a small room with chairs and a TV. "Sit." She pointed at one of the chairs.

I took two quick steps forward into the room and whirled around. "Catherine," I said. "Mckerney. Auto accident. They just brought her in. I have to see her."

"Yes," the tank-like nurse said. "She's alive and she's being well-taken care of. She's across the hall in the ER. She needs blood. Can you donate?"

I shook my head, dancing on my toes. "No. Veins clog up. Too narrow, I guess. Besides we aren't compatible, blood-wise." I started toward her. Then the nurse's words registered. "She's alive! She's gonna make it? "I need to be with her, now."

The nurse didn't budge from the doorway. "In a minute. Happens we all know her. She has a contract here."

Like an apparition, a gowned figure materialized behind the nurse. The figure wore blue scrubs, a cap, a mask across its face, and booties. I couldn't for the life of me have identified the figure as male or female. Its gown was spattered with blood on the front. A lot of blood, it seemed to me. It murmured something in the nurse's ear. She nodded. My stomach did flip-flops and I felt nauseous.

I saw the nurse frown and then lean toward me. The room swam in crazy circles and suddenly I was looking at a very fuzzy ceiling. The next thing I knew I was sitting on a chair with my head hanging between my knees and a voice I didn't recognize was repeating, "Breathe slowly, breathe deeply."

The Case of the Stolen Case

I raised my head and looked around. How long had I been out?

The blond tank was gone. A different nurse was crouched beside me. He had very short dark hair and molasses colored skin. His expression was one of polite concern. "What's goin' on," I mumbled? "I want to see Catherine Mckerney."

"Sure. Can you walk?"

"You damn right." I put a hand on his shoulder and levered myself out of the chair. Everything seemed to work. "Did I pass out?" I said to the nurse beside me.

"No, man, not quite. You just turned a little green. Come with me."

He put a hand in the small of my back and walked me across the hall. There were two beds, both occupied and the room was busy with doctors, nurses, technicians and lots of complicated machinery. I recognized CM's long dark hair and shuffled to the foot of her bed. The doc and the other glanced at me sympathetically and went on with their tasks. Catherine had an oxygen tube in her nose and other tubes in both arms. There was a big white bandage on one side of her forehead, but I didn't see any blood.

"Mister....Sean," said a man I took to be an ER doc. "You're the person Ms. Mckerney lists to be notified in case of emergencies." He said this matter of factly. I was surprised. I hadn't known she'd done that. Then I was pleased, for a moment.

"Doctor, how is she?"

He nodded. "She's lucky. The split on her forehead bled copiously, but the EMTs took care of that and except for two black eyes, numerous bruises and miscellaneous contusions, she's going to be all right. Fortunately, she's healthy and in good physical condition. The only question is her concussion. We'll keep her here overnight just to monitor her."

My pulse began to slow down now I knew CM was going to be okay. The doctor and I had stepped into the hall where there was hurried traffic, but no one paid particular attention to us. "I want her moved to a private room as soon as it can be arranged." The medico raised his sandy eyebrows at that.

"No need. She can stay right here until tomorrow morning."

I shook my head. "Trust me, doctor. She needs a more secure place. A private room."

He shrugged and nodded. "I'll arrange it."

I went to the admitting desk and leaned over. I fished my card case with my license out and waved it at the man sitting there. For a moment, the phones weren't ringing and the radios were silent. "Has anybody been inquiring about the female accident victim who came in an hour ago? Mckerney?"

The man looked through a bunch of message slips. "Two," he said.

"The family requests no information be given out. Stonewall if you have to. Nothing to nobody. Okay?"

"Sure. No problem."

I looked in at Catherine again and then found a telephone. I called assistant prosecutor Jerry Ford.

Quickly I explained what had happened and cut through his expressions of concern and said, "Jer, as a personal favor, can you arrange to have a cop on her room? They'll release her tomorrow morning and I'll be here until late, but I could use some relief between midnight and six am. I know we're in Minneapolis but—"

"What's the deal, Sean?"

"Jerry, this was deliberate. I saw the truck come out of the alley. He was aiming for her."

"Damn! I'll get right on it."

"Thanks." I hung up and looked at my hand on the receiver. It was trembling and I could feel the little waves of muscular tremors running through my body. It wasn't reaction to Catherine's crash. I was mad and getting madder. Damn mad.

28

It was six a.m. and I was sitting an uncomfortable chair outside Catherine's room waiting for the off-duty Minneapolis cop to come back from the cafeteria. He said he was going to stay until we got a reading from the docs on her condition. I didn't know this cop, but he exuded sympathy, so I figured he must have had a heads-up from his watch sergeant or his precinct captain or somebody who knew Catherine. He had checked my ID when I showed up on the floor and it took him several seconds to decide I was OK after I offered to take over his chair while he went to get coffee or something to eat and visit the men's room.

I heard a rumble of male voices as the elevator doors partway down the corridor across from the nursing station slide open. The uniform was back, accompanied by Detective Ricardo Simon. Simon came up and stuck out his hand. I stood up and he grabbed my shoulder in kind of an awkward hug.

"Hey, man, I was real disturbed to hear about the crash. How's she doin'? Are you okay?"

I squeezed his hand and said, "I don't think the doctor has been to see her yet this morning, but he was pretty upbeat last night. I think she's going to be all right but she hasn't waked up yet."

"Wrong, wrong wrong," came a strong voice from the room at my back. "I'm definitely awake."

I whipped around and went into her room to find Catherine looking a little wrung out and tousled, but definitely awake and alert. CM flicked her eyes over my shoulder and recognized detective Simon.

I leaned over her bed and kissed her undamaged cheek. Her hands lifted, she winced and grabbed me. She squeezed me around the neck, and I saw as I bent closer that it was painful to do.

"Where am I and what happened, to coin an original question," she said.

"HCMC."

Simon leaned against the door frame, a wide grin on his face. "It's nice to see you again so soon, Ms. Mckerney. You look pretty good in white."

"It's nice to be fawned over, but you could have given me some warning." She dragged the bed sheet up to her chin and stuck her free hand into her disarrayed hair. Her questing fingers encountered a large bandage wrapped around her head. "What's this thing?" She wrinkled her forehead and looked beyond me at the uniformed cop now standing in the door. "Am I under arrest or something?"

I opened my mouth to explain when a husky voice from the hall said, "Excuse me officer, can I get through here?" A tall white-coated figure wearing a stethoscope around her neck and a nametag that said Doctor J. Spizer pushed into the room. "You gentlemen can vacate the premises while I check my patient." She impatiently waved us out and bent over Catherine as I closed the door.

In the corridor, I shook hands with the cop and assured them things were definitely looking up. They elected to leave and I sat down, suddenly feeling a wave of relief falling over me. A few minutes later, the doctor called me back into the room and I took CM's hand when I reached her bedside.

"You're going to be fine," Doctor Spizer said smiling down at Catherine. "We'll release you in an hour or so and then I suggest rest and minimum exercise until some of the contusions begin to fade. You'll be so stiff and sore I don't think you're going to want to move around much. A few days should do it. Meanwhile, Mr. Sean can take care of you." She smiled, nodded and left the room.

"Okay, what happened to me?"

"You got hit broadside by a truck. It came out of an alley on

France and slammed into the Miata, knocking you into a light pole."

"How bad is the car?"

"Totaled. Thing is, it wasn't an accident."

CM looked silently at me for a minute. "So that's why you're so wired. I thought when you first came in it was just no sleep and lots of coffee, but it's more than that, isn't it?"

"Yeah. Since you don't make the kind of enemies who send marauding trucks after you, I think it's pretty clear somebody's trying to get at me through you. I can't decide if this was a warning or a failed attempt to do serious damage. Maybe they thought I was in the car with you, but that's not likely. Either way, we're not taking any chances. Security is good enough in your building and you're just going to have to stay at home until I can get this sorted out."

CM shifted in the bed and I could tell from the expression that passed over her face the movement caused her some pain. "I really can't sit up. I mean I can. Everything works but there's a lot of soreness. The doctor is prescribing Percodan, but here's an idea. One of the instructors at the school has a h—vehicle that will accommodate a gurney. Why don't I call him and arrange for him to drive me home? That way, I can be as comfortable as possible."

"Okay." I wondered what she wasn't telling me. I handed her the telephone and she connected with her school office. A man named Kent came on the line, although I didn't actually hear the guy's voice I could tell it was a guy. When she hung up she smiled at me and said, "He'll be here in an hour." He was. He was tall and good-looking. Of course, from my perspective, most people look tall. When he shook my hand, I could tell he had a lot of upper body strength. He was probably a masseur. He was wheeling a gurney very like the ones the hospital used.

"I couldn't park at the pick-up entrance," he smiled.

A nurse showed up and Catherine signed some papers. Kent and I flanked the nurse wheeling the mobile bed expertly down the hall and into the elevator. On the way, Kent explained that he'd had to park at the rear entrance, next to the emergency ambulance station. When we exited the hospital, I figured out why. His vehicle was long and black and shiny and even though it had creamy fringed curtains on the rear side windows, the thing was unmistakably a hearse.

The nurse smothered a grin. Catherine chortled and I just shrugged. I turned to a grinning Kent. "I can't say I'm surprised they wouldn't let you park in front. You'd give the hospital a bad name."

The nurse had collected two orderlies and the three of them maneuvered CM and her gurney into the hearse with a minimum of bumping and discomfort. I watched them drive off in stately fashion, Catherine waving gaily through the side window. Now that I thought of it, it wasn't such a bad idea for her to leave in that fashion. If anybody was watching the floor or the main entrance, they'd miss her.

I went through the building and collected my car from the street. There was no ticket on the windshield. I didn't detect anybody looking at me with suspicious attention. Nevertheless I went around a couple of aimless blocks and then beat it for the apartment. As I'd instructed, the hearse was waiting in the garage right next to the elevator entrance. Kent and I helped CM into a wheel chair because even the back elevator wasn't big enough for the gurney. Kent packed up and I took Catherine upstairs.

Inside, we managed to get her into bed with a minimum of painful hassle, but she was obviously in a lot of discomfort. I gave her the pills and a glass of juice. Then I went into the other room and called Detective Simon. I'd previously arranged for a loose tail while we moved Catherine from the hospital, just in case.

"Our guys didn't see anybody, Sean. The hearse threw us for a few minutes but we had one car within sight the whole way. I think you're clear, but if you need anything just holler. Give Catherine my regards."

I brought her a glass of cool water and said, "I've been thinking. I can't tell whether that truck was aimed at both of us, or just at you. But It makes sense for us to stay apart for a while. I've arranged for some protection here. Now I'm gonna go to the office for a couple of hours. Then I'm going home. I'll check in frequently, but I do have some things to do now."

She smiled and said, "I'm fine, Sean. You don't have to baby me. The doctor said all I need to do is rest to let the bruises and soreness retreat. You go on. Besides, the way you're simmering, I can almost hear you humming. It'll do you good to do something."

I kissed her gently and started out the door. "However," she called me back. "I don't want to learn about any speeding tickets or assault charges."

I nodded and went out thinking she knew me too well. To say I was royally pissed was a vast understatement. I expected the occasional bumps and contusions. It came with the job. I even, though rarely, got shot at. But when somebody targeted people close to me who were not involved, I took umbrage, vast and intense umbrage. I was going to find whoever set up Catherine and make them pay. Big time.

Twenty minutes later in my office out on Central, I was on the phone with the Minneapolis PD trying to collect whatever they had on the fugitive truck. It wasn't much. Since the cops agreed with me that it was a deliberate hit and run, they had canvassed the neighborhood and come up with some witnesses. Of course, the wits didn't agree on much of what they'd seen. It was a big flat-sided truck with white, gray, light blue walls. It had duals or singles on the rear and was or wasn't a diesel. The sides of the box were clear of lettering or it said Acme Moving Company. Nobody knew what color the cab was, although my memory said it was faded green.

Some of the good folks on the scene weren't even sure of the color of Catherine's wrecked red Miata. One person reported what may or may not turn out to be a partial license plate. It was a Minnesota plate and the first three letters were probably GRR. The police were running the info by the motor vehicle people in St. Paul, but they weren't hopeful. Neither was I.

Since I had only one active case at the moment there was no question in my mind the car crash and the Frogtown fire were connected. The telephone rang.

"It's Sal," said the voice. "I just heard. God, Sean, I am desolated. Is Catherine all right? Will she be all right? I just can't believe this. Is it true they think it was deliberate? Such a charming lady. Can Catherine possibly have such enemies? Who could possibly be involved in such a thing?"

I'd never heard him so agitated. "You, for one," I said. That got his attention.

"What? Excuse me? You think I'm involved?"

"Sally, Sally, what kind of a dolt do you think I am? You hire me to look into Mordecai Marsh and George Beechy, both of whom get dead. I get warned once and threatened once, even if it comes in the form of a warning. What's more, the tone of your voice leads me to believe you know that the stolen case is the key to this whole business and somebody doesn't want me to pursue this any more."

"But Sean, how can you even suggest I'd be involved? You know how I adore Catherine."

I knew that, but I also knew that if it came to a choice between his friends and his well-being or his money, which came to almost the same thing, he'd give up anybody. I liked Sal Belassario, but I didn't trust him all that much.

"All right, enough. I've been chasing the real estate scam more than the other thing but now I'm mad. I'm gonna find those obnoxious thugs who stole that case I recovered and I'm gonna deal with whoever smashed into Catherine. In a similar fashion. An eye for an eye and all that."

"To do that, you have to find 'em first."

"Yeah." I thought I heard a small measure of satisfaction in Sally's voice, but I was concentrating on my task. "Gotta go, Sal. Stay in touch."

"Count on it. But I wish you'd get email." He hung up.

I called Ort at the bar and several more street contacts. I wanted to get my hands on Annette Campbell. An hour passed and the phone rang.

"Sean, my friend. I've had word from several directions that you have an urgent need to congregate with my temporary ex-roommate." Her voice was provocative enough in person. On the phone, it was enough to turn the head of a life-long celibate.

"Yeah, I do, Laura. And I am exceedingly impatient. Did you hear about Catherine's accident?" I called it that only to reduce my emotional baggage. I was convinced it had been a deliberate attempt to murder her. Or us. I'd got the message all right. But my reaction wasn't going to be what was expected.

"I did, love. But you can't see Ms. C. until tomorrow. Pick me up at the corner of Tenth and Fourth, in Southeast. Shall we say elevenish?"

"You got it." I called Catherine. She didn't answer so I left a message. I drove home.

The red light was again blinking. CM had returned my call. "I was in the shower, love. I think I need to come over there and spend a few days soaking in your hot tub. Call me."

I did. First I checked in with the team I had watching the perimeter of her building. Catherine hadn't wanted anybody else in her apartment. She hadn't wanted any minders at all. "Sean, I see you've ignored my wishes again and put some people outside."

"You noticed. Very astute. It just makes me feel better to know you aren't so vulnerable when I'm not there."

"That's very sweet. Actually, I didn't see them. But I know you." Her chuckle tinkled down the line. Made me feel warm.

"I'm going to do a few things. If it gets too late, I'll stay here. I've going to see the Campbell woman in the morning."

"All right. But call if you aren't coming over. And please be careful. I know you're still angry. I can hear it in your voice. Love you." She hung up.

She was right. I was still angry. Dangerously angry.

29

I opened my safe and retrieved the aluminum case. I could still opt to deliver it unopened to Sal, whether he wanted it or not. Or I could chuck it in the river. I wasn't going to do either. I was gonna open it. And I had pretty much decided that subtlety was overrated in this particular circumstance.

I examined Beechy's case closely. I even used a magnifying glass on the seam and the locks. Then I weighed it. It weighed enough that I knew it wasn't empty, even though it made no noise when I shook it.

I measured my case and took several Polaroids. Digital cameras are nice and convenient, but I didn't have one. I made sure the pictures were sharp and clear and the background was completely nondescript with nothing to identify anything, least of all where the case was when the pictures were taken. Or when. I also made sure the locking mechanism was cleanly visible in one of the shots so anybody could see the case hadn't been tampered with.

Then I started tampering. The seam between cover and body was very tight and I could just barely get a razor blade into it. That was no help. I examined the seam opposite the handle and locks. I judged there was likely to be a pair of hinges on that side. I got out my hand drill and a diamond-tipped concrete drill bit and went to work. It was tough going, but after a few minutes the drill sank into the interior. When I pulled it out, there was a bit of paper stuck to the drill that looked an awful lot like Uncle Sam's currency. The air that leaked out of the hole I'd drilled smelled pretty stale. It smelled like paper currency as well.

The second hole, next to the first, hit pay dirt, in a manner of speaking. I figured I'd hit a hinge so I drilled a larger hole. Then I went after the hole with a hammer and cold chisel. By the time I'd knocked the hinge out, the back side of the case was a mess, but I didn't care. My anger over the attempt on Catherine and the resistance of the case fueled my strength and made me careless. When the first hinge finally gave up and the cover popped up about a quarter inch, I didn't hesitate. I own a large pry bar about six feet long. It's made of hardened steel and it has a flat blade on one end. I have no idea what its original purpose was, nor where it came from. Didn't matter.

I knocked together a rough wood frame to hold the aluminum case and clamped it to the bench. After I jammed the blade of the pry bar into the seam, I hit it a few times with a small sledge hammer. All at once the case gave it up. The other hinge split and the cover flew open, spewing portraits of various dead presidents into the air and all over the basement floor. It was a mini confetti storm. There was a lot of money. After the paper storm subsided, I got a broom and swept the money into an untidy pile in the corner of the basement and out of the way.

The aluminum case was a mess. Now for my quickly forming plan.

I was going to prepare a trap.

I called around and found what I needed on the fourth try. An outfit in Columbia Heights had a variety of new and used cases and trunks for sale. Then I called the Revulons to be sure one of them would be available in a couple of hours. They assured me they'd wait all night, if necessary.

Victor's Luggage—New & Used, in Columbia Heights, had a good-sized hard-sided bag that would not only hold Beechy's now badly beat up aluminum case, but a few surprises as well. Next door to Victor's is a used bedding store. There I cadged a few old bed spring coils and some smelly down pillows they were going to discard. On to the hardware store for duct tape, extra glue sticks for my glue gun, and several big mousetraps.

Then I went to the office to talk with the Belinda and Betsy Revulon.

"Here's what I want to do," I told them. "I want to send a couple of pictures and a short message to several locations. Some of these outfits have websites or email and the rest have a fax number. I could use a courier service, but I'd rather do it electronically."

Four Revulon eyebrows went up in unison. "Electronically?" said Betsy "Sean Sean on the Internet?" said Belinda.

"Yeah, listen. Just because I'm not up to date everywhere, doesn't mean I don't see the advantages, sometimes. But it has to be done so the message can't be traced back to you. Possible?

"Sure. We'll scan the pictures, create a file and send it to the address you want through an anonymous remailer. Nothing to it. We can do the same thing with the fax messages."

True. The message will contain these two pictures and a way for the right recipient to respond."

"No problem. The anonymous remailer will take care of that. But to do a search to try to find an email or website address for your targets, we need someplace to start."

"I understand. I want the message to go to every general contractor or construction company in the southern twin cities. I looked. There can't be more'n twenty-five. Here, let me write down what I want." I didn't know which company Armond Anderson was affiliated with, but I was pretty sure my scatter-gun approach would work. So the complete message with the two pictures of the clean undamaged aluminum case said only "Your missing case?" And it was signed, George Beechy. I might get a few wise-ass answers but only one would be right. I thought.

While we were identifying the addresses and looking for websites, Betsey scanned the two Polaroids and then ran me a couple of larger prints. I left them to their labors after reminding them to be sure they were well-insulated from any blowback. I wasn't too worried. I knew that someone with good cyber savvy could eventually trace the messages, but it was my intention to take down Anderson and the Talbot's enterprise before that happened. I glanced back as I reached the door to the stairway. The two cousins were standing side by side in the door of their office, watching me go. I could see identical looks of concern on their faces. Damn, I was gonna have to practice outward calm or I'd never pull this thing off.

Back in my basement, I assembled my device. With a hammer I smashed the case that had held the money back into some semblance of closed after I filled it with as much of the cash as I could cram into it. Then I glued it into the bottom of the larger container, which was almost a small trunk. There was plenty of clearance on the top of the smaller case but very little on the end or sides. I wired three bedsprings in fully compressed positions and nailed them to a piece of scrap wood. The wood I secured across the top of the beat up original aluminum case, wedging it in and adding generous dollops of glue in the bargain.

Then I glued the three mousetraps into the bag beside the case I'd lifted from Beechy's basement and baited them with a couple of hundred dollar bills each from the pile on the basement floor. I was wearing thin latex gloves so I wouldn't leave any finger prints and I'd already wiped down the insides of both cases with some cleaning fluid. The basement stank. The sterile package was just in case something went wrong with my plan.

While things dried and hardened, I went upstairs and had a drink. If Catherine had known what I was doing she would have labeled it a bad idea and scolded me. She would have been right. I knew it was a prank, but I also figured if it got delivered to the right place, and my timing was right on, it would give me the distraction I was going to need.

After I had a drink, I went back to the basement. The rest of the cash and the contents of the two old pillows went into the bag. With heavy black thread, a couple of screw eyes and a lot of trial and error, I assembled a trigger mechanism. It was rigged so when the bag was unlatched, the compressed bedsprings would throw the cover back. I thought the quick release of the cover would suck the loose paper and cash and feathers into the air, distracting the thugs. As an added fillip, I carefully mixed some torn newspaper with more of the cash and laid it carefully over the mousetraps. That was sort of insurance. If one of the thugs put an incautious hand into what looked like paper packing, they might snag a mousetrap.

After placing all this assorted stuff and springs in the bag, I closed down the cover. I had to use a screw jack originally designed for leveling house beams to close the bag cover the last inch.

As a final measure, I used two old straps to secure the lid in place. When I picked it up and shook it, I could hear the paper rustling inside, but nothing else. Good. Then I sat down to wait. I figured I wouldn't have to wait long and I knew I wasn't in a waiting mood.

30

I didn't sit still for long. There really wasn't much I could do now that my trap was baited, in a manner of speaking. I had to wait for some results and there was no telling how long it would take. I was picking up Laura Lipp at eleven to go see Annette Campbell. By the time my altered trunk was finished I cleaned up and then it was time to take a leisurely drive into Minneapolis and pick up la Lipp. I saw her from a quarter block away, standing tall and blond in a gray pantsuit that did everything for her lithe figure. Even some of the traffic on tenth seemed a little sluggish as it passed her corner. I slid over, paused and she hopped in.

"Where to?"

"Annette is no longer bunking with me, Sean. We decided mutually that she should get a place of her own."

"Okay. Where do I go?" I figured there was no sense discussing that decision with Laura. Annette knew there were people looking for her and so did Lipp. The Campbell woman had the wits to stay out of sight and Lipp wasn't going to give her any grief about an independent decision.

"There's an old development of row houses out in Mounds View. I've sent people out there before. You'll want to get out to Highway 10 and go north."

So I did that.

* * *

North of Minneapolis, a little south of Anoka, is a series of older communities along what used to be a principal highway that ran northwest into vacationland and on to North Dakota. They were mostly blue-collar working family places that support the gaggle of commercial establishment that have grown up along the highway.

We drove in complete silence up Central Avenue and then northwest on Coon Rapids Boulevard. I didn't mind the silence. It gave me time to reflect. I was making progress but now that I had the stolen case and most of the players lined up, I needed to find some definitive proof of Mordy's killer. I was hoping Annette Campbell would provide some answers, although my last interview with her hadn't been too productive. I'd sensed she'd been holding back and I hadn't wanted to irritate her right then. Then there were some other intriguing loose ends. I still had two keys to two unknown locks. I had tenuous links to an apparently wealthy construction company in Bloomington and I had a ton of somebody else's money. I was counting on the money to bring me some of the answers.

We arrived at an older development called Apple Gardens out in Ramsey. La Lipp directed me down the main road which ran at right angles to the highway. These were all single-story places with two-car tuck-under garages. Each had a short narrow driveway sort of parking place that led directly to the front stoop.

I didn't see any cars parked at front doors. Vehicles were either in the garages or occupants of the houses were out. At work, maybe. You know, day jobs. I glanced at Laura who was just staring serenely through the windshield, relaxed in her seat. Halfway down, I caught a flash of reflected light off one of the garage doors as it swung open. A green late-model Buick nosed out of the garage and then abruptly fishtailed onto the drive and roared past us. I didn't recognize the driver who was hunched over the wheel, staring straight ahead. Late for work maybe? Overslept? In my rearview mirror, I saw the Buick's taillight flash briefly and the driver screamed left onto the highway, heading back toward Minneapolis.

"Strange," said Laura, "I think that car came from the place where Annette is staying.

I horsed my Taurus into the slot by the front door of 1288 and I got out into the hot sun. Laura didn't wait for me to come and open her door, she promptly exited and headed for the front stoop.

"Wait a minute, I said, "your legs are longer than mine."

No reaction. She grabbed the screen door and pulled it open then she banged on the not-too-solid-sounding front door. It gave under her pounding.

"Wait a minute," I said again. "There could be trouble here." Lipp hesitated and then pushed inside with me right beside her. I had one hand on my holster, just in case. Two steps inside the small living room and I stuck my left arm across her body to stop her. We just listened for a minute.

"Sean—"

"Shhh. Listen," I whispered. We did and I could hear the sound of water running and then a toilet flushed somewhere toward the back of the place. A door opened, footsteps clacked down the hall toward us and Annette Campbell came into the room. She stopped, obviously startled at our sudden appearance. The she smiled and said,

"Well, this is a surprise. I guess you've been looking for me."

"As a matter of fact, I have. Sit down, please. I indicated the mall divan shoved into one corner. Annette did so without objection and I grabbed a straight chair and placed it in front of her. Then I glanced at Laura.

"I'll just make us all some tea," she said, walking to the tiny kitchen. But I knew she'd be listening while she did so.

"Is there anybody else here?" I asked.

"No."

"But there was. Somebody who just left your garage," I pointed out. "In a dark green Buick."

"Oh. That was George. He brought me some clothes."

"I assume you mean George Talbot. I thought you were quits with that crowd."

"Well, gee, I mean, now that Mordy is gone, I got nobody ta turn too, you know? I gotta look out for myself."

So much for loyalty and grieving.

"All right. Let's talk about Mordy. What do you mean gone? Where is he? Have you seen him since that night we found you at his place? Where is he? Did you kill him?"

Annette's face turned pasty white and for a moment I thought she might pass out.

"Damn, you, Sean," she said in a broken voice. "I really did love him. No! I didn't kill him. I been either at that funky place you put me in out on the south side or with Laura or here."

"What do you mean? You just said he was gone."

"George told me Mordy left town."

31

"You bastard!" she snapped at me.

I didn't much care. I was through dancing around and dealing politely with these people. From the corner of my eye I caught Laura peeking at me from the kitchen. The look on her face was not one of approval.

"Well?" I demanded. "Here's another question. See this key? I fished the lock box key out of my pocket. "I'm pretty sure this is a key to a safe deposit box Mordy had somewhere. Trouble is I don't know which bank. Do you?"

Campbell bit her lip and looked at me from red-rimmed eyes. Then she heaved herself out of the couch and stalked into the back of the house. Toward a bedroom, I assumed. Her high hard heels rang on the uncarpeted floor a little like pistol shots. In a minute or two she came back, still stalking. I wouldn't have been surprised if she'd been carrying a gun and aiming it at me.

"Here," she snapped. "Maybe this will help." In her hand was a small untidy stack of envelopes and bankbooks. I shuffled quickly through them. Mordy apparently had accounts at three banks, one in downtown Minneapolis, the others in the suburbs.

"Thank you," I said. "At least I now have something to go on."

"Look," said Annette. Honest to God, I don't know anything. I told you the first time we talked that Mordy was trying to get me out of the gang. He had something set up so I was gonna disappear, you know? Then he'd come and join me after the gang moved on. That's what he told me. That's all I know."

"When Mordy went underground, he went to a place called the Shelton Hotel. Do you know it?" I was watching her closely, but I couldn't tell if she'd heard of the place.

"I that where he—where he was found?"

"Yeah. With a bullet in his forehead."

She closed her eyes and swayed slightly.

"Did you know he was there? Did you tell anyone that's where he was hiding?"

Tears trickled down her cheeks. I didn't care. Well, I did, a little. Especially is she was innocent. At least innocent of this particular beef.

"I swear to you. I loved Mordy. We were gonna get married. I never would betray him. I didn't know where he'd gone. And besides, nobody asked me until now, you know?"

That was interesting. I ran the sequence, what I knew of it, through my head. Yes, it was possible, likely even, that she'd been hidden by Catherine and me and then by Laura Lipp during the crucial time. Knowing Mordy, he could have tripped over his own feet and let somebody find him.

"How did Talbot find you today?"

"I called him. I was outta money, running low on food and I didn't know what to do. With Mordecai gone, I didn't know anybody else in this town. I had no way to get hold of you. What did you expect me to do?" She was crying steadily now. I handed her a box of tissues I found on a table. I didn't bother to point out that if we'd stayed in Richfield, as I'd told her to do, I'd have been in touch with her days earlier.

"All right, tell me everything you and Talbot talked about," I said.

There wasn't much. She'd called him that morning at a number she had. No, she didn't know where the phone was located, but it wasn't a cell number. She told him what she needed and he said he'd bring some stuff right over after he went to the store. Groceries and stuff.

When he got there he was pissed, Annette said. He belted her one, like he used to then he calmed down and said Armond was ready to dump the whole thing and move on. Talbot told her they were giving up on the case Beechy was supposed to keep for them, and the gang was a little nervous because of the arrests of the local real estate scammers.

She stopped and wet her lips.

"And?" I prompted.

"That's about it. He said they had to do something about Jake, because he'd be pissed if they just left him in jail, but he still had almost four years to serve. He said for me to sit tight and he'd call when they were ready to leave town."

So, I thought, the heat's getting to them. Even after trying to take out Catherine, they were going to cut and run. Prudence was one of the reasons this group hadn't been caught before. It just meant I had very little time.

Okay." I said. Now, name some names." Who's in this group?" She rattled off the names of the same men she'd given me days earlier.

"What about Armond Anderson?"

Blank look. "Who?"

"You don't know anybody by that name, is that what you're telling me?"

"You got it sug--." she bit her lip and more tears rolled down her streaked face.

I started to say something and Lipp walked in with a tray and some tea in a steaming pot. She'd timed her entrance perfectly. It looked like Annette was neatly compartmentalizing things. Talbot had named Anderson to her and she'd repeated it to me without even realizing it. To her, Armond Anderson wasn't part of the gang, and she hadn't connected his name to the "boss" she and the others referred to in earlier conversations.

Lipp poured tea for Campbell and herself. I declined and went to the telephone handing on the kitchen wall. I called Catherine who sounded pretty chipper.

"I wish you'd reconsider staying away from me until this thing is finished," she cooed into the phone. Cooed?

"You're cooing," I said in a low voice.

"I know. It's my cooing you to come home, voice."

"I don't think it will be too long but I don't want to take any chances. Bet I stay away for now." She cooed some more and I hung up.

Then I called Revulon central. Betsey answered. "Okay, Sean. Here's the deal. We have sent an anonymous message to all the construction companies with email addresses in the southern suburbs. None of them can tell who else got the message with the two pictures of the case and an offer to sell. By the end of the day we expect all the addressees will have seen the pictures. So by late tomorrow I bet you'll have an offer."

"Excellent," I said. "I'll be in touch."

Then I ripped the telephone off the wall.

"Hey!" said Campbell.

"I can't take any more chances," I said. I can't shove you in jail and I won't tie you up. But you're not gonna get in touch with your new boyfriends until this is over. Then, if there's any reasonable way, I'll help you get out of town."

I thought for a moment and said to Laura. "You got a cell phone, right?"

Wordlessly she fished it out of her purse and extended it to me. "Just punch send after you put in the numbers."

I looked at Annette. "Why was Talbot in such a hurry when we arrived?"

She shrugged. "You mean 'cause he tore out of here? He drives like that all the time."

I called a friend of mine in St. Paul, a guy who worked for the phone company and moonlights as an occasional bodyguard. He used to be a defensive tackle for the Minnesota Gopher football team. Yes, Greg was available for a few hours and overnight. I gave him instructions and after he arrived, I explained I wanted Miss Campbell isolated, but he shouldn't try to defend her if men with guns showed up unexpectedly.

Annette looked unhappy, but I couldn't decide if it was because I appeared ready to giver he up, or because I'd hired a babysitter. All I knew was that I wasn't going to lose her again. I also figured that as soon as I laid hands on Mordecai Marsh, I was gonna transport him forthwith to this same location where he'd be placed under similar house arrest.

The Case of the Stolen Case

"Can I just go to a store occasionally?" Campbell whined.

"No. You make lists, Greg here will communicate them to me and I'll get whatever you need. The operative word there being need. Don't pout. It won't be very long."

I was pretty sure I could keep that promise. As soon as the word I had the vagrant aluminum case, I was sure Armond or his henchmen would be in touch.

I grabbed Laura and we left. She was uncharacteristically quiet on the ride back to southeast and her place.

"Thanks for hooking me up with the Campbell woman."

"Sure, Sean, but I'm not happy with the result. I just thought you wanted to talk with her, not put her under house arrest."

"Listen, I'm not happy about it either. I don't usually treat women that way and she's been through a lot," I said, pulling up to the curb in front of her building. I knew it was her building, not just where she lived, but her building. I'd done a little research on the woman and she had more than one or two nice real estate holdings around town. "She's been a pain ever since we found her at Mordy's. She'll be a lot safer staying in that house instead of out on the street where her former associates could get at her. I don't want any distractions. Right now I want that gang focused on getting their hands on their money. I think it'll only be a few days anyway."

I drove off and headed for my office. Since I hadn't talked to Catherine for a couple of hours I called her. She said she was fine. She'd invited the boys into the apartment.

"Excuse me?"

"Sure. I knew you'd put some of your friends here to watch over me so I went and found them and invited them in."

"I hope everybody is alert."

Catherine giggled. "We're playing cards." I heard low laughter in the background.

"Yeah?"

"Strip Poker. I'm wining."

"Yes? Those goons are probably deliberately letting you win."

32

The following morning I had a call on my machine. I didn't hear it. I must have been in the shower. Betsey Revulon said. "We've had a dozen inquiries overnight. So far they're all cranks. Except for two. Call us."

Instead I went to the office. Down the hall in their office I listened to a voice I'd never heard before. It sounded young, but it had the right information and the right tone of menace I'd expected. But the second one they played was a voice I recognized. It was the man who talked to me in the dark of the night. That was the night I took my late night stroll after the party.

Armond Anderson. The developer, raconteur, prominent man of local society. Killer? I wondered? I also wondered what his real name was. Because I was now sure this business was long standing and widely spread. And in my world that meant some folks, especially the weasels at the top would be masquerading behind aliases. "Mr. Sean," the message said. "I understand you have something of ours. Something you'd like to return to us with a minimum of hassle."

A 'minimum of hassle?' Give me a break. Then there was a number to call. It was all melodramatic, but if that satisfied them, I was cool with it.

I called the number and talked to a machine. Of course. I called from the payphone hanging in the hallway of my building. It was one of the few such phones still left in this era of cell phones and computer connections.

Then I called Ace Cartage. AC employed some people I knew and others I knew about. It was run by an ex-con with the unlikely name of Ace. He was from Illinois and employed several other ex-cons. I wanted some muscle around as backup. And I didn't want anybody on parole who wasn't supposed to associate with felons. Ace knew me and I knew Ace, so my special needs weren't questioned. It pays to work in a town where you know people, people with attitude and special skills. They sent me Harlan and his crew. Harlan no-last-name had three spectacularly muscled assistants. We weren't introduced. Seemed like a lot of meat for one rather light if unwieldy box. The more the merrier, I sometimes say. Harlan was much taller, had his hair in a very short buzz-cut, and sounded like he might have lived in New Jersey at one time.

They put my box on their two-wheeler and lugged it to their truck.

The deal was I wanted them to store the box for a few days while I set up the exchange and to create the right atmosphere. If I'd been too easy and just popped over to whatever location the boys suggested, it might have looked like a plot. I couldn't have that. We already had too many plots.

So I planned to negotiate for a day or two. Meanwhile the aluminum case was out of harm's way. I thought.

The next day, around noon, Ace called me. "We have a problem."

"What!" I guess I sounded a bit agitated. That's because I was. Agitated.

"Yeah, the boys made a mistake when they logged in your freight last night."

"Meaning...."

"Meaning when I went to look for it I couldn't find it."

"Has it been stolen, purloined, spirited away? What?"

"No it's here, somewhere. See the thing is, we brought in several shipments yesterday, both before and after yours. Somehow the numbers on the bills of lading got messed up. When we store stuff, even for a short time, like with your crate, we assign it a place in the warehouse that goes with the number on the paperwork. This morning I noticed the place I thought I'd assigned to you was empty."

"No crate," I said.

"No crate," Ace agreed. "I know you didn't come get it."

"You're right about that. How long to find it?" I could almost hear him shrug.

"Couple days."

Barely within my schedule limits. "How hot is the warehouse?"

"Pretty warm. Depends on the day, you know?"

"Oh, I knew all right. Ace cartage leased space in a huge warehouse on the north side of downtown Minneapolis. It was not air conditioned. Normally not a problem, except that I had specified a low floor for storage, which was how Ace happened to notice my box was missing. If, perchance, my box was on an upper floor and it got overheated, some of the glue and some of the cheap triggers I had installed could melt. That would set off the package which I definitely didn't want to happen. At least, not before I was ready. Now there was a chance Ace would have a messy and hard-to-explain explosion in his warehouse.

"It is imperative you locate that box and keep it in a cool location, as I specified."

Long silence on the other end.

"Look dude," said Ace finally. "If this box stinks up my warehouse, and my business, I'm gonna be lookin' for you. You dig?"

"Just find the box."

After we disengaged it occurred to me that Ace might have jumped to an erroneous conclusion. Maybe he thought I'd stuffed a body in the box. I crossed my fingers and went back to negotiating. I was impatient to get the business done, but I couldn't let on to Armand the developer or whatever his name was, that I had lost possession of the case. I had to remain cool and distant, as if I didn't give a rat's ass whether he got the thing back today, tomorrow or never.

Armand and I had another conversation on the telephone. It was interesting that now I wasn't working through his layers of intermediaries. We were negotiating principal to principal, if not face to face. This was a long conversation. I'd bought one of those cheap throw-away-cells that drug dealers sometimes use so I had an untraceable connection to these guys, should anything untoward happen. I could almost hear the hiss of audio tape passing over the recording head of a small tape recorder in his office. That's what I would have done in his place. Once he asked me to speak up, couldn't I find someplace a little less noisy from which to call?

"Sorry, my office isn't soundproof."

"I'm sure that's the case, Mr. Sean, but I doubt very much your office is as busy as it sounds from this end. A coffee shop perhaps? Maybe a local bar?"

He was letting me know he was keeping a sharp eye out. "Suppose we arrange a transfer of possession tomorrow sometime," I said.

"That would be most satisfactory. I am becoming anxious to have this business concluded."

"You have business elsewhere, I assume."

"One could say that."

Why don't you call me tomorrow, shall we say eleven in the morning? I'll give you a number to call." He agreed and I gave him the cell number.

* * *

The following morning, precisely at eleven he called. Not exactly. One of his minions was the voice on the phone. Understandable. I was to take the package—that's what he called it, "the package," to a place in Bloomington where I should wait in the parking lot of a building there and receive further instructions. Then he asked something I was waiting for.

"Didja open it?"

"Open what?" I said.

"The case. The package."

"I tried, but couldn't manage it."

"Okay," my caller said.

Then I called ACE. Of course they hadn't located my box, but they were making headway, he said.

"I need it by one today," I said tersely and closed the phone. I still didn't like cells, but they were handy in some situations.

I rolled home again and opened my gun safe. Chose my favorite, the 1913 Colt 45 caliber semi-auto. Inserted the loaded clip in the handle and slammed it home. Picked out two more clips and loaded them with fresh ammo. Phone rang.

"We found it."

"What?" I said.

"Your missing package, dude. The label must have fallen off, the one that routes packages to places. Anyway, we got it."

"Good. I'll be there in twenty." I hung up my real telephone and stashed weapon and ammo in a small black aluminum case I had made for just such occasions and left for Ace storage. The package was waiting for me on their small loading dock at the side of the building on Twelfth Avenue North East. I couldn't see any external damage. I loaded the thing into the trunk of my car and drove to the designated parking lot in Bloomington.

After half-an-hour of dozing and waiting, I almost decided to bag it and head home. Then my damn cell buzzed. "Yeh?"

"Drive west and into the parking lot of Bloomington Construction. They have a big building there with lots of offices. Ninth floor front. Armand Construction Services. Don't make any detours."

Since the caller Abruptly hung up, I made no response. I blinked my lights with the remote key controller and wheeled out to my destination. It was a short drive. Of the four cars following me, I wondered which were the bad guys and which might be somebody else. I couldn't tell from the brief glimpses I had of the occupants.

I parked and hauled the package out of the trunk. Looking around was no help so I didn't, except once. I didn't see anything or anybody that set off alarms. I strolled into the back entrance and took the elevator to the ninth floor. I was alone in the elevator. At the ninth floor the elevator door slid quietly open and I saw a large sign for ACS down the hall in front of me. I stopped and shifted the package to my other arm so my right hand was a little freer in case something threatening came down.

I took my time getting to ACS's front door. They were being so open about the exchange, I assumed they didn't expect me to be leaving after they verified the contents. I knocked and opened the door, juggling the package in front of me. I hoped nobody intended to shoot me through the package. That would have been embarrassing. Nobody did. The outer office was empty except for a table. I set the package on it and backed toward the door.

A man I didn't know came out and eyeballed me. "No wire," I said. "You wanna frisk me?"

He looked at me and a voice I knew said from the inner office, "Don't bother, he wouldn't be that stupid. Bring the package here, John. Mr. Sean. Just wait right there, if you please."

Right. The door swung wider as the guy picked up the package. "It doesn't need all five of you to open the box." I said it as casually as I could manage, watching carefully for any signs of weaponry.

The door swung closed and I stepped quietly to one side, reaching back so my gat was in easy reach. There was the sound of ripping, a muffled curse or two. Then, "What? Look out!"

A loud rattling commenced, followed immediately by a terrific bang from the flash grenade attached to an inside flap of the box. I could visualize exactly what the scene was like. I have a well-developed imagination, you see. Plus, I'd set off one of these surprise packages in the past. Little white ping pong balls flew everywhere and a big puff of thick white smoke issued forth. The combination of floating ping pong balls, the flash grenade with smoke and noise created a satisfactory pandemonium. I heard a loud crack as a door somewhere in the other room was smashed off its hinges, allowing several large loudly shouting members of Bloomington's finest to pour into the room. A single thug made it back into the room where I waited. The look of confusion and terror on his face was extremely satisfying. I stuck out my red Ked-shod foot and tripped him as he raced by. He slammed face first into the outer office door and bounced into the arms of several more Bloomington cops. Did I fail to mention that? I was covered six ways from Sunday since I'd left ACE storage in Minneapolis.

The smoke cleared and the staff of Armand Construction Services were brought out in handcuffs. When their leader approached, I stepped forward and smiled. "Mr. Armand, you can mess with me, but don't ever threaten my lady." I smiled what I hoped was a shark's smile. Melodramatic? Sure. Why not?

33

"As I understand it, this Armand was using the cover of a legitimate construction company to operate his real estate scams." Catherine slid down on the couch beside me and stretched her long slender legs onto the footstool in front of her. I admired the view.

"Correct." I sipped from my heavy tumbler of 40-year-old single malt. I was treating myself after a satisfactory conclusion to a nasty case. "Unlike a lot of law-breakers, Mr. Armand took the long view. He expected to make huge killings after testing his theories and gradually building up a nice little nest egg."

"Tell me again how this all works." Catherine said, snuggling closer.

"It's quite simple, really. There are appraisers, and loan officers, and people called closers at Title Insurance companies. Let's say a loan officer knows that a client of his bank or S&L is selling a home and wants to be sure the client realizes a chunk of cash from the sale. But, said client is heavily mortgaged, so even when selling, client isn't going to realize much cash in hand. Our bent loan officer gets the people involved in closing or finalizing the sale to inflate the final cost of the property, maybe only a point or two. Because of the way the real estate business runs, it's a very person to person business. An acquaintance at the title company agrees to inflate the sales price and not mention the add-on to the lender, that is the bank taking a mortgage on the property."

"So the mortgage is for more than the property is actually worth."

"Right."

"And the checks for the amount over the original loan are written to the seller by the Title Company?"

"Again, correct. Which means the bank, the lender never knows about the change in the amount unless someone compares the original offer and the appraisal with the final documents. But since everybody involved knows and trust everybody, and they're all busy with lots of deals, nobody compares and the deal slides through. One single deal, on a house in Eden Prairie, say, might not realize huge amounts of cash, probably only a couple of thousand. But multiply that by a dozen deals, especially multi-million-dollar business properties and you are talking about some significant amounts of money."

"Didn't you say Armand also did some insurance fraud?" Catherine asked then.

"Yep. They torched a couple of south Minneapolis businesses to collect on the insurance, apparently because Armand ran short of cash to pay for his operations."

"So why did it fall apart?"

"Mr. Armand made a few fatal errors. His principal one was believing he'd persuaded his gang to be patient. But then he expected them to support themselves for months, years even. Most criminals are always looking for people to rob or scam, right? So they assume everybody around them is the same way. So there's not a lot of trust among thieves, as we're fond of reminding ourselves.

"Then, of course, they ran into Minnesota Nice."

Catherine frowned. "What?"

I smiled at her. "Your cousin, Mordecai. He was just supposed to be a local contact, a driver, a go-fer, maybe even a fall guy or screen if things got dicey. But he met Annette and fell for her and decided he'd help her go straight, gentleman that he was."

"Poor Mordy," Catherine sighed. "Maybe things would have been different if I'd heard the phone ring."

"We'll never know," I said reaching for her.

Made in the USA
Middletown, DE
15 January 2017